# OUR LIFE IN A DAY

Jamie Fewery is an author, columnist and copywriter. He has written for the *Daily Telegraph*, *Five Dials* and *Wired*, and works for a London-based marketing and creative agency. He lives in Berkhamsted, Hertfordshire with his wife and son. *Our Life in a Day* is his first novel.

# OUR LIFE IN A DAY

# JAMIE FEWERY

ORION

An Orion paperback

First published in Great Britain in 2018 by Orion Fiction
This paperback edition published in 2019 by Orion Fiction,
an imprint of The Orion Publishing Group Ltd
Carmelite House, 50 Victoria Embankment
London EC4Y 0DZ

An Hachette UK Company

1 3 5 7 9 10 8 6 4 2

A CIP catalogue record for this book is
available from the British Library.

ISBN 978 1 4091 7816 3

Typeset at The Spartan Press Ltd,
Lymington, Hants

Printed and bound by Clays Ltd,
Elcograf S.p.A.

MIX
Paper from
responsible sources
FSC® C104740
www.fsc.org

www.orionbooks.co.uk

*For Alice.*
*Thank you for all the love, support and courage.*

# PROLOGUE

It wasn't supposed to be a special evening. That, Tom assumed, would be tomorrow. On the actual day: 21st June. Ten years since they had met and walked home together in the small hours through the quiet, early-summer London streets.

But when Tom opened the door to the flat they shared in West Hampstead, he knew right away that Esme had been planning this for a while. Everything was covered in her fingerprints. From the confetti, torn and chopped from pages of their favourite books and placed on top of the doorframe so that it would rain down on him as he stepped inside, and the hundreds of photos, clipped with tiny wooden pegs to brown string, so as to form a sort of pictorial bunting through the small hallway. To the album he could hear playing softly in the living room, the one they had danced to three years ago when they'd bought the place and it still smelled of the previous owner's weed habit and boxer dog. *Making Movies* by Dire Straits – the only CD he could find in the forty or so boxes that dominated their small flat for months after they moved in.

'Hello?' he called out, dropping his bag at the foot of their coat rack and hanging up his lightweight black raincoat, still damp from the summer shower he'd been caught in on the walk from the Overground station to Islay Gardens. 'What's going on?'

'In the lounge,' she called back.

The flat was so small that just three steps took Tom from the hallway into their living and dining room. Where Esme was waiting for him.

She had dressed up, wearing a dark blue cocktail dress and grey heels. Her face was made up just enough to accentuate her big, dark eyes and thin lips. Her mouth seemed ever ready to lift into a shining smile or collapse into a tearful frown. Her hair was in the pixie cut that had recently replaced her shoulder-length brown waves. Part of the 'new Esme' look she had decided to cultivate since her – their – difficult start to the year.

'What's all this, Es?' he asked. 'I thought we were just going to pack tonight.'

'A surprise.'

'Oh. So what, dinner?'

'Not quite.'

Tom looked around the room. A candle on the coffee table illuminated the off-white walls, the expensive wall clock showing 7.03, and their couch, torn in strips down one side by their cat, Magnus, who had apparently never agreed with its deep red colour. In the corner she had set up their flimsy drop-leaf dining table for two. A bread basket sat in the middle, emulating a restaurant, and on Tom's normal side was a small, wrapped gift. No more than a couple of inches square, and maybe a centimetre high.

'Shit, Esme. I haven't even wrapped your present yet,' he said, feeling slightly guilty because a more accurate description would have been 'haven't even bought'. He was intending to do so tomorrow, before they set off west for their anniversary mini-break. She had booked a nice hotel in the Cotswolds on a whim. But for a while, celebrating their ten-year anniversary at all had been up in the air. Recently very little had gone as they'd wanted or planned.

2

'It's not a present as such,' she said. 'Just an idea I had.'

'An idea?'

'Yes. Sort of. Tomorrow you'll get your real present. Tonight, I'm giving you the gift of time travel.'

She was being playful with him. Tom was sceptical.

'Look, sit down. The first course is almost ready,' she said.

'Can I change first? You caught me off guard a bit and I look like shit,' he said, glancing down at his tatty jeans (second-best pair), rain-soaked New Balance trainers and tired blue linen shirt. Along with everything else, he had been intending to sort out his hair tomorrow morning, getting the cheapest barber in north London to tidy his shapeless mop of brown hair and perhaps even trim his short, grey-flecked beard.

'Fine. But hurry up. You're already late.'

Tom wondered how he could possibly be late for something he didn't know was happening, but said nothing as he hurried into their bedroom to find the white cotton Oxford shirt Esme liked him in, and a different pair of jeans to replace the ones he'd been wearing all day.

Looking at himself in the mirror and trying to pluck out the nose hair that had been annoying him, Tom wondered why she had done all this – despite it being typically Esme. Had she discovered something?

Tom shook the question from his head. He was determined not to spoil the night. It was too important for both of them. Instead, he took a deep breath, then made his way into the living room where she was waiting at the table, smiling.

'So,' he said, taking his seat. 'Are you going to tell me what all this is about, then?'

'Open it.'

'This?' He picked up the small parcel, and started to pick away at the Sellotape as she beamed at him.

Inside was a stack of Post-it notes, on the front of which was written: *Our Life in a Day*, with a drawing of a clock, stuck at twelve. It could be midnight or midday. Tom leafed through the small yellow pages, expecting to find a story or a little sketched flick book. Things that would be characteristically thoughtful of Esme. But each note was blank, except for a time and another smaller drawing of the clock.

'Sorry, Es,' he said. 'I'm not really getting it.'

'It's a game.'

'A game?'

'Yes. I made it up. An Esme Simon creation. Especially for Tom Murray.'

'And what happens in this game?'

'Well, if you play it right, over the next couple of hours you'll revisit every significant moment from the ten years we've spent together. You'll experience every moment of us,' she said, smiling at her own cleverness. 'You see what I mean now? Time travel.'

'Right,' he said. Tom was surprised. This was the kind of thing the Esme of a few years ago would've done. But it was somewhat out of character for her now. 'And are there any rules to this . . . time-travel game?'

'Just one. The instructions are on the back.'

Tom turned the stack over. Esme had taped a folded-up piece of A5 paper to the Post-its. He unfurled it and began to read.

*Welcome to Our Life in a Day. A new game devised by Esme Simon, for Tom Murray, to celebrate our ten years together.*

*Each Post-it note represents an hour. You have to think of the twenty-four most significant moments of our life together. One for each hour of the day.*

4

*There is only <u>one</u> rule: the moment had to have taken place roughly during the hour shown on the note. For example:*

*3–4 a.m. When Esme had to pick me up from Milton Keynes station because I'm an idiot and fell asleep on a train (March 2011, if you remember?).*

*The game is only complete when you have a moment for every note. At which point you will receive your prize . . .*

*Have fun! Love you, Es xxxx*

Tom looked up at Esme, her face lit by the candle between them and a broad, satisfied smile. He hesitated for a moment.

What did he consider the twenty-four most significant hours of his and Esme's relationship to be? What about the hours she'd forgotten, or the things she didn't even know about? The things she couldn't know about?

Tom's palms were clammy and he could feel his heart begin to beat a little faster. This gift could mean more than she might ever have expected. But only if he was able to tell the whole truth.

He glanced at the deck again, and then back up at Esme.

'Ready?' she said.

# PART 1

# CHAPTER ONE

**2 – 3 am**

# THE NIGHT WE MET
## June 2007 – Stockwell, London

'So when are you leaving, then?'

'I didn't say I'm actually going to go,' Tom said.

'You literally just did.'

Tom shook his head.

'"Part of me thinks the problem is London. I might move to Edinburgh,"' she said, mimicking his voice. 'Verbatim quote. Besides, you don't actually know anyone there. All of your friends are either here or in Lowestoft.'

'My grandparents live in Leith.'

'Oh good! And you, a twenty-five-year-old man, will spend your weekends and evenings hanging out with people three times your age. Tell me, Tom, how's your bridge game?'

'I said I *might* go. It means I'm not sure about it.'

'Jesus, you're difficult.'

'I know,' he said sadly, leaning up against the chipped, light blue kitchen worktop, careful to avoid the slick of stale spilled beer, and taking a sip from his half-full can of warm Diet Coke.

'Sorry,' Annabel said, touching his arm in sympathy. 'Probably shouldn't have said that.'

Tom smiled. He wasn't sure how much longer he could stick the party. The music was a terrible mix of nineties indie and execrable house courtesy of Ali's friend Mem, who had offered his DJ skills for the evening, claiming that he had turned down a slot at Fabric to do so. The lounge was full of Ali's ad agency workmates, who were doing lines of cheap cocaine off a framed replica of Magritte's *Golconda* that belonged to the landlord. While the 'roof terrace' (or more accurately 'the roof') had been taken over by an amateur photographer, who was insisting that partygoers hold an empty frame in front of their faces for him to capture their portraits against a naff backdrop of the London skyline. And, worst of all, Tom was in a minority of two oddballs who'd chosen not to wear fancy dress, surrounded by upwards of fifty people dressed as Iron/Super/Bat/ Spider/Bananaman, three as Wonder Woman and a bloke who'd covered himself in painted green sponge to become the Hulk – a decision he seemed to regret more with each passing hour.

According to Annabel (herself dressed as someone called Jean Grey) the only other 'normal' at the party was Esme Simon: a friend of Ali's and former girlfriend of his flatmate, Angry Matt – a drummer for a moderately successful hardcore rock band, whose relentless touring schedule meant he'd been absent from the flat for the last eleven months.

Esme was pretty. Her hair was shoulder length, wavy and dark brown. Her eyes gave life not just to her face, but to her whole body. She hadn't stopped smiling for the entire evening, despite the fact that she was wearing jeans, red Converse and a checked shirt, while all around her were poor facsimiles of the incredible, the amazing and the invincible.

However, according to Annabel, who had noticed Tom looking at her, Esme was 'not right for you'.

'Hang on,' Tom said. 'One: why? Two: who said I was even interested in her anyway?'

'Right. One: she's constantly upbeat. Unlike you. One-point-five: she's too *good*.'

'What do you mean, *good*?' he said, echoing Annabel's tone, making good sound a quality to be avoided rather than aspired to.

'She does, like, child speech therapy or something. A *nice* thing. Devotes her life to helping others. You're a selfish artiste.'

'I'm not sure a covers-band-musician-slash-teacher could be termed an artiste. But fine. Anyway. I don't see how those particular two types of people are incompatible.'

Annabel sighed. Tom could tell she was preparing one of her well-meaning 'lessons'. She was always looking out for him, which often meant telling him not to do certain things. Though given recent events, that was probably fair enough.

'Okay, what?' Tom said.

'It's not just about whether you'd be a good fit. It's whether *this*,' she said, obliquely gesturing at Esme then back at Tom, 'would be a good idea. After everything.'

'I think you're reading far too much into a couple of exchanged glances at a party.'

'I'm just saying my piece. I'd be a bad friend if I didn't.'

'And your piece is?'

'That you're too vulnerable. I know you think you're alright now. But it's barely been two months.'

Tom said nothing. There was a little more than a kernel of truth in what Annabel was saying. But he had a long and not-too-proud history of ignoring the red flags friends and family raised on his behalf. For better or worse.

'Don't worry.'

'I do worry. Because I can tell that you like her. You've only listened to half of what I've said when she's in view.'

'Who are you to judge, anyway?'

Annabel sighed, visibly irritated by him.

11

'Tom. How long have I known you? Fourteen years?'

''Bout that.'

'And during that time, how many functional relationships have you had?'

'One. No, two.'

'The correct answer is zero, Tom. Zero.'

'You liked Tansy. Everyone liked Tansy.'

'Except you.'

Tom said nothing to this. It was, of course, perfectly true. Tansy had been his first serious girlfriend, in a relationship lasting just six months of the early noughties. Like Annabel and himself, Tansy was from Lowestoft on the Suffolk coast. Her parents ran a doughnut and tea stand on the pier, which was rumoured to reuse tea bags up to three times during the lean winters when holidaymakers were scarce. Tom and Tansy had met at sixth-form college, struck up a frosty friendship, based mainly on ribbing each other before, during and after lessons. Eventually the friendship became a relationship, the ribbing became vitriolic arguments and, on the night of their college dinner dance at a local seaside hotel, their relationship ended with Tansy throwing a can of cider at Tom's head.

'Tansy was difficult,' he said. 'You never really knew her.'

Annabel opened the oven, which had been crammed with ice and beer cans, pulling out another Carlsberg, the sight of which made him feel a little on edge. Tom had been apprehensive about being here around all the booze and narcotics. He had promised Annabel that he'd come, but maybe it was too soon.

Tom wondered how many of the other partygoers knew. Had word got around?

He looked over at Esme again, aware that Annabel could see him doing so. There was something about her. The kindness and humour in her face, maybe. The fact that she seemed almost innately happy. He liked her, there was no denying that.

'Tom.'

'What?'

'Again?'

'No.'

'I'm not blind. Or stupid.'

'I don't know what to do.'

'Well, since you seem totally determined to ignore my advice, you have two choices. Either move to Edinburgh, live with your grandparents and play cards. Or find true love with Esme Simon.'

'Those are both a bit extreme. Going home seems like the safest option,' Tom said. It was a joke, but he knew it was also true. It had been a turbulent year. Everyone said he must take care. Balance was important.

'Probably. But clearly you're not going to do that.'

'What do you think? Like, really, what do you think?'

'Other than that I wish I'd never forced you to come to this party?'

'Come on, Annabel.'

She groaned. He was sure he heard her mutter 'for fuck's sake' under her breath.

'Really, I'm not sure it's a great idea,' she said. 'But I don't think you're going to listen to me. And, even though I don't think she'll like you—'

'Thanks.'

'Pleasure. As I was saying. Even though I don't think she'll like you, or vice versa, I'd prefer that you actually talk to her and prove me right than stand here staring while pretending to listen what I'm saying.' She took a long drink. 'Besides, her friend has gone for a fag.'

'And?'

'Your moment has arrived, Tom Murray.'

Tom watched the girl Esme had spent the last half-hour with make for the door, leaving her alone.

'Tom!' Annabel said.

'What? I've literally never approached someone at a party before.'

'And?'

'It's pretty high risk,' he said.

'So now I'm supposed to pep you up to do something I don't think you should be doing?'

'I didn't say that.'

'Well, if it helps, I'd say she's looked over at you at least half as many times as you have her. Though maybe that's because she thinks you're weird.'

'Really?' he said, disbelieving. Though he *had* caught her glance once or twice. 'No. It's daft. What are the odds that we'd hit it off?'

'As I said, incredibly low. One in a million.'

'A million what?'

'I've no fucking idea, Tom! Just bloody say hello or don't. It's driving me mad. I've told you what I think, but you don't care. You've been terrible company for most of the evening. So at this point I would honestly rather see you crash and burn than I would keep talking about what she *might* be like,' Annabel said. 'Look, that joke you told me earlier about the fancy-dress shoes? It was sort of funny. Use that.'

'*Sort of* funny?'

'Go,' she said, pushing his arm, which immediately attracted Esme's attention and forced his hand.

Tom felt as though he'd been shoved out onto a stage in front of a thousand people without a script to read from, caught under a single spotlight shining down on him. An expectant audience waiting for him to make them laugh.

But, really, there was only one person looking at him: the girl standing by herself in the corner of the kitchen. The one in plain clothes, just like him, with a kind look about her. Who, for all his better instincts and his friend's advice, Tom was unable to ignore or

14

look past. There were maybe four steps between the two of them, but to Tom it felt like an entire ocean.

Immediately aware that he was standing still in a sort of kitchen no man's land, on a patch of chipped linoleum between Esme and Annabel, Tom gathered himself. With all the nonchalance he could muster, he took a sip of his drink and ran his fingers through his messy hair.

Then, after almost three hours of circling, Tom finally made his approach.

'Hi,' he said.

'Hello,' she said.

'It's Esme, right?'

'Right. And you're Tom?'

'Yes.'

'Nice to meet you,' Esme said. At which, and for no reason he could understand, Tom reached out, grasped, and awkwardly shook her hand. She looked surprised.

'Oh. Very formal.'

'Sorry.'

'It's fine,' she said, as Tom began to notice some little things about Esme. The way her mouth relaxed into something that wasn't quite a smile, nor neutral. That she spoke well, every consonant and vowel there to be heard. How her glasses made her look slightly lopsided, because one of her eyebrows was almost imperceptibly higher than the other. He wondered if she was seeing the same in him. His unshaved face, the little turmeric stain on the collar of his shirt, or the red mark of a spot that he'd tried to cover up by rearranging his fringe.

'Oh, thanks, by the way,' Tom said, attempting a rescue.

'For what?'

'Not wearing fancy dress. I thought I'd be the only one.'

'What do you mean?' she said. 'I'm Lois Lane.'

'Oh . . . ?' Tom stuttered, his internal monologue a litany of swearwords directed at Annabel for allowing him to go over. 'Fuck. Sorry. I'm not too up on these superhero things.'

'And I'm taking the piss,' she said, smiling to herself and looking around the room at the various superheroes and infamous characters from stage and screen.

Tom allowed himself a laugh. Though he wondered if this was Esme signalling that she wasn't interested. Kindly batting him away before she had to make her feelings explicit and embarrass him. He looked round for Annabel. She was now being flirted at by a man in a Teenage Mutant Ninja Turtles costume, who would soon enough discover that she was gay and make some half-arsed excuse to stop talking to her.

But that smile. In itself a reason to say something else, to try to hold Esme's attention for a little while longer.

'Have you noticed it's always the shoes that let the costumes down with fancy dress? Like, over there you've got Spiderman. And it all looks good. Until you see that he's wearing a pair of black loafers.'

Esme chuckled, told him he was right, and his heart lifted a little. Tom tried to stop collating a mental list of all the possible reasons why Esme would want nothing to do with him. To the point that even as she gamely continued his joke by pointing out a Wonder Woman in court shoes and an Iron Man wearing desert boots, he was wondering if this – tonight – would be it. That they'd share a few laughs at a party and then go their separate ways.

He needed her to take charge. To ask something or give him the tiniest bit of confidence that there could be a spark. But the superhero-shoe joke gently died, and the uncomfortable silence of two strangers with nothing to say to each other began to surround them.

'So, you're Tom Murray then?' she said, to his relief. Though he might have imagined it, Tom was sure that there was a hopeful tone to her voice. 'Ali's friend from back home?'

'I am.'

'The musician?'

'Well. Sort of. I play a bit, compose a bit.'

'Compose?'

'Nothing exciting. I'd like to get into making film scores.'

'Oh wow,' she said and for a moment Tom wondered if she'd misheard and thought that he actually did write film scores.

'But mostly I teach and play in covers bands,' he said. 'It's a bit shit, really.'

'So, you can play a load of instruments?' she said.

'No. But I have a very clever keyboard that can.'

Esme laughed and Tom felt that lift again, levelling up in this ridiculous game they were playing.

'Do you want another drink?' he said. 'I think there's still a few in the oven-fridge thing.'

'I would. But I was just about to leave. Work tomorrow,' she said, looking over to the ad agency coke heads who had turned on one another with accusations of unfair consumption and withholding stash. 'Besides, this party looks like it's dying out. Or kicking off. Either way . . .'

And just as quickly as he had been up, Tom felt everything drop. Despite the promise of the last few minutes, Annabel may have been right. Really the only thing they had in common was a lack of fancy dress. It wasn't exactly enough to carry them through an awkward first date, let alone a relationship.

'Oh right. Yeah. You're probably right. Another time maybe,' Tom said, disheartened and anticipating the silence again. The reminder that they were still strangers.

'Sure.'

'Huh?'

'Another time.'

'Sorry, I—'

'Maybe we could do a drink another time.'

'Yeah ... I mean ... sure,' he said, surprised and tripping over syllables as well as words. While Esme took her coat from a hanger on the kitchen door and made herself ready to leave into the cool summer night.

'So you are actually going now then?' he asked.

'I am.'

'It wasn't, like, an excuse then. Not to talk to me.'

'No. I really am going. Unless you can give me a brilliant reason to stay, that makes it worth being so tired tomorrow that I'll end up having to finish all my work on Sunday?'

'Well, that photographer on the roof is still kicking about.'

'Nice try.'

Tom caught Annabel's eye; she was observing him with the worry and hope of a parent dropping their toddler off for its first day at school. 'Fine,' she mouthed at him.

'I think your friend wants you to leave too,' Esme said.

'Oh yeah?' he said, feigning confusion while making a mental note to send Annabel an arsey text when he got home. He was worried. Having had this whole exchange go more or less exactly as he had wanted it to, he was panicked and felt out of his depth. It was classic Tom Murray behaviour. He had no idea how he continued to surprise himself.

And now there was Esme, standing right in front of him, wearing a red trench coat and a thin, light grey scarf. She looked somehow expectant.

'Where do you live then, Tom Murray?' she said, buttoning herself up.

'Camden. Near the locks.'

'Right. Well I'm in Pimlico. And I'd say that's on the way, wouldn't you?'

'Well, sort of. I mean not entirely ...'

'Good,' she interrupted. 'You can walk me home then.'

With that, she led him out of the party, past a drunk Wolverine kissing an equally drunk Catwoman on the stairs, and out onto St Martin's Road in Stockwell. Where, at 2.59 a.m. precisely, Tom felt their arms brush together, the tips of her fingers lightly touching his, then, eventually, the wonderful feeling of Esme taking his hand for the first time.

## CHAPTER TWO

**7 – 8 am**

# OUR FIRST DATE OR SECOND?
## June 2007 – Pimlico, London

The feeling of her bare thigh against his made Tom jolt.

'Morning.' Esme reached across his chest to hold him.

'Morning,' he said, shaking off the momentary confusion about where on earth he was, and scrambling to recall the unlikely series of events that had brought him to Pimlico. Tom was suddenly hyper-aware of their proximity – the light, soft hair on his chest pressed down by her arm. He never knew what to say in this kind of situation. What could he? He had woken up next to women before, but past experience suddenly seemed useless to him. 'You alright?' he said.

'Bit tired.'

Esme yawned, one side of her mouth stretching a little further up her face than the other, Elvis Presley like.

'You've only just woken up.'

'I didn't really sleep.'

'Shit. I didn't snore, did I? No one's ever told me that I snore,' Tom said, realising that he should clarify. 'Not that there are many to . . . well, you know.'

'No, it's fine. It's not you, it's me.'

'Little early for that, isn't it?'

Esme whacked him playfully on the arm. 'I mean that it's *me* who has the problem with sleeping. I struggle if there's someone new in the bed,' she said. 'Not that it happens... well... often.'

'Of *course*.'

'Tom!'

'I didn't say a word.'

'Well, I don't. This is... a rare occurrence, shall we say?'

'If you like.'

'I just mean that every time I've had a new boyfriend or... partner,' she said, prudishly, 'I can't sleep for the first two or three times – *nights*.'

Esme moved away from him a fraction, across the bed and back onto her own red-and-white striped pillow, which clashed with the yellow bed sheets. He thought back to last night, when they'd stepped into her bedroom for the first time and she'd told him to 'ignore the mess' despite there not being any. At least not compared with his own studio apartment, which was permanently strewn with clothes, bags, instruments and discarded pizza boxes. If his flat wasn't so high up he would almost certainly have a mouse problem.

Tom felt odd the instant they were no longer touching. Flat, even. As if any distance between them was suddenly and immediately unbearable. He wondered if she felt it too. But it was a sentiment that, if expressed, might make him seem more weird and clingy than hopelessly romantic and spontaneous.

'So what,' Tom said. 'You've just been lying there, awake?'

'And thinking,' she said, a little coy.

'There's no way I'm playing the pathetic "what are you thinking" game, Esme.'

'Oh God, neither am I.'

'But...' Tom said, after a moment. 'What *are you* thinking?'

'Ha! I knew it.'

22

'Fine. I'm everything I've come to hate,' Tom said, waiting a moment before turning back to her. 'Well?'

'If you must know, I was thinking about ground rules.'

'Rules? Because of what happened last night?' Tom said. He was referring to the moment Esme's flatmate had found him in the kitchen wearing only his underwear. She had turned the lights on, screamed, and inadvertently summoned an upstairs neighbour who fancied himself as a bit of a hero. Albeit armed with a cricket bat rather than a utility belt.

'No. For, like, *this*.'

'Ohhh.'

'What?'

'I thought you meant rules for your flat.'

'No. And again, sorry about my housemate.'

'I was only getting a glass of water.'

'It was my fault. I should have texted to let her know I was having... company.'

'Is that what you call it?'

'Tom. I said no jokes about... that. I don't make a habit of doing this. As in, like, *never*.'

'Well, that does make me feel very special.'

'It should,' Esme said, the jokiness suddenly gone and replaced by sincerity, as she took hold of his hand beneath the duvet. It put him in mind of the first time it happened, the other night after the party. Now it felt familiar. As though these hands were always meant to link.

Tom shifted his head on the pillow. He was on the right side of the bed, the side Esme never slept on because it was 'too close to the wall'. The pillow was plump and barely used, there for decoration and symmetry rather than function.

'Anyway,' he said. 'These rules of yours.'

'Ah yes. Okay, so, these are basically things that should govern our relationship. From day one until, well ... day whenever.'

'Relationship?' he said, smiling.

'Exactly. And that's rule one. No asking if we're together, when it should be perfectly clear if we are,' she said, pausing for a second. 'Assuming that you want to?'

'I do,' Tom said. And just like that, there they were: an item. It was as if a wand had been waved – although to Tom the process felt a tad more administrative than that. Every one of his ill-fated relationships had been preceded by weeks of preamble and uncertainty; questions over whether or not sex meant partnership; second-guessing if the connection was strong enough to be labelled with something other than the vague headers of 'seeing each other' or 'dating'. Before eventually being defined by a conversation about exclusivity that always implied a lack of other, better options. Tom had once suggested to a girl that he might 'change my relationship status on Facebook', rather than actually asking outright if they were together.

'I hate not knowing where I am with things,' Esme said, by way of explanation. 'I always think it's easier just to put a name on it. Then in three weeks, if it turns out it's all wrong, it can change.'

'You have a confusingly optimistic and pessimistic way of looking at things.'

'I like to think so. Glass half full *and* half empty.'

'Do we have to arrange a check-in at three weeks? Like a proba-tion period or something.'

'Trust me, you'll know if we do.'

Tom laughed and said, 'So what about rule two.'

'It's a big one.'

'Okay,' Tom said warily.

'Rule two is that you have to – *have to* – accept that when I'm working I'm working. I've been with two men who constantly

24

arranged things or told me I was boring for catching up on the weekends. One of whom was a trust-fund idiot who never understood the idea of working and *really* didn't get that if I skipped or rushed it might literally affect how some poor kid communicates.'

'How long did that last?'

'One month.'

'What about the other one?'

'That was Matt.'

'Angry Matt?'

'I hate that people call him that.'

'Well I've only met him twice. But it was pretty clear that he is quite an angry person. What did he do, anyway?'

'Oh, loads of things. He would come off tour and expect me to have all the time in the world. Once, he booked tickets to Alton Towers for a Friday afternoon when I had three therapy sessions back to back. Then turned up at a school to pick me up. I think that was when I realised it wasn't going to work.'

'And did that make him . . .'

'Shut up,' Esme said, with a smile. 'Anyway, I care about my job so that's that. And I'm starting on my paperwork at nine today, so you'll have to bugger off before then.'

'That's fine. I like that you love your job,' Tom said, trying to remember exactly what it was that she did. Something to do with kids, he knew that much.

'It's also that I'm still learning,' Esme said. 'I think you always are when you work with people. Especially children.'

'I bloody hate teaching kids.'

'Tom!'

'Every week, I sit through an hour of a nine-year-old boy trying to play "Merrily We Roll Along" on the piano. He never gets any better. Never gets any worse. Every. Bloody. Week.'

'That does sound awful.'

'It is.'

'Though maybe it's the teacher's fault?'

'Oi.'

'Anyway. I don't *teach*, as such.'

'No . . . of course.'

'You've forgotten. Haven't you?'

'Child psychologist?' Tom said hopefully.

'You're not a million miles off.'

'Psychiatrist?'

'Speech therapist,' Esme said. Right away Tom remembered her telling him. He felt bad that it had slipped his mind and he started to think about other things he might've forgotten. Her middle name for sure.

'I look at why a child might struggle with language, or can't talk at all,' Esme continued. 'I work with a lot of autistic children, and kids with learning difficulties. Sometimes it's really sad. Especially to see the parents. But mostly it's just uplifting and nice.'

Tom shuffled closer to her. The overpowering vanilla and thyme scent of the diffuser on the bedside table was stronger on her side of the bed.

'How'd you get into it, anyway? Kids' speech and all that.'

'I did English Language at uni and always found the way words develop the most interesting thing about it. Then an MA in early years speech development and things went from there. Got my first job at St Bart's.'

'But now you work in a school?'

'Some school stuff. Some NHS. It's bits and pieces, really.'

'It sounds amazing,' Tom said. 'And important. Unlike being say, a guitarist in a pub band.'

Esme laughed.

'You're making a difference in your own way I'm sure.'

'I like to think so,' Tom said. 'So you're not, like, a doctor then?'

'Just a therapist.'

'Cool,' Tom said, a little distracted, his own history with therapists suddenly front of mind – the small rooms he had been in; plush offices with plump sofas in unassuming urban townhouses. And the more functional, plasticky NHS rooms, their walls plastered with peeling posters raising awareness of flu jabs, meningitis, asthma.

'You alright?' Esme asked, noticing his sudden blankness.

'Fine. So what's rule number three then?'

'Eeerm.'

'Are you making these up as you go along?'

'Not at all!' Esme said, in such a way that it was impossible to completely believe her. 'Rule three is that I hate – no, *despise* – words like *holibobs*, *nom*, *foodie*. Basically any word or saying that might appear on the side of a fruit smoothie bottle. Use them and we'll have problems.'

'I've never even heard of most of them.'

'I keep a list of them on the fridge. Laura adds some she hates, too.'

'Seriously?' Tom pictured an A4 piece of paper with these words scribbled angrily out in red pen.

'Absolutely. There's a place in hell reserved for people who use those words.'

'Bloody hell,' Tom said.

'You mean to tell me that there are no words that literally make you want to kill someone?'

'No. I mean, there are words I dislike.'

'Like what?'

'I don't know. Can't think of any.'

'Well think harder then.'

'Fine,' he said, half thinking of something. 'Okay. I don't like it when people say things like "it's wine o'clock".'

'Urgh.'

'But I wouldn't necessarily *hate* someone if they did.'

'You'd be entitled to. Awful. Consider it on the fridge.'

'I'm honoured. Can I ask where this aversion to certain types of word came from?'

'There's a woman I work with who uses them all the time. Angie. She makes me grind my teeth.'

'I've never heard of her either,' Tom said, picturing a slightly overweight woman wearing boot-cut jeans and a slogan T-shirt.

'That's probably for the best,' Esme said.

Tom laughed. As he did a shard of sunlight crept through the gap between where a grey curtain met a magnolia wall, lighting up the varnished oak floorboards and Esme's slightly tatty, blue and white striped rug, onto which was dropped Tom's jeans from the night before. The sight reiterated the unusual nature of this situation. He was not the kind of person to often wake up in a stranger's bed. And he knew that Esme was the same, as she had been at pains to point out. So was this, he wondered, a collective, excited impulsiveness? Or was it what they both really thought and hoped it was? They would come to know the answer soon, he thought, as Esme stretched and reorganised the Glastonbury 2005 T-shirt that constituted pyjamas.

'Now,' she said, looking up at him. Her brown eyes locked on his and he knew he would find that comforting and wonderful every time it happened. 'Rule four is a serious one.'

'*Serious* serious? Or are you winding me up?'

'*Serious* serious,' she said, sitting up in bed. As if to say it was impossible to have a proper conversation about something like this while lying down and staring wide-eyed at each other.

'Okay.'

'I don't want to get into full histories, big issues and where they come from right away. But you should know that I *hate* lying and I can't forgive cheating. Like ever. I know some people can get over that stuff. But for me it's non-negotiable.'

'Right.'

'Not saying you will, obviously. But I'm just putting it out there. That kind of thing sort of fucked up my family.'

'I'm sorry.'

'It's fine. It was a long time ago. These things just have a way of lingering, don't they?'

'I suppose they do,' Tom said, unsure of what to say next and letting a brief silence descend until Esme took over again.

'I've always thought that if you talk about things before they become a big problem you can work your way out of them. Whatever it is. Unless the thing is that you're a career criminal or something.'

'Well, about that . . .'

'Seriously? You know I could see something in your eyes.'

'Two years for armed robbery.'

'Damn.'

'Well it's been nice while it lasted,' Tom said, pretending to climb out of bed, before Esme grabbed his arm and he fell back in next to her.

'My point is,' she said, clearly keen to return to the topic. 'I've always known that I couldn't live with it if that kind of thing happened to me.'

Tom nodded. He wanted to tell her it wouldn't be a problem. But he didn't. Instead he kissed her – a tacit okay if not an implicit one. As soon as they parted, Esme started again.

'Which sort of brings me onto the next thing.'

'Oh?'

'Marriage,' she said.

'This isn't like the relationship thing, is it? You're not going to tell me that we're engaged because we had sex and you're in some mad Christian cult.'

'Not really. The opposite in fact,' Esme said, looking down at the duvet, refusing to meet his eyes. 'It's maybe daft to say it, but I want you to know that I never want to get married.'

'Never?'

'Never. And I mean it, Tom. I'm not one of those "never until he asks me" types. I'm a never never type. And I know it's early to bring it up. But some men get really dickish about it when they find out.'

'Well,' Tom said, a little surprised that the topic had come up. More so at why. 'You will be pleased to learn that I am not that man.'

'You don't mind?'

'I sort of don't care. I've never really thought about marriage and long-term stuff like that,' he said, knowing in himself that there were a number of reasons behind that.

'Good,' Esme said, seeming to relax. 'It's good that you don't care. Because I really do. If not in the way most people do.'

'Rule five,' Tom said, taking her hand. 'No marriage.'

'Good,' Esme said with a smile. 'By the way. What if I was in a mad Christian cult?'

'Oh. Well, I suppose I'd have to join up, wouldn't I?'

Esme laughed and said, 'So romantic.' And as they fell into a contented silence, Tom found himself thinking back to how they got here.

They had spent the day before in St James's Park, arranging to meet at two in the afternoon, having parted on her doorstep only eleven hours earlier. He bought them coffees and ice creams as they circled the ponds and sat on benches overlooking the pelicans, ducks and geese.

Later, she went with him to the gig he was playing in a dodgy Kentish Town pub called the Goat and Boot with a covers band called Top Gunz. He spent their entire set looking out to the back of the room, where she was sat at a tall table, watching the drunks dancing in front of her to 'Chelsea Dagger' and 'I Predict a Riot', which the singer belted out with gusto, and the band utter indifference.

After that, he had expected that he would return home for another sleepless night thinking about when he would next see Esme. But, to his surprise, she suggested they take a cab to hers, where they sneaked quietly into her room, fell onto her bed and, with all the clumsiness and hesitance of teenagers, undressed each other in the half-glow of orange street light which pierced the tatty curtains. The sex was nervous and uncertain. The second attempt, half an hour later, was informed by the mistakes of the first time, and all the better for it.

Everything was moving fast. The kind of fast that Tom had told himself he wouldn't allow to happen that year. The kind that other people had told him he shouldn't allow to happen that year.

But what if this was normal now? What if he had found Esme at just the right time in his life, and she had found him at just the right time in hers? Tom hadn't felt as excited and hopeful as he did that morning in years. Having spent a long time scrambling to find a life that worked for him, perhaps he had finally succeeded.

Now, with their early-morning pillow talk lulled, Tom considered telling her a few things about himself. Stuff she should know. Had a right to. But, he thought, what would be the sense in spoiling the mood? They were happy now. *He* was happy now. Besides, they had time. Plenty of it, if they stayed on this course. There would be a moment for all his stuff, and it wasn't just yet.

'Okay. No more serious,' Esme said, speaking up and settling the debate for him. 'Do you want to know about rule six?'

'Depends on how many more there are.'

'Last one, promise. But probably the most important,' she said. 'Rule six is that whenever we're staying together, you have to get up first to make the tea. I like mine medium-strong. The colour of a Caramac bar.'

'Hang on,' Tom said. 'What if my rule number one was that *you* always have to make the tea?'

'Well, it clearly wasn't. And even if it was, I got there first. So that's that.'

'Right. So am I to understand that if we're together for, say, fifty years, I have to make you tea every single morning.'

'Yes. Although I'd hope that by the time I'm in my mid-seventies someone will have invented some sort of home-help robot.'

'What if I've got a broken leg?'

'You'd have to buy a Teasmade. Or keep a travel kettle and some little sachets of milk by the bed. Anyway, have you got a broken leg?'

'No.'

'And clearly you already know where the kitchen is. So . . .'

'Now? Literally on my first morning in your flat?'

Esme nodded. She had a playful look about her. 'Tea bags are in the cupboard next to the boiler. Milk in the fridge. Use the posh mugs on the tree, though not the one that says *Darling Daughter*. Laura will probably go and borrow that cricket bat if you do. Oh, and put some clothes on,' she said as Tom climbed out of her bed, feeling the chill of the draughty flat.

Tom picked his jeans up off the rug and found his shirt under a chair piled with clothes and books. He put them on and looked back at Esme, who was now sitting up in the bed. The antique brass alarm clock on her bedside table showed 7.45.

'Very sexy,' she said, while he looked in the mirror and pushed his messy brown hair around until it looked vaguely presentable. 'Though I'm not sure who you're hoping to meet between here and the kitchen.'

'It gets all tangled,' he said, defending his vanity. 'Also, I never got to tell you my rules.'

'Do you have any?'

'Not as such,' he said, about to open the bedroom door. 'But I do have a question.'

'As long as it's not about the relationship thing. I know it's fast. But I just—'

'No. It's not about that. I'm happy with the ... *relationship* thing,' he said.

'Good. Then I grant you your question, Tom Murray.'

'Okay. So we met on Friday.'

'Yes.'

'Or Saturday morning, really.'

'I suppose.'

'And we hung out yesterday. Then ... well ... you know.'

'I do.'

'So. Is this our first date, or our second?'

'Good question. What do you think?'

'No,' Tom said. 'I'm asking you.'

'Fine. Well I'd like to say second. Because, you know ... First date and all that,' she said, motioning to the bed around her. 'But I don't know. We can decide when you're back with my cup of tea.'

Alone in her kitchen, Tom allowed himself to drift back over the past day and a half again: from the moment he approached Esme at Ali's party, to now, and everything in between. The unlikely, the surprising, the wonderful. He reminded himself to text Annabel later to explain in no uncertain terms just how wrong she was. She'd disapprove, of course. But then she didn't know what it was like.

The boiled kettle clicked as the front door slammed shut. Footsteps creaked down the corridor, and quite soon he was no longer alone in the kitchen.

'Oh. You again.'

It was the blonde girl he had met in the early hours of the morning. This time she was wearing running leggings and a vest, carrying a copy of the *Sunday Telegraph* under her arm. Laura. Esme had told him about her yesterday. She was a junior political reporter who, according to Esme, was a 'complete and utter Tory' and based her style on Samantha Cameron. Despite all that, Esme assured him, she was lovely.

'Morning,' Tom said brightly, lifting tea bags from the mugs and holding them in a spoon.

'Bin's in the cupboard under the sink.'

'Ah. Thanks.'

'I see she's got you making tea already.'

Tom smiled and said, 'Laura, isn't it?'

'It is.'

'Tom.'

'Nice to meet you again, Tom. And sorry about all that last night.'

'It's fine.'

'We don't have many gentleman callers, you see,' she said, apparently trying to break the tension with deliberate over-formality.

'Honestly, it's fine,' Tom said, thinking back to the last time someone had stayed at his. January, after a gig date at the Hope and Anchor in Islington, during Tom's ill-conceived three months on *Guardian* Soulmates. The next morning was, at the very best, awkward and quiet.

'Can I make you anything?' he asked, shaking Julie (or was it Julia?) out of his head.

'No. I'll sort myself out.'

She took a tin of expensive-looking coffee with 'LAURA ONLY' written in marker pen across the front, and cleaned out the filter of an espresso machine.

'You're the fancy-dress party guy then?' she asked. 'She texted me about you.'

'I suppose.'

'And is this the second date or first? Or shouldn't I ask?'

'Actually we were just discussing that. Undecided so far.'

'Well, either way it must have gone well,' she said, tamping down her coffee. 'If I know Esme, anyway.'

'I guess so,' Tom said, picking up the two mugs of tea, hoping that he'd made hers right. He was about to go back to Esme when Laura said his name.

'Yes?'

'Listen, I've never done this before and I'm not the sort of person to ... well ... go around telling people what to do,' she said, completely dishonestly if her reputation as a journalist was anything to go by. 'But I just wanted to tell you to be nice to her. Esme is kind and giving and clever. And if you're good to her, she'll be the best friend you ever make,' Laura said, glaring now. 'Trust one who knows. Okay?'

Tom nodded.

'Good,' Laura said abruptly, taking her breakfast to the flimsy dining table set up at the end of their small, all-white galley kitchen. 'I suppose I'll see you around.'

Back in the bedroom, Esme had opened the curtains, throwing light onto the Lichtenstein print behind her bed, the grey and slightly stained rental-flat carpet, and her pine chest of drawers, piled with a laptop, more books and an overly loaded jewellery tree. In the corner of the long, narrow room was his guitar, leant precariously against a wardrobe to which only one door was fully attached. Her full-length mirror was obscured by the green floral dress she wore yesterday, hung up before they went to sleep.

The window was open slightly. Tom could hear the muffled coos of London pigeons which sporadically settled on Esme's windowsill, and the nearby hum of traffic from the Vauxhall Bridge Road. The sun was shining, its rays beaming across the rooftops of the white stucco and yellow brick townhouses of Pimlico. The tops of the trees outside swayed gently in the breeze. It was a perfect day.

Esme was sitting up in bed now, grinning. Tom sat down next to her and passed her a mug. She pulled his face near with both hands and kissed his lips.

'Happy?' she asked.

'Happy,' he said, sitting against the bedhead and taking a sip of the slightly too hot tea.

'That took a while.'

'I met Laura again.'

'Oh God. She didn't say anything, did she?'

'No,' Tom lied. 'Nothing. We were just chatting.'

'No one chats with Laura. They get *told* things and occasionally, if she's in the mood, they get to tell her something. But that's pretty rare.'

'It was fine. Honest.'

'And did you decide?'

'Oh. The date thing. First, I think. Really to call it a second there'd have to be a day or so in between.'

'So those eleven hours were, like, an interval?'

'Exactly.'

'In a thirty-six-hour first date.'

'Yes.'

'Well, that's fine with me.'

'Good,' Tom said. He passed Esme her tea and looked into her eyes. He had never really believed that it was possible for his life to change so quickly. But then he had never expected to meet Esme Simon at half past two in the morning, at a party in Stockwell that was winding down around them. He'd never expected to walk her home through south London and across the Thames. He'd never imagined that she would want to meet him again later that day. Of all the things he hadn't expected, at the very top of the list was waking up in Esme's bed on a bright day in late June, knowing so clearly and so absolutely that he was in love with her.

'But I do have one question,' Esme said.

'Go for it.'

'What will that mean for anniversaries? Do they stretch across a day, or two days, or—'

'Let's worry about that next year, shall we?'

'Okay,' Esme said, and shuffled closer to Tom. 'We've got plenty of time, haven't we?'

THE BEST VERSION OF MYSELF

October 2007 – Hampstead, London

# CHAPTER THREE

9 – 10 pm

# THE BEST VERSION OF MYSELF
## October 2007 – Hampstead, London

'Right. Nine o'clock exactly,' Neil said, looking at his digital watch. 'Where is she?'

'She'll be here.'

'Well, it's been half an hour. We're beginning to wonder if this brilliant girlfriend of yours actually exists.'

'Fuck off, Neil,' Tom said.

'Annie, you've met her, right?'

'Yeah. Couple of times.'

'A couple?'

'Before she was with Tom,' Annabel said, taking a sip of her Guinness and black.

'Hmm,' Neil said, theatrically stroking his chin. 'So it's entirely possible that Tom saw this girl at a party, fancied her, and decided to lie about her being his new bit.'

'Bit?' Padraig – or Pod, as they called him – said.

'Slang term, isn't it? For girlfriend.'

'No. Or at least not to my knowledge. How long have you been saying it?'

'Dunno.'

'You mean all this time you've been calling various partners of friends and colleagues "bits" while everyone looks at you like you've gone mad.'

'Maybe I am mad?' Neil said, picking a flower out of the jar in the middle of the table and positioning it in his hair.

'You're a dickhead. Not quite the same as being mad,' Annabel said, silencing Neil for all of two seconds before he started up again, like a spoilt child after more attention.

'Anyway. You do have to admit that my theory has some weight to it. Murray here meets the girl of his dreams, concocts a relationship and invites us all to meet her at some posh Hampstead boozer, never thinking that we'll say yes. And in about ten minutes he's going to pretend he's had a text saying she can't come. Stuck at work. The lab has exploded or something.'

'She doesn't work in a lab, Neil. She works at a hospital and at a school,' Tom said wearily, thinking back to his school days and Neil's remorseless winding up, hazing and piss-taking; the time spent in a headlock with his knuckles rubbing his skull as he forced Tom to admit to ridiculous things like how he fancied the headmaster, had no balls or was gay – the last of which stopping only when, at fourteen, Annabel confided in the two of them that she was 'bisexual, at the very least' and Neil became the only British schoolboy in the mid-nineties to take a fierce stand against homophobic put-downs.

'Same difference.'

'What?' Tom scoffed.

'Lab. Hospital. Same difference. Science. White coats.'

'And the school?' Pod said.

'Don't be pedantic.'

'You know,' Tom said. 'Sometimes I wonder if the only reason we're still friends is that we're the only people from our school year to have moved to London.'

'You could hang out with Ben Merriweather if you're looking for other Lowie Londoners,' Neil said, reprising the term he had daubed them with years ago when they moved from Lowestoft to the capital. Neil was the first to arrive in the city, to take a job on a graduate scheme for a bank. Followed shortly by Annabel, who had fallen out with her parents. Then, finally, a couple of years later, and for very different reasons from the other two, Tom himself.

He thought about saying something back but decided against it. Neil was one of those people there was no point arguing with. He was always right and when he wasn't would make up facts to amend the truth in his favour.

'My point is that you drag us all here—'

'You live five minutes away, Neil.'

'I'd say Golders Green is more like ten minutes on the Tube. Fifteen on the bus. Anyway, Pod here has come all the way from Lowestoft. Just to meet this girl!'

'I was in London anyway,' Pod said, with a mix of innocence and bemusement. 'With work. I thought that's why we'd decided to meet this evening?'

'Just ignore him,' Annabel said.

'It's alright for you. You've already met her.'

'Whatever. Anyway. If Tom here had followed my advice, we'd not even be here. You could still be at home in Golders Green playing your stupid Xbox.'

'PS3, thank you very much.'

'Whatever, gamer geek. I'm going out for a fag. Drives me fucking mad that you can't smoke in pubs anymore. Now all you can smell is the stale piss from the toilets,' she said, getting up from the table, as Tom looked at his phone again, wondering where Esme had got to, or if he had missed a text to say she couldn't make it.

But there were no more messages, just:

**Tom: How about the Rosslyn Arms? xx**

**Esme: Perfect. See you after Spanish xx**

Tom thought about another message. But he'd already sent too many:

**Are you okay? Xx**
**Anything up? Xx**

And a sort of casual yet desperate:

**Let me know if you can still make it xx**

What else was there to say?

Was Esme having second thoughts? They were just over three months in – perhaps the cooling-off period had begun? Tom had been here before; he knew the signs. Last week she'd cancelled a trip to the cinema at the last minute. In return he had told her he couldn't stay over on the weekend after a gig. Now this.

'What did she mean by that?' Neil asked, when Annabel had gone. 'About her advice.'

'Oh,' Tom said. He didn't want to tell them, but knew that if he didn't, Annabel would. 'She sort of told me not to get involved. With Esme, I mean. Because of what happened.'

'Why? Is Esme—'

'No. It's nothing to do with her. More to do with me. Annabel thought it might be too soon.'

'But you're alright? With her, I mean. Esme,' Neil said. Tom had known him for so long that he could see the change in his demeanour, hear it even. Gone was the ribbing and joking. In its place an incongruous seriousness. This was how things went now.

'Fine, mate,' Tom said. 'Annabel was . . . just worried. You know? I don't know. Maybe she had a point.'

'What do you mean?'

'I mean maybe she was right. It was too soon and all that. I don't know. I've just been thinking.'

'Tom. Come on, mate. From everything you've said—'

'From everything I've said you lot think she's the bloody girl of my dreams.'

'And what's wrong with that?'

Tom thought for a second. There was absolutely nothing wrong with that. This new thing with Esme was incredible. From the first time they met there was an undeniable and unstoppable attraction that seemed to pull them together. Ever since then things had been pretty well perfect.

So where had all these doubts suddenly crept in from? Why had he made an excuse not to see her? Tom had done this before – chipped away at the foundation stones of a friendship or relationship enough for it to crumble. He didn't have to do anything big and dramatic to ruin things. He also didn't want to believe that he was doing it with Esme now, too.

'Nothing, I suppose,' Tom said finally. Neil went to speak again, but Tom interrupted him. 'It's just that a few months ago I was thinking of leaving London altogether. Starting fresh somewhere else.'

'Edinburgh?'

'Yeah. Or anywhere, really. Somewhere new. I wanted a clean break. I told Annabel—'

'We remember. You've made similar plans about fifty times,' Pod said.

'Fine. But this time they were more serious.'

'Really?' he said, disbelieving.

'Yes. I'd look at flats online and everything.'

'Mate. I look at flats online all the fucking time. It doesn't mean I'm going to move to these places.'

'The point is, I was going to get out. Now I'm still here and I'm with Esme, and I'm—'

'Happy?'

'I was going to say committed. But...'

'Fuck commitment for now. Are you happy, Tom? With Esme?'

Tom stopped for a moment and thought. The answer was obvious.

'Well, yeah. I am.'

'And you love her, right?'

Rather than answering, Tom nodded. In the almost twenty years they'd known each other, the subject of actual, proper love had never come up. Even when Neil was telling them about his plans to propose to his university girlfriend (they broke up three weeks after graduation).

'Okay. So what's the fucking problem?' Neil said, continuing with his liberal swearing. 'You're happy, you're in love, she loves you back. And here you are wondering if you made the wrong decision by staying in London instead of buggering off to the arse end of nowhere.'

'Neil. Edinburgh is not the arse end of nowhere.'

'You know what I mean. The point is, why the second thoughts?'

'Because it's me, isn't it? When am I ever properly sure about anything?'

'Literally never. But for once in your life it looks like you've made a genuinely good decision.'

Neil took a swig from his beer as Annabel took her seat back at the table, still exhaling her last mouthful of cigarette smoke with a sidelong glare at the barman, who she apparently blamed for the recent smoking ban.

'Still no sign then?' she said.

'Not yet. She'll be here,' Tom said, thinking that he'd perhaps been too casual about the evening. *Meeting some friends. Would be great if you could come along.* He hadn't made it sound like an actual plan.

'What are you talking about, anyway?'

'We were talking about Murray here, and this Esme. And how he should actually go for it instead of having second thoughts about the whole thing.'

'I'm not having—'

'Seriously?' Annabel said.

'I'm not.'

'Tom.'

'It's fine,' he said, taking a sip from his Diet Coke and staring down at the light cast by the candle across the stained wooden table.

'He said you might've had a point. That it was too soon.'

'I think I did have a point.'

'And I disagree,' Neil said. 'This is the happiest he's been in bloody ages. Why not just go for it?'

'Fine. If that's what you think,' Annabel said. 'But I'll still worry that it's too soon.'

'I am still here, you know,' Tom said.

'Okay,' Annabel said firmly. 'One question. Does she know yet?'

As soon as she said it, Tom fell silent. Instead of answering immediately, he started going back through the moments he could've said something but had chosen not to. Most recently at the reverse fixture of this evening: meeting her friends for a Thai meal in Soho.

That time Tom had been late. Which was bad because, unlike everyone else at the table, he had absolutely no excuse to be, having worked at home for most of the day (save for an hour-long lesson in the plush living room of a wealthy Primrose Hill family, who had bought their uninterested son a guitar Tom could only dream of being able to afford).

When he eventually arrived at the restaurant, Esme and her friends were sat around the table, already deep in conversation. For a moment he waited in the doorway, watching them while they couldn't see him. In the rush to get ready, Tom had masked his nervousness about doing this. The whole thing felt very adult. Something real people without big problems in their lives did. He wasn't sure if he was cut out for that kind of thing; if it was for him.

Tom collected himself and started towards the table. He hit pause on his iPod in time to hear a high-pitched voice call, 'Here he is!'

'Cara,' Esme said, like a school teacher admonishing a child. 'Give him a minute.'

'How'd you even know what he looks like?' the man next to Cara asked.

'Facebook,' she said, at which everyone else groaned. 'What? Everyone does it. I bet you all bloody have.'

'Absolutely not!' another girl said. She was wearing Thai fisherman's trousers and had braided hair. Tom guessed that this was Philly, who Esme mentioned had recently returned from a year travelling around South East Asia and was taking her time getting over it (and herself).

'Come on,' Cara said, and the group lapsed into lightly argumentative chatter about the rights and wrongs of Facebook stalking (as well as who'd done it). Tom was relieved that their attention had been diverted. He looked over at Esme on the far side of the table. Perhaps sensing his discomfort, she got up, took him by the arm and led him to their seats.

'Sorry I'm late, Es,' he whispered as they took their place, watched by her friends like they were bride and groom entering their wedding reception. 'It sounds ridiculous but I had literally no idea what to wear.'

'You only have three shirts.'

'Exactly. I didn't know which one of the three to wear.'

'You look great,' she said, holding his hand. 'You always look great.'

Esme went around the table so that Tom could meet each of her closest friends and their partners one by one, which was fine except that by the time he was introduced to friend Y he had already forgotten friend X's name.

Of the eight, those he remembered were the ones that appeared most frequently in Esme's stories and anecdotes. Laura, her flatmate, he already knew. Then there was Jam, short for Jamilla – a half-Kenyan girl Esme had met at university.

'Jam likes to live in places that are about to be gentrified so she can complain about gentrification when it happens. While still enjoying her nice coffee and freshly baked bread,' was Esme's unsparingly honest description of one of her closest friends.

And Martin, Esme's best male friend, who Tom was pleased to discover was an overweight man with long, dank hair, who chose to wear walking boots, cargo trousers and a Simpsons T-shirt to a nice restaurant.

The first direct question came just as he poured himself a glass of water from a bottle so heavy he almost dropped it.

'So what part of Camden is it you live in, Tom?' Jamilla said.

'Near the lock. It's a studio. Not much, really.'

'I know someone who lives near there. Says it's nice but touristy.'

'That's about right. Though I don't go out much during the day so I can pretty much avoid the day trippers.'

'How long have you been in London?'

'Nearly four years. I'm originally from Lowestoft.'

'Is that in Wales?' a voice asked from the end of the table. Tom was about to answer when Martin fielded the question for him, with the wearisome, patronising voice Tom would go on to learn he used for everything and everyone.

'East, Philly. By the coast.'

'Wales *is* by the coast,' came the reply.

'And Esme says you're a musician?' Jamilla said, pulling Tom's attention back towards her.

'Yeah. That sounds pretty cool,' another girl, either Sophie, Chloe or Siobhan, added.

'It probably sounds cooler than it is. Mostly I teach.'

'So you're a music teacher?' she said.

'Well, sort of,' he said. 'I do a bit for the school near me. Lessons and that sort of thing. But I'm not, like, a *teacher* teacher.'

'Oh,' the girl said, sounding slightly confused.

'Otherwise it's private stuff for rich kids, and I play in a couple of bands.'

'Any we've heard of?' Laura chimed in. As ever, her tone when asking questions was never quite kind. For a while, Tom thought this was something to do with him. But eventually he realised that she was completely unable to leave her day job behind. To the point that she could make the most innocuous question cause genuine panic in whoever she was talking to.

'Probably not,' Tom said, desperate to move the conversation away from himself, which he knew would be hard, given that the sole reason for the dinner was to meet and get to know him. 'A couple of wedding bands. Sometimes in the summer I fill in for an Oasis tribute act called Supersonic.'

'Fuck, I think I've seen them,' Cara interrupted. 'Some corporate do a couple of years ago. Are you Noel?'

'Nah, the other one. It probably wasn't me anyway. I only do a few gigs a year when one of the usual guys can't make it. The Noel and the Liam are pretty much the only ones who do every gig. They have the right haircuts.'

'No one knows who the others are anyway.'

'Exactly. It's easy work – I just have to wear a polo shirt and refuse to smile for an hour or so.'

The few who were listening to him laughed, which lifted Tom's confidence a little. But he was happy to hear another conversation quickly bubble up and begin to dominate the table, this time between Philly and Laura, who was silencing the gap-year stories with a diatribe about how she could never do the gap-year thing 'because of all the hostels'.

Eventually, just as Tom was beginning to settle into the evening, came the question he had been dreading. The one he knew how to answer, but always hated nonetheless. He had hoped that no one had noticed. But they were too polite for that. And so came the first time he would lie to this new group of potential friends.

'God. Sorry, Tom. I've just seen that you haven't been topped up. Red or white?' Jamilla said.

'Oh neither. Thanks.'

'I can get you a beer if you'd rather?' Martin said, holding up a bottle of Singha.

'No, it's fine. Thanks,' he said, nervously. 'I'm on these tablets. Can't drink with them. Just a Coke for me.'

'You know you *can* actually drink with most tablets,' Laura insisted. 'It's a common misconception. Doctors just tell you not to in case you throw them back up.'

'I'd rather not risk it. Coke's fine.'

Even as he said it, Tom was convinced that everyone had seen through him; certain his flimsy, clumsy, off-the-cuff excuse gave away the lie instantly. It was months, maybe even a year, since he'd last had to lie like that. He was out of practice. He tried to dry his clammy palms on his jeans and was about to escape to the bathrooms when Esme leant over and said, 'You didn't tell me you were on tablets.'

'I'm not,' he whispered back. 'It's easier than saying I don't drink. People think you're weird.'

'They don't,' Esme said. 'My friends are nice.'

'Please. I've had it before. As soon as you tell someone you don't drink they always ask something stupid like "How do you have fun then?" I just can't be bothered with it.'

'Okay,' Esme said, sensing the frustration in his voice and returning to a conversation with – or rather a rant from – Laura about the recent promotion of Gordon Brown to Prime Minister.

Tom, meanwhile, took a breath and settled himself, feeling that he'd got to the edge of something and just about managed to avoid falling off. And that was where he stayed for the rest of the evening – one minute the centre of attention, the next quietly observing others – until he and Esme left arm in arm at 10 p.m., turning down the offer from Jamilla to go on to a pub around the corner. At which point, he found himself back on the ledge again.

'That was alright, wasn't it?' Tom said, as they walked towards Tottenham Court Road Tube station.

'Fine, Tom.'

'And I came across well?' he said, asking himself as much as Esme.

'You were good. But this wasn't about you impressing my friends. It was about them impressing you.'

'I know. But they all know each other so well. I think that—'

'What was the drinking thing about?' she said abruptly.

'What drinking thing?'

'The tablets excuse. You're not on tablets. Why not just say that you don't drink?'

'I told you. People think—'

'But you haven't told me, have you?' Esme said, releasing his hand as they began to climb the grotty steps down to the Tube, stepping over trampled, sodden copies of the *Evening Standard*. 'All you've ever said is that you don't drink because you don't like the way it makes you feel.'

'Es.'

'Actually no. Once you told me it's that you don't like the taste of beer or wine. And if that's true, then fine. But last month you had a non-alcoholic lager thing. So I really don't know where I am with you on this.'

He said nothing. Instead he cursed himself for not being careful enough. This kind of thing required continuity.

'Why tell people you're on tablets, Tom?' she said. 'Why lie?'

He was about to answer when he saw the Tube train's lights illuminate the black hole of the tunnel. Seconds later came the rumble of carriages on rails, the ugly, piercing shriek of brakes, and the fuzzy voice of the announcer asking them to 'Stand clear of the doors, please, stand clear of the doors.' They were staying at his that night, heading north to Camden Town.

Tom was grateful for the interruption. The forced break in a conversation that was headed only one way. He gathered his thoughts as Esme got on the train ahead of him, finding two seats between a fat, sleeping man in a pin-striped suit and two young boys eating foul-smelling burritos from foil wrappers.

Esme sat down heavily, the weight of the day and the evening seeming to finally take its toll on her legs. He sat next to her, placing the battered brown leather satchel he took with him everywhere in the gap between his calves and the fan heater, blowing musty warm air into the carriage. As the doors slid shut, Tom said nothing, hoping that Esme would move on.

'No one thinks anything if someone doesn't want to drink,' she said, as the train pulled away. Her tone had softened. Gone was the exasperation, the vague anger and irritation. In its place a certain sympathy, a kindness and acceptance.

'I know,' Tom said.

'So why the tablets thing? Or the taste thing? If something happened you can tell me. We've all had bad experiences.'

'I know.'

'Tom, you have to give me something more than "I know".'

Before he answered, Tom hesitated. Here it was again. The old question of how much of himself to give? What to offer her? This time informed by the fact that he had to say *something*.

'It was,' he said.

'Was what?'

'A bad experience. A couple, really.'

'What, like throwing up? Blacking out?'

'Sort of... actually... well, both really,' he stammered. 'I mean, that kind of thing,' Tom said, his palms sweaty again, his heart swollen to the size of a basketball, pushing on his ribcage and throat.

'And that's what made you stop?'

'Yeah... I think so. It made me realise, you know? That it's... not for me.'

Esme said nothing when he finished speaking and they pulled into Euston. As if she was letting the words settle like thick snow on cold pavement. The few seconds of silence seemed to last hours. All the while Tom wondering if there'd be more questions, or if this was it.

'Okay,' Esme said quietly. She took his hand as she spoke. 'You know we've all been there?'

Tom nodded at this. He wanted to say that, no, we haven't all been there. Certainly she hadn't. His 'there' was an altogether different place from her drunk night out that ended with a friend holding her hair back as she threw up.

'And it's fine to decide that, Tom,' Esme continued. 'It really is.'

'I know,' he said. 'And I'm sorry, Es. I guess I think people might... judge.'

'And so what if they do? It's your life, your choice. I'm proud of you for not just doing what everyone else does. I love you for it.'

Esme leant over to kiss him. He kissed her back.

\*

'You can't be fucking serious, Tom,' Annabel said, almost slamming her pint glass down onto the table. She was angry. Tom knew she had the right to be.

'Annabel, I'm—'

'I really can't believe you sometimes.'

'Leave it, eh?' Neil said.

'It's not as if it was just a dose of the flu, Neil.'

'Look. If he doesn't want her to know at the moment, it's not up to us. He'll tell her when the time's right.'

'Neil.'

'Topic off-limits. Along with Murray's ex-girlfriends,' Neil said, as Tom checked his watch again, trying not to look worried.

'Oh, I was going to kick off with an ex-girlfriend story when she got here!' Pod said. 'Town-wide manhunt. Murray found in a compromising situation with the geography teacher's daughter when he should've been at his Saturday job.'

'Pod,' Tom said, sensing Annabel's annoyance growing.

'What? How about when you nicked that scarecrow, dressed it up and tried to sneak it into the nightclub as your date?' he said. 'Or when you almost got arrested for throwing a snowball at a police car.'

'None of it,' Tom said. 'I don't want her to think I'm—'

'A prick?' Neil said, which Tom ignored while the others laughed.

'I'm really pleased you two find this so funny,' Annabel said, sounding like a disapproving teacher.

'Could everyone just stop?' Tom said firmly. 'I don't want her thinking I'm someone . . . else. You know? An earlier version of myself. What you said earlier about making a go of it. I do want to. It's just I'm always a bit scared about myself, you know?'

His friends went quiet. They knew what he was referring to, the particular part of Tom that died that evening five years ago.

'I love her. She loves me. If things go right this *could* be amazing.'

The table went silent. The banter and jokes now gone.

'Fine, Tom. But you know deep down that *not* telling her isn't going to help things "go right". You have to realise that.'

'Annie, come on,' Neil repeated, jumping in to defend Tom.

'Do you think it's okay, honestly okay, that she doesn't know?'

'It's Tom's choice.'

'How long have you been together now?' she said, turning back to him.

'Almost four months.'

'And she knows none of it?'

'I said, she knows bits.'

'Bits.'

'Annabel.'

'I think it's wrong,' she said, as the door opened.

'Stop,' Tom said.

'No, Tom. If you're going to make this work I really—'

'I said *stop*,' he said firmly, and Annabel looked around. 'She's here,' he said.

## CHAPTER FOUR

8 – 9 am

# BUILDING A HOME TOGETHER
### April 2009 – Belsize Park, London

Tom had been awake for almost an hour already, shocked into consciousness by an explosion of glass which turned out to be the bin men emptying last night's bottles from the pub next door. Now he was in a terrible mood it was impossible to get back to sleep from, despite Esme next to him still snoozing soundly.

It wasn't as if he hadn't raised the possibility that this might happen.

'It's is a single-glazed maisonette, ten metres from the Essex Arms, Es,' he'd said eight weeks ago when they were on the bed in his tiny studio flat discussing what it would be like when they finally moved in together. 'And I'm a really light sleeper.'

'The agent said you can barely hear the pub at night.'

'How many nights do you think he's spent there?'

'Tom, please. It's nice. It's in Belsize Park. It's got that period charm I like.'

'Along with thin walls and a draught. Also, the communal hallway looks like a murderer's den.'

'You are impossible to please,' she said.

In fairness, Tom had presented an alternative: a two-bed at the bottom end of Finchley Road, with a window that looked out onto train tracks popular with both rats and the city's lesser pigeons. If he was honest, the only good thing about it was the quietness, though for Tom that was always the most important quality in a house. He knew that she'd hate it the moment he found it online.

Esme, meanwhile, had found loads of potential properties, each more unsuitable for Tom than the last. There was the one in Muswell Hill, which he had vetoed for being 'too cut off and above a branch of Pizza Express'. A place in Camden was condemned because the door led out onto the high street and so, Tom worried, would be coated in piss every Friday and Saturday night. And then there was the big, top-floor flat in West Hampstead that seemed perfect, until the weird neighbour came over to introduce himself during their viewing.

They'd spent a grand total of three weekends at the beginning of the year touring wintry north London's property barrel scrapings, driven about in a series of estate agency-owned Mini Coopers to view grotty flats full of other people's stuff.

Until they found this place.

For Esme, it was 'the one'. For Tom it was 'the closest to the one' that he had thus far seen. It was nice and it was homely. Both important qualities, because – although he never properly admitted it before they started looking – the idea of moving in with Esme terrified him.

The thing was (or *one* of the things was) she had lived with her previous partner and therefore already understood the politics of it; the unspoken things that people just did so they could rub along fine. Tom, on the other hand, didn't know anything about that. It was all new to him: from the decision to move in together, to picking out the flat and sharing its space.

Aside from living back with his parents for a couple of years, he had been a stranger to cohabiting since his solitary year at the

University of Hertfordshire, when he was squeezed with seven others into a run-down 1970s block that smelled of vinyl flooring and cheap furniture polish. Again, Esme had had an entirely different experience of university halls. Higher education – and the cohabitation that came with it – accounted for five years of her life, and she'd loved every moment: three at Oxford, studying English Language, plus another two at UCL to complete her training to become a child speech therapist.

For all his fear, uncertainty and doubt, the debate was eventually settled in a branch of Starbucks in Queen's Park. They were sipping hot chocolates and looking over the one-page brochures for the four places that comprised their shortlist when Esme confronted his prevaricating and nit-picking.

'Look. Do you even want to live together?' she had asked, after he'd complained about the fees attached to the move and suggested, again, that they spend a few months living in the relative safety of his studio, instead of getting their own place.

'Yes. Of course I do,' he had said, withholding again the fact that moving out of a place he was comfortable in calling home terrified him. As did the intimacy that would come with living with Esme.

'Then you have to get over the fact that nowhere we live will be perfect. Christ, Tom. This is London. We'll probably only be there for two years before the bastard landlord hikes the rent up and we're forced to leave.'

'Well...'

'So could you stop finding some ridiculous fault with every single place we see?' she continued, before he could find something to disagree with. 'There's nothing wrong with any of the flats we've looked at, really. Except the pissy door place in Camden.'

'I know, Es. I do.'

'So what is it then? Knowing you, I'm guessing that you're scared about this whole thing. It's new, it's removing you from somewhere you feel comfortable. But it's fine to be hesitant about this stuff, Tom,' she said, taking his hand. 'Jesus, I'm scared too.'

'You?' Tom said, surprised, this admission being entirely contrary to the established architecture of their relationship: him the awkward, socially inept one; her the sound, level, determined picture of a life well lived.

'Of course I'm bloody scared. There'd have to be something wrong with you if you weren't. Christ, Tom. With most people, you only see maybe twenty per cent of what they're actually like. When you live with them, it's a hundred per cent. All the pretty bits and all the ugly bits. The nights when I don't want you to come over because I'm in jogging bottoms and wearing a face pack? Well, you'll be there. When I'm ill and want to be left alone, you'll be there. We're going to share a bathroom, for God's sake! Which is just about the most horrendous thing imaginable.'

'I suppose,' he said, smiling.

'When you share a life with someone, you share the whole bloody thing. Not just the bits you want someone to see. But what's the alternative?'

'You're right,' he said. 'I know you're right.'

'Good. Now pick one,' she'd said, holding three sheets of paper in her hand, like it was a card trick. 'Because I'll tell you now I am not going to beg you to live with me, Tom. I'm not.'

Something in her expression warned him now was not the time to raise other concerns about his innate fear of change. Esme, he realised, was not just asking him to pick somewhere to live, she was seeking confirmation that they had a future together. That there was something to build on for the years to come. That this was not one of those relationships that ticks along for a year before falling apart at the first sign of commitment.

They'd got too close to that once already.

'This one,' Tom said, pointing to the Belsize maisonette. 'If you like it?'

'I do,' Esme said with a smile, and took out her phone to call the agent.

And now, there they were.

Esme still asleep and the noise outside growing, with engines of sports cars taken for weekend spins, slamming doors, the *bleeps* of reversing trucks. At one point he heard a posh voice yell, presumably to her dog, 'Oh, Digby, not there,' and hoped that 'there' did not mean his doorstep.

Stacks of branded cardboard boxes pilfered from various north London supermarkets sat against almost every wall. But instead of being full of Monster Munch, Fairy Liquid and Pedigree Chum, they contained the worldly possessions of Tom and Esme – collected yesterday from their now old homes in Camden and Pimlico, and driven (uncertainly by Tom) in a van through the centre of the city.

Her alarm clock said 8.30. Meaning nothing had stirred her now for over an hour and a half. This, he could foresee, was how it would be: him up early most days, never quite getting used to the noise, but putting up with it as he would a broken doorbell or a loose floorboard. Those things that are initially annoying, but are eventually forgotten, and oddly missed when they're gone. Esme asleep, soundly curled up in the foetal position with the duvet pulled up to where her neck met her jaw.

Giving up on waking her himself, Tom climbed out of bed and went into their little living room, separated from the kitchen by a breakfast bar and a cheap plastic dining table to accompany the most basic furniture the landlord had bought for the flat. Their new home was in various stages of chaos. On the kitchen worktops sat the remnants of last night's takeaway Chinese, alongside the three cheese graters, two kettles and four colanders they now owned – the result of the coming together of their material lives.

He was looking through a small stack of Esme's books when she shuffled into the living room, wearing her red-chequered pyjama trousers and his large, dark blue hoodie, cuffs rolled up to the elbows.

'Morning,' Tom said cheerfully.

'How long have you been trying to wake me up for?' she said groggily.

'What do you mean?'

'The nudging, the music,' she said, stopping to yawn. 'The stamping around.'

'What, you were awake?' he said. She kissed him on the cheek, yawned and ran her fingers through her hair. Then began opening cupboards, looking for something that clearly wasn't there before eventually giving up and trying the fridge, from which she took a piece of bread and put it in the toaster.

'I was *drifting*,' she said. 'Why do you keep bread in the fridge?'

'The fridge is where bread goes.'

'The bread bin is where bread goes.'

'We don't have—'

'Add it to the list,' she said, pointing to a piece of paper fixed to the fridge, on which she had detailed everything they were missing and would need within the next day or two: an ironing board, more plates, teaspoons, a bathmat. Tom had argued against the latter, insisting that they could just lay a towel on the floor. But Esme had insisted that she, as an almost thirty-year-old woman, refused to live like a student or a grimy bachelor.

'I'm making tea,' Tom said. 'You can finish the job while you're making breakfast.'

'No thanks,' she said. 'Rule six, remember? Also, I'm making *me* breakfast. You can sort yourself out.'

'This is how it's going to be, is it?' he said, taking her faded and chipped Oxford University mug down from the cupboard she had designated for glasses and cups. 'Every man for himself. Or herself.'

'You know, I didn't know where I was when I opened my eyes,' she said, ignoring him.

'You are Esme Simon,' Tom said, sarcastically and slowly. 'I am Tom Murray. And this,' he said, gesturing around the room, 'is our flat in Belsize Park, London. The year is 2009—'

'Shut up. Idiot,' she said, spreading marmalade on her toast and taking it into the living room without a plate. They couldn't find the plates and had eaten last night's Chinese straight from the foil boxes.

She dropped down onto the couch and took a bite. Tom placed her tea down on the boxy IKEA coffee table that adorned every rental flat he had ever seen. She looked at the colour of it, as she did every time he made it.

'You know it's bloody noisy here,' Tom said.

'It's fine.'

'Every morning the bin men collect the bottles from that pub.'

'We've only been here for one morning.'

'Fine. *Some* mornings the bin men collect the bottles from the pub.'

'And?' she said, pushing herself upright.

'It sounds like the end of the world.'

'Don't be melodramatic, Tom.'

'There are also people talking outside. They're noisy too.'

'Yes, how *awful*. People *talking*. Perhaps we should write to the council?'

'Barking dogs. Runners.'

'Okay. Tom, you are aware we live in London, yes?'

'I know. But—'

'Your last flat was four floors up. It's always going to be quieter when you're away from street level.'

'Hmm.'

'Are you trying to tell me that you don't like it here? Already?'

'No! I—'

'Because it took us long enough to find it.'

Tom stopped. His uncertainty, reticence even, was still there. But he knew that it was important for her and for them that he dulled it.

'Esme, no. I'm not . . . I'm happy here. I just wish there were fewer people in Belsize Park.'

'I'm sure everyone who lives here thinks the same. That's London, though. Isn't it? Nobody wants to live anywhere near anyone else. But nobody wants to leave to live nowhere near anyone else.'

'I have no idea what you just said.'

'Think about it,' Esme said. She stretched her arms out and yawned, signalling the end of that debate.

'Also,' she said, 'you've brought too many CDs with you. We'll have to get rid of some. There's that hospice shop over the road.'

'Right. You can stop that now.'

'What?' she said, as Tom sat down on the floor and motioned to a box marked 'FICTION A-M & VASES (FRAGILE!)'.

'If we're talking about having too much crap, then what about your books? Four boxes of them. Most of which you've already read. Why can't *they* go to the charity shop?'

'I might want to read them again,' Esme said bluntly.

'Seriously? What is the likelihood of you ever reading . . .' he said, picking up a book at random, '*The King of Torts* by John Grisham.'

Esme went to defend herself but Tom cut her off.

'While we're at it, why *did* you ever read *The King of Torts* by John Grisham?'

'On holiday! I like to read page-turners on holiday.'

'So you're basically admitting that you will never read this again unless you happen to suffer long-term memory loss when we're in bloody Marbella or somewhere.'

'No. Look, I probably won't read it—'

'So let's chuck it out then!' Tom said, preparing to throw the book onto the ever-expanding charity-shop pile they should probably have taken care of before they moved. But Esme grabbed his arm.

'No! I will decide when I throw books out. Not you.'

'But—'

'No,' she said again, picking up his copy of *Faded Seaside Glamour* by a band called Delays.

'What are you doing with that?' Tom said.

'Let's make a deal. One for one?'

'Absolutely not,' he said.

'CDs are worthless now anyway. Literally no one will own them in, like, two years.'

'Except me. The record stays.'

'And stop calling CDs records. Records are cool. CDs are pointless.'

'*Stop calling CDs records*,' Tom repeated, in a high-pitched, whining voice.

'Childish,' Esme said.

'I might listen to that again. You know you won't read *this* again.'

'That's not the point.'

'No. The point is that you hate chucking stuff away. Even when it's bloody useless.'

'I could say the same about you,' Esme said, as Tom began to laugh. 'What's funny?'

'You look like you're about to throw that CD at my head.'

'I'm keeping it away from you. Anyway, I might if you don't put the book down.'

'No chance.'

'Fine. We'll play a game to settle it.'

'Oh come on.'

'Each of us picks up one thing that we think should be thrown out and asks a question about it. If the owner gets the question right, it stays. If they're wrong, it goes.'

'Only if I can go first,' Tom said, ending their Mexican stand-off by turning the book over to read the blurb on the back. 'As a side note, I find it strange that you are so good at coming up with games on the spot.'

'I am a loss to television,' she said, still holding the CD.

'Okay. So, who is the main character in *The King of Torts*?'

'Clay Carter,' Esme said, without so much as a thought.

'How the fuck do you know that?'

'How do you forget a name like *Clay Carter*? I win. The book stays.'

Tom threw the book down on the floor next to Esme, where it joined hardback editions of the Winnie the Pooh books and signed copies of the first three Harry Potters, for which the keep/chuck game was not necessary.

'My go,' Esme said. 'I want you to name track three on this CD.'

Tom drew a blank. He had not listened to the album since he'd bought it some years ago. If he was being honest, it was doubtful that he'd played it the whole way through.

'You have no idea, do you?'

'Hang on,' he said, prepared to take a punt on anything. 'Erm.'

'Five seconds.'

'Es!'

'Three. Two.'

'Shit.'

'One. Answer please.'

'Fine. Pass. I have no idea.'

'The answer is "Long Time Coming". Know it?'

'Actually yes. It was the single. Only good song on the album.'

'Well, you might want to give it one last play,' Esme said, beginning a separate pile next to the books. 'Because it's gone.'

They played the game three more times, during which Tom lost albums by Elliott Smith and Ryan Adams, while Esme gave up a yellowing, beaten copy of an Ian Rankin novel adorned with a '3 for 2' sticker from a long-defunct bookshop chain. Then he realised that Esme was working down towards CDs he either really liked or had some sentimental value. Gifts bought by friends. Signed copies. Even a limited edition or two.

'I'm not sure I like this game,' Tom said, just as he was about to relinquish a copy of *The Three EPs* by the Beta Band. 'And I'm rubbish at it.'

'I think it's good.'

'Well you would. You've only lost one book.'

'I have a talent for games.'

'For games you've made up.'

'Maybe so. But all of my games have a message behind them.'

'This one being "relieve Tom of his stuff".'

'Or better still "memory and compromise". Good qualities when you're building a life together, don't you think?' Esme said. 'For whatever's next for us.'

She smiled at him and he smiled back. From outside came the noise of a loud car stereo and a group of kids laughing. A dog barked, a truck reversed. All sounds he'd have to get used to if this house was going to become a home.

'Ignore it,' Esme said, handing him a book. 'It's my go.'

# CHAPTER FIVE

6 – 7 pm

# OLD SECRETS AT OUR FIRST CHRISTMAS

## December 2007 – Lowestoft, Suffolk

Anne Murray rinsed out the gravy boat the family only used at Christmas and passed it to Tom. This, as much as anything, was one of their Christmas traditions. Tom's dad, Gordon, would have a brandy and a cigar (marking the only time of the year he was allowed to smoke in the house). Sarah, his sister, and her fiancé, Nathan, would choose some music and set up the dining table for games. Tom and Anne would wash up and talk and tell each other what they might want from the year to come.

Today, however, something was different. There was a third person in their post-Christmas lunch clean-up line.

'Where does this go, then?' Esme said, displaying a large crystal bowl that had been used for fruit salad. Tom noticed his mum wince as Esme held it up.

'Top shelf of the larder, love. There's a box for it.'

Tom took a stack of plates over to the cupboard where the best china was kept, storing them away for another year. Esme meanwhile joined Anne at the sink and picked up a damp tea towel.

'Is it strange,' Anne said, 'being away from your family at Christmas?'

'We only left them this morning, Mum,' Tom said.

'I know. I mean on Christmas Day.'

'We were—'

'No. Not at all,' Esme interrupted. She was firm but polite. Determined to stop Tom snapping back again with that exasperated, irritated tone people use when they think their parents are saying something daft.

'I just hope we've been a nice change. Not too annoying or weird,' she said, permanently convinced that her family was difficult and unruly, rather than normal.

'It's been lovely.'

'What normally happens at yours then? Around now. Don't tell me you're all doing something intelligent while we just loll about like a bunch of gluttons.'

Esme laughed. 'Nothing really,' she said. 'In Hungary people celebrate more on Christmas Eve. It's about the only thing my parents still do traditionally. On Christmas Day they might go for a walk or watch a film. But that's it.'

'So no turkey or anything?'

'Carp,' Tom said.

'Sorry?'

'They eat carp. Like from the river.'

'Carp?'

'He makes it sound awful. But it's really nice.'

'You had it too?' Anne said to Tom, sounding a little surprised. Perhaps unable to imagine her son – who as a child refused any food that was not breadcrumbed – eating carp.

'I did,' Tom said.

'Carp,' Anne said again, slightly disbelieving.

'Well Hungary *is* landlocked, Mum. Harder to get hold of a piece of cod than it is here,' Tom said, repeating what Esme had said to him a week ago with an authoritative tone.

'We also make gingerbread and wrap it up for the neighbours. Then go to church for midnight mass.'

'Oh. You're ... well ...'

'Religious? Not really. We just like the carols at Christmas.'

'Lovely, isn't it? Did you take Tom with you?'

'No,' Esme said, smiling at Tom, who by 10 p.m. had eaten too much stuffed cabbage and poppy-seed cake and fell asleep in an armchair in front of the Christmas Eve *Top of the Pops* re-run, waking up at 3 a.m. with a blanket thrown over him. 'He stayed at home with my dad.'

Tom remembered waking up in that cold living room. It was a strange place, but he had never felt so immediately at home anywhere. Tamas and Lena Simon had taken him in, told him stories about meeting and living in a foreign city in their early twenties, given him gifts and brought him a little way into their family.

'Is there anything else I can help with?' Esme said, dropping a handful of cutlery into a drawer beneath the hob.

'You've been quite helpful enough,' Anne said. 'Go and sit down. Tom here can finish up.'

Esme put a tea towel featuring a crude, primary-school illustration of Rudolph the red-nosed reindeer down on the kitchen worktop and left Tom and his mum.

He turned the radio up a little. 'The Fairytale of New York' rang around the kitchen for what felt like the ten thousandth time that winter, as Tom filled his mum's wine glass from the enormous bottle of prosecco she was keeping cool in a paint-splattered bucket full of ice and cold water because it wouldn't fit in the stuffed fridge.

'Well then?' he said.

'Well what?'

'Well what d'you think?'

Tom's mother paused for a second, grabbing a ladle from Tom before he put it in the cutlery drawer rather than the utensils pot.

'She's perfect, Tom. Just perfect.'

He smiled and went to thank her. But before he could, Anne was off with a list of Esme's virtues.

'She's clever and funny and nice to have around the place. Oh, and ever so pretty, Tom. Ever so.'

'I'm glad you like her.'

'And you do, too.'

'Well, yes. Of course.'

'I mean more than *that* though, don't I?' she said, loading all sorts of implications, emotions and possibilities into such an ordinary word. 'I can see it. She's different, this one. Not like Niamh or Emma, or . . . who was the other one? The Australian.'

'Carla.'

'Yes, Carla. Esme's different. Something more. Your dad thinks so, too. So does your sister. And Nathan,' she said, referring to his sister Sarah's fiancé.

'Nathan?' What the bloody hell does he know? He never met the others.'

'Oh, he just likes to feel included, doesn't he?' Anne pulled off her rubber gloves with a snap. 'And what about her family? You get on alright?'

'Fine, yeah. They're nice. Really nice.'

'You don't sound very convinced.'

'No, I am. I like them. Yesterday was fun.'

'Must've been strange. Celebrating on Christmas Eve like that.'

'It's good, though. Means we always see both families over Christmas.'

'Hmm,' Anne said, reorganising the cupboards where Esme had either put things in the wrong place, or balanced one thing a little too precariously on top of another.

'What?'

'The way you said that. "Always see both families".'

'And?'

'You make it sound proper. Like there'll be more Christmases.'

'There will, I hope,' Tom said.

The mention of it, the thought, sent him a few years into the future. He saw an older version of himself in Esme's family home with her parents. For a brief second he even pictured someone else entirely. A child maybe, their presence signified by a scooter by the door rather than any physical manifestation. Tom quickly shook it away. It was too soon to think of anything like that. Maybe that kind of thing wasn't for him at all.

'That's nice, Tom. And do you think she's . . .' Anne said, turning away from the cupboard above the cooker to mime slipping a ring onto a finger.

'No. Esme's not like that.'

'Not like what?'

'She doesn't like marriage. Hates the idea of it.'

'Why?'

'She just does, Mum. And it's not one of those things you should ask her about.'

'Okay,' she said, in a way that suggested she wasn't about to leave the topic alone.

'Mum,' Tom said.

'I just think it's sad.'

'It is what it is.'

'But you've talked about it, then?'

'Only to confirm that she's not interested.'

Tom saw her trying to resolve her clear liking for Esme with this distaste for the more traditional elements of the family that she had built her own life around.

'Well,' she said. 'Maybe she'll change her mind.'

71

Tom thought about arguing back against this, but knew there was no point. Esme had been clear with him about her feelings on it and he didn't care enough to try to change her mind.

'Sarah will be starting soon, won't she?' Tom said, thinking about his sister, who was in the process of setting up decks of cards and gambling chips from a set that only ever saw the light of day at Christmas time.

'In a minute,' Anne said, her voice now serious. 'There's something I want to ask you, Tom.'

He knew what was coming. He had been expecting it. But before he could answer they were interrupted by a voice from the living room.

'Rummy! All set up.'

'We should—'

'Not yet,' Anne said firmly.

'Mum.'

'Tom. We have—'

'Not now,' Tom snapped, and left her alone in the kitchen.


Fifteen minutes later, the Murrays were halfway through a game when Esme quite deliberately caught Tom's eye.

'You okay?' he mouthed. Her answer came in the form of a smile and another large sip of red wine. Then she laid down three aces and a run of hearts – five, six, seven, eight.

'Again?' his dad cried. 'That's the fourth in a row!'

'I would say I'm sorry. But . . .'

'Are you sure you've never played this before? You're not some sort of card shark we're going to lose our life savings to? In five pence pieces, admittedly.'

'I'm saying nothing,' Esme said, dragging a stack of six small silver coins towards her, adding to the pile that she had already amassed.

Though he joined in with the mock exasperation and frustration,

Tom was in fact quite happy. Esme had worried about this for weeks. So had he. There is a particular type of familial assimilation Christmas at a relative stranger's home requires. Get it wrong and one or both of them would be trapped for hours, if not days, in a maze of traditions they could neither understand nor break.

Between occasional glances over at his mum (who was joining in happily now, the scene in the kitchen apparently forgotten), Tom had been watching Esme, looking for any signs of discomfort or stress. But at no point did she look anything except content and at home. She had told Sarah and Nathan about her work in early years speech development. Then told Nathan specifically about Angry Matt, the drummer she had dated for a few months before meeting Tom and whose band he was a fan of. Gordon asked her about studying at Oxford, as if it was a different planet rather than a university. Anne gave her a potted history of Lowestoft, told primarily through gossipy anecdotes concerning her friends and their friends.

He thought back to when they almost vetoed the idea.

'Maybe it's a mistake,' Esme had said one evening in mid-December, while she was wrapping presents and drinking mulled wine in her Pimlico flat, with Tom watching on.

'What?'

'Using Christmas as the meet-the-parents time.'

'I'll be fine.'

'Oh that's good,' she said sarcastically. 'I'm actually talking about me. If I screw up at Christmas they'll remember it for ever, won't they?'

'You won't screw up.'

'I might. What if I drink too much and say something stupid?'

'Well, just don't drink too much. I won't be.'

'What about the games? You said they play games.'

'*We* do.'

'Well, like what?'

73

'We play cards. Sometimes have a quiz.'

'Right,' she said nervously, then fell silent.

'What now?'

'I'm worried that I won't understand the rules. I'm crap at learning new rules, Tom.'

'Esme, you've got a degree from Oxford. You're probably the smartest person I've ever met. I'm sure you can remember the rules to Old Maid.'

'What's Old Maid?'

'We might not even play it,' Tom had said.

For a moment she went quiet, bowing to the Kate Rusby album Tom insisted on listening to because he believed it contained the only truly good festive songs ever recorded. But then her worries bubbled up and over again.

'Do you think they'll like me?' she asked.

'Of course. Why wouldn't they?'

'Well, did they like your last girlfriend?'

'Niamh?' he asked, thinking back to the almost embarrassingly quiet and shy Irish girl he had brought to Suffolk for the long (*really* long) Easter weekend two years ago. 'Hard to say.'

Esme took a deep breath.

'They'll love you, Esme,' Tom said. 'How could they not?'

And now everything seemed so right. So fitting, he thought, as he looked over at Esme again, holding his gaze until she looked back. She smiled and took a sip of wine, draining her glass.

'Another?' Tom asked.

'We've run dry,' Gordon said.

'It's fine. I'll grab a bottle.'

Tom got up from the table and went into the kitchen. The wine was stored on top of the fridge in a small, six-by-six bottle rack, along with the bottle of Smirnoff his mum kept for the occasional vodka and tonic she'd drink on a Saturday night. The bottle that always used to last her a year, until her son grew up and started to sneak mouthfuls, and then Coke bottles full of it.

He pulled down a bottle of red. Screwtop. Maybe as recently as six months ago the feel of it in his hand would've been different from what it was now. But the temptation was gone. Replaced by a kind of unfamiliar satisfaction with life. He was looking at the bottle when he heard the soft patter of slippered feet.

'You didn't answer me earlier,' the voice behind him said. He turned to see his mum in the doorway.

'Answer what?'

'You know what I mean, Tom,' Anne said. She looked serious – braced to bring her most hated topic of conversation to the surface.

'Mum, please. Can't this wait?'

'It's been bothering me ever since you got here,' she said, fixing him with a stare.

'Well it shouldn't.'

'It wouldn't if I thought she knew. Because if I had to guess by the way you ran off, I'd say that she doesn't.'

He stopped, unsure of how best to answer this. The truth would annoy or upset her. Perhaps it was kinder to tell a white lie. Harmless, really. But then Tom looked into his mother's eyes. The same ones he'd seen distraught beside his hospital bed.

'She doesn't,' he said. 'Not exactly.'

The news seemed to hit her like a punch to the gut. And Tom knew why. For all the talk of this relationship being different, there were a lot of things about it that looked the same as the others.

'Not exactly?' she said, echoing him incredulously.

'She knows that I don't drink,' he said.

'But you've not told her why that is?'

'Mum—'

'She *deserves* to know, Tom.'

'I know.'

'Well you should—'

'Please, Mum. All I'm saying is not today. I need you to give me some time, okay? It's Christmas.'

'I don't like talking about it, either. You know that. Especially at Christmas.'

'So why are we?'

'Because there've been others, haven't there? They've stayed around for a couple of months. But they didn't know. And I always say, Tom,' she said, holding up her hand to thwart his interruption. 'I always say that to know *you*, they have to know *all of you*. That included.'

'She will. I promise that she will.'

'When?' she said firmly.

Tom hesitated. It was impossible to put a time on it. To plan that kind of conversation. He had thought about saying something on the drive up. But instead he'd talked about growing up in Lowestoft and pointed out banal personal points of interest, like the pub where he spent his eighteenth birthday, or his old secondary school.

'Soon,' he said. 'When the timing's right.'

'And what if it's never right? I know it's such a hard thing to say.'

'Harder for me,' he said, which he knew was a little cruel. They had argued when his mum had told him she'd kept things from his grandparents. Not wanting to upset them, he was told. It wasn't fair to her to bring that up now.

'Sorry,' he said. 'But I've told you this is different and I don't want to mess it up. You have to let me do it my way.'

'Yes. But in the past your way hasn't been that honest, has it?'

'Mum,' he said, almost hissing, desperate to keep their voices down. 'I will. That's why it's different. I'll tell her.'

'Everything?'

Tom sighed.

'It has to be everything, Tom. All of it. Otherwise it'll all come out when you don't want it to.'

Tom hesitated again.

'It will be.'

'Promise me.'

Tom nodded. Then, without warning, Anne Murray went over to her son and embraced him. She was crying when she let go, tears creeping down the gentle lines of her face.

'What is it?'

'I want it to be different, too.'

'I know,' he said.

'I know it's silly,' Anne said, collecting herself. 'But I've been thinking.'

'What?'

'I know it doesn't work that way. And you'll get annoyed at me for thinking it.'

'Mum, please don't.'

'I've just been wondering, you know? If she can help you. Make you . . . better.'

'Mum.'

'No . . . not *better*,' she said, admonishing and correcting herself. 'Happier, I mean. So you're not—'

'It's not as simple as that, Mum. You know it isn't.'

'Of course I bloody know,' she snapped. 'My son tried to kill himself.'

The words stunned them both. Until a few years ago Tom had never seen his mum like this. Now, these moments of raw anger came out occasionally. He knew he was to blame. Still, it shocked both of them, trapping them beneath a silence akin to a heavy winter quilt.

'I just always hope,' she said, softening, the moment having passed. A flash of anger rather than an argument. 'When I see you like this. It's just so different, Tom. So much better than you were.'

Tom watched her face fall as she stepped away from him. Despite everything he had told her, every link he sent for her to read and every news story about the condition, Tom knew that his parents would always seek a cure. It annoyed him.

'I am happy,' he said. 'And she is helping.'

His mum nodded. She was lightly biting her bottom lip to keep herself from crying again when a look of surprise overtook her. She seemed to be looking past Tom now.

'Everything alright?' Esme said from behind him.

'Fine, love,' Anne said. 'Got a bit of Fairy Liquid in my eye. Daft of me. I'll go and sort myself out,' she said, brushing past Esme in the doorway. 'Tell Sarah to deal me in.'

Tom turned to face Esme. He worried that the emotive nature of his talk with his mum was still obvious in his sad eyes or a worried look. Obvious tells that she might pick up on.

'You sure everything's alright?' Esme said. 'You've been ages.'

'She's fine. We were just chatting.'

'Sarah told me to come and get you.'

'We should go back,' Tom said, picking up the bottle of wine he had been dispatched to get. He went ahead of Esme, who was still in the kitchen doorway.

'You know if there's anything—'

'There isn't,' Tom said.

'I know. But if—' Esme began, as the kitchen cooker beeped and the red-lit digital clock showed 17:00.

# PART 2

# CHAPTER SIX

3 – 4 pm

# ONE DOWN, TEN LEFT
## June 2008 – Just outside Whitstable, Kent

'*Tom*,' Esme hissed. 'Don't. They're all looking at us now,' she said, directing his attention to the surrounding cars.

Tom thumped the car horn again, his head craned out the window in an attempt to spot the problem on the road ahead, before slumping back into the seat of the sickening, blueberry-air-freshener-scented Vauxhall Corsa they had rented for the day. The traffic had barely moved ten metres in the last hour.

'This is a bloody disaster,' he said. 'As soon as we turn off we'll have to go home again.'

'We might get a couple of hours.'

'Yes, but it was meant to be the whole day, wasn't it? Lunch, beach, dinner. We'll be lucky if we see the tide go out.'

'Come in.'

'What?'

'Come in. The tide comes *in* at night. Didn't you grow up by the sea?'

Tom said nothing. Instead he turned the radio up for another traffic report, during which an overly cheerful woman he could only assume had never sat in a stationary car reminded them again of the reason their anniversary trip had so far mostly been spent on the M2, fifteen miles from the junction that would take them to the coast.

'Fucking camper vans,' Tom said, referring to the Volkswagen the traffic news had told them was quietly smouldering in the middle of the two lanes, its engine having blown up, spilling oil across the road three miles away, near a village called Boughton-under-Blean.

'Come on. It's not their fault.'

'Four fire engines, she said.'

'These things happen. At least no one was hurt.'

'Probably some bloody hippy who didn't bother to look after it,' he mumbled. 'Couldn't give a toss about anyone else.'

'Tom.'

'And what kind of place is bloody Boughton-under-Blean anyway? Who names a fucking town Boughton-under-Blean?'

'Tom, I'm serious. If you keep on like this I'm going to make you stand with the dads,' she said, pointing at a group of middle-aged men who had absconded from their family estate cars and collected around the bonnet of a Volvo. 'Maybe you could borrow one of their copies of the *Daily Express*.'

'Hey!'

'Well, you sound like someone ranting on a radio phone-in show.'

Tom didn't say anything to this. Mostly because Esme was right. Instead, he sat back and considered how their hopeful trip to Whitstable on a sunny Saturday had instead become four hours stuck in a small rented car with no air conditioning, quietly broiling as half the population of the South East made for the Kentish seaside at once.

The whole thing had been his idea. Instead of dinner or a picnic on Hampstead Heath, they would go somewhere new. Get out of London for the day. Rent a car that gave them the freedom of where to go and when to come back. Celebrate the three hundred and sixty-five days that had passed since their meeting at Ali's costume party and the strange, heady, exciting hours that followed it.

Whitstable was picked from a Google search of 'best beaches near London'. Tom needed little more than a *Time Out* article to convince him that this was the place, and his plan was immediately in action.

'It'll be nice,' Tom had said when he told a slightly dubious Esme about his idea. 'Oysters, a walk on the beach, seeing a new town. Then fish and chips for dinner.'

'Only if you're sure you don't mind driving.'

'Not at all!'

But that wasn't quite the truth.

Indeed, the trouble had started at the very beginning of the day, when Tom had collected the car from a muddy yard in Kilburn, the dealer a man whose demeanour gave Tom the instant impression of a career thief and conman. He had eschewed a more reputable rental firm for this one, which was cheaper and recommended to him by the drummer in one of his covers bands. *Never trust a drummer*, he'd told himself as he waited for the grizzly clerk to find the keys to the Vauxhall Corsa they would be driving.

Tom hadn't driven for a while, and never in London. Having grown up and learned in an area without so much as a motorway, suddenly being thrown into lane after lane of slow-moving – yet somehow perilous – traffic was something he'd always been desperate to avoid. Even when playing gigs in Greater London he refused to drive, instead arranging for a band member to bring his amplifier to whichever backwater town pub or community centre they might be playing at.

So when he found himself on Vauxhall Bridge Road, reckless cyclists one side of him, a police car on the other, and the turning towards Esme's flat two lanes away, Tom started to realise that his idea of a little jaunt down to the coast was possibly going to be a little more fraught than he had anticipated. Nonetheless, after a few diversions and changes in direction, he eventually made it to Denton Road in Pimlico, pulled up five doors away from where Esme lived, and took three or four deep breaths to get rid of the kind of bubbling frustration that only driving can create.

'You're not ready?' he had said, when she answered the door in jogging bottoms, flip flops and a loose-fitting T-shirt. Her hair was tied up, and she was wearing glasses instead of the contacts she still put in whenever she was seeing Tom. The kitchen table was piled high with beaten-up NHS case folders. Next to it all sat a mug of tea and an opened grab bag of Milkybar Buttons.

'Ten minutes?' she said, as Tom stepped inside her flat.

'Five.'

'Tom, there's literally no chance I—'

'Try.'

'Alright. Moody.'

'Es.'

'Will the car be okay?'

'Probably,' he said, as he spotted a yellow-jacketed traffic warden turn onto Denton Road. 'Shit.'

'I'll come out,' Esme called, as Tom ran back to the car before the warden got there to begin the most absurd game of cat and mouse, in which he drove extremely slowly from one end of the road to the next, before performing a three-point turn and going back again, repeatedly for twenty minutes.

When they eventually escaped London Tom's nerves were shot, and Esme's good nature was about to turn. The anniversary playlist had been ditched in favour of banal weekend radio and a frustrated silence had settled over the car. At which point, they arrived at a sea of red brake lights, stretched out towards the horizon.

'I feel sick,' Esme said, sticking her head out of the window, having clearly had enough of the noxious and nauseating blend of car fumes, baking asphalt and the air freshener stuck on the dashboard.

'I'd offer you a mint,' Tom said. 'But we don't have any.'

'Oh God, Tom! Would you just snap out of this? You're driving me bloody mad.'

'I'm frustrated.'

'I know. Me too. But you don't have to be a prick about it. I don't want to sit here next to some whinging middle-aged man who's obsessed with the sodding traffic.'

'I'm not middle aged. I'm not even thirty.'

'In attitude, Tom, you're right there. Forty-three, bored, sat in an estate car, wishing you had a Sky Sports subscription. That's you, Tom. You are the noughties edition of Mondeo man.'

'Ouch.'

'It's true,' she said, pulling up her light summer shirt and cleaning her sunglasses with its hem, before slumping back into her seat and looking out of the window.

'It's just that it's our anniversary. And instead of being on the beach, we're in a car and it's bloody miserable.'

'Yes. It is. Which you are at least fifty per cent to blame for.'

'Well, sorry if I—'

'Tom!' she snapped, loudly enough for the dads to divert their attention away from the small transistor radio playing commentary of the European Championships football.

Esme got out of the car and stormed over to the side of the road, where she found a place to sit on a barrier. As soon as she left, Tom knew that he would have to go and join her, that he would have to make the walk of shame in front of the dozens of cars that had witnessed their argument. Past the dads, who'd be saying stuff like 'been there' and would make jocular comments in his direction as he went to offer his apology. Finally summoning up the courage, he opened the door.

Esme was staring at the sky, at a single seagull hovering and swooping on the summer air thermals.

'Sorry,' Tom said bluntly, sitting down next to her on the warm metal barrier. 'I don't want to be that person.'

'Which one?'

'The bored, Sky Sports, traffic-moaning one.'

'No one does. But looking at them I suspect it's easy to lapse into. That man there in the cargo shorts and the faded yellow polo shirt? He used to be a playwright. The *Guardian* called him the 'enfant terrible of British theatre'. Now look what's happened to him. He's the area sales rep in Essex and Kent for a bathroom tiles company. All because of traffic.'

'And two kids, probably.'

'Traffic, Tom. Traffic,' she said.

Tom gave a gentle laugh.

'And that one. Him with the T-shirt that's at least a size too small. He—'

'Oh don't,' Tom said. 'You're making me feel sorry for them.'

'Don't worry. They're happy,' she said. 'Or they're not, but they're able to repress it enough to carry on with their lives.'

'*Es*! They can probably hear you.'

'Nonsense. They're listening to that radio.'

They sat for a moment in silence. Tom took Esme's hand and kissed her cheek.

'I am, though. Sorry. I'm just frustrated about what today was meant to be and about what it is.'

'Me too,' she said, shifting slightly closer to him. 'But you've got to remember that it's not just about today. It's the whole year we're celebrating. It's always dangerous to plan these things too carefully.'

'I know,' he said. 'And you're right.'

'Besides, the whole day doesn't have to be wasted. We could do something here.'

'Here?' he said, looking around at the parked cars, the bored children looking hopelessly out of the windows at the central reservations, the van driver and his mate who had decided to seize this opportunity to sunbathe on the roof and share a copy of *Nuts* magazine.

'Yes, here. We don't need Whitstable. We can make our own fun in . . . wherever we are.'

'Near the Blean place. No man's land,' Tom said. 'Fuck knows.'

'Exactly. Fun in Fuck Knows. Look at it this way, we'll always remember it as the time we spent our anniversary stuck on the M2.'

'What do we do, though? I brought some food but I reckon that hummus has turned in the heat.'

'Not food. I was thinking of a game.'

'Of course you were,' he said, a little apprehensively. A large grey cloud hovered on the horizon, which he decided not to mention to Esme.

'What?'

'I'm not really in the mood.'

'Well, I am. And remember, you are still making things up to me.'

'Really?'

'Really. The rules are that we each name a highlight and lowlight of our first year together. Then a plan for next.'

'Why don't we just do highlights?'

'Because I want this to be realistic. The first year is exciting and lovely. But it's also when sex goes from being all amazing and new and different, to finding out what works and that becoming normal. It's when you talk about each other's flaws to your friends in private, in the hope that you can bear living with them in the future. There's a lot of compromise and downsides to the first year. Anyone who pretends it's just champagne and roses is a bloody idiot.'

'How very pragmatic. And sorry about the sex,' Tom said, immediately developing a complex about it and wondering if and when he had let Esme down. And, equally, if she had faked anything so that he wouldn't know. It was one of those things he wanted to ask about. But knew it was best not to.

'Forgiven. Anyway, you have to think of three for each category. You'll get a point for each.'

'Hang on,' Tom said, turning to look at Esme. 'How can you award points? If they're my highlights then they're my highlights.'

'Yes. But the way this will work is that I'll say "highlight", "lowlight", or "plan" and you have to answer straight away. No hesitation. If you umm or err or can't think of anything, you don't get a point. Then you ask me.'

'You're making this up as you go along.'

'I am.'

Tom laughed, though was in truth a little apprehensive. Worried that what she might think of as fun would trip him up in some way. That he'd say the wrong thing.

'Everything's a game to you, isn't it?' he said, as he mentally filed through as many memories of their first year together as he could, trying to separate the things that had gone well from those that hadn't.

'Well noticed. But you don't get a point for it. Ready?'

'Shit. My turn first, is it? Well, I'd say a high—'

'Ah, ah, ah!' Esme stopped him. 'I choose, remember. Lowlight,' she said, talking quickly, like a gameshow host keen to catch a contestant off guard.

'What?'

'Lowlight. Come on.'

'Well . . . er . . .'

'No points.'

'Come on. You've got to give me a second,' Tom said.

'Rules are rules. Right, now you ask me.'

'Fine. Highlight.'

'Ha! So predictable. First night you stayed at mine. You got up at four in the morning because you were thirsty. Laura finds you in the kitchen, thinks you're a burglar and Joe from upstairs turns up with a cricket bat.'

'That was *awful*.'

'It was hilarious,' Esme said. 'In hindsight.'

'Who comes down with a cricket bat anyway?'

'Someone who fancies the girl who lives downstairs and thinks it might be his moment.'

'Isn't he married?'

'And?' Esme said.

'So that's your highlight, is it? From everything we've done together in the last year, that's what really sticks in your mind?'

'Afraid so. Anyway, my go again . . . Highlight.'

'Our trip to Amsterdam,' Tom said, a little too quickly, as though Esme had a gun to his head.

'You have to be more specific.'

'Fine. The boat trip.'

'That's a rubbish one.'

'Better than yours. At least no one was nearly killed.'

'No. You see mine was about you. It was a memory of Tom. Yours was just that you enjoyed a boring boat trip in Amsterdam. I had nothing to do with it.'

'I can be more specific.'

'Yes. But that would just be about the architecture or the weather or something. The memory has to be about you and me. Not a thing you and me did.'

'Bollocks,' Tom said, looking up again at the black cloud, drifting ever closer. 'I'm not very good at this sort of stuff.'

'Just be creative,' she said, whacking him on the arm. 'I'll give you half a point for Amsterdam because it *was* nice, and it was hilarious when you couldn't work the audio tour and had to listen to it in German.'

'Ja.'

'Anyway. Your go.'

'Lowlight,' Tom said.

'Food poisoning. Missed you playing in the tribute band at that Irish festival in Victoria.'

'Fucking hell, Es. How do you come up with this stuff so quickly?'

'I have a good memory.'

'So, really, the game is rigged.'

'Not at all. My go again. Lowlight.'

Tom said nothing. He was distracted by the droplet that had landed on his hand. Followed by another, and a few more soon after.

'You feel that?' Esme said.

'I did. I was thinking about making it one of my lowlights – rain during our anniversary celebrations. But now I realise that the real lowlight is probably still the motorway.'

'A sort of lowlight within a lowlight?'

'Exactly.'

'I guess we'd better . . .' Esme said, motioning at the car, as the rain began to come down heavier, causing the gaggle of dads to scatter back to their estates.

She ran first and Tom followed her over to the little Corsa. But when they got there, the doors wouldn't open.

'Tom, bloody unlock it!' she shouted, pulling the neck of her dress over her head as he padded around his pockets, desperately searching for the keys. 'Tom!'

'I can't find them.'

'If you've locked them—'

'I *definitely* brought them with me.'

'Then open the bloody car. I'm getting soaked,' she said, over the noise of the water that had begun drumming against the tin-like roof of the Corsa. 'And people are looking.'

'Shit,' Tom said, patting himself down frantically now, before scuttling back to the barrier they'd been perching on to find the keys on the side of the road.

'Got them!' he called to Esme, sprinting back and finally unlocking her door. Inside the pleasant, fresh smell of summer rain was instantly overpowered by the awful, noxious blueberry air freshener.

'Don't,' Esme said. 'Before you even start. Don't.'

'They must've fallen out of my pocket.'

'I'm soaked.'

'I am sorry, Es.'

'And they were all looking. All the dads.'

'Well, you know ... Pretty girl, wet clothes.'

She whacked him on the arm again. And again, as he chuckled to himself.

Tom turned on the car and set the heaters high for Esme to dry her hair. The radio promised 'two hours of all the show tunes you've told us you love in our one hundred best musical moments', which he immediately silenced again. Outside the rain continued to fall, beating down hard against the windscreen. When she'd done what she could with her hair, Esme slumped back in her seat, looked over at Tom and smiled.

'Worth the journey?' he said.

'Oh, absolutely.'

'You don't sound convinced.'

'Well, I could say something trite and romantic. Like "oh Tom, it's just so perfect!".'

'But it's not.'

'Exactly.'

'And that's okay?'

'More than okay.'

'I love your optimism, Es,' Tom said. 'I just wish I could borrow a bit of it sometimes.'

'It's not optimism. I just think it's things like this that we'll remember. I know it's not necessarily what we planned, or what you wanted.'

'And, anyway, who's to say a day on the beach in the sun would have been better than four hours stuck in traffic?'

'I mean, I think life's better when it surprises you. It's like when people try to over-plan a wedding and it ends up being really boring in comparison to one that's just a bit slap-dash. The things you do as a couple should represent who you are.'

'And we are four hours stuck in traff—'

'Oi,' she said.

The rain began to ease a bit.

'So shall we call this a glorious failure?'

'Glorious is a bit strong, Tom.' He smiled, knowing that she was right. 'At least we'll never forget it, will we?'

'As hard as we might try.'

Tom leant over to kiss her. Her face was still wet from the rain and her lips tasted like cherry lip balm.

He thought about the drive back: the hours on the motorway; the looming battles with London's cabbies, cyclists and cars; the return to the rental place in Kilburn that, at night, resembled the setting for the denouement of a television crime drama. Then he caught Esme smiling, joyful even now, in the menial surprises of life. He became suddenly aware of their togetherness, himself one half of a whole – that the things he lacked, she had, and vice versa. He could stand a few more hours like that, wherever they spent them.

'Your go to ask, isn't it?' he said. Esme looked surprised that it was him who'd suggested carrying on with her game about their first year. Although Tom didn't say it, he wanted to relive more and remember more; to appreciate things he might not have noticed in the moment.

'Oh right. Highlight, then. But it can't be this,' she said with a smile.

'Fine,' Tom said, sitting back in his seat, content to drift back through his last twelve months with Esme.

# CHAPTER SEVEN

2 – 3 pm

# LEARNING MORE ABOUT YOU
## March 2010 – Oxford

Tom picked up a stone from the small pile he had assembled between his feet and threw it as hard as he could. He could never get enough whip on it. That was the problem, he was sure. Undeterred, he picked up another and tried again.

'Imagine if you had to do blue plaques for the life of Tom Murray,' Esme had said, when explaining the idea to him a couple of years ago, when they had given up on the idea of a hot-weather holiday because neither of them could afford it. 'Where would they be?'

'What do you mean, blue plaques?'

'Those round memorial plates they stick on the side of buildings where someone super important or famous lived. *Johnny Important, Scientist, Lived here in 1881.*'

'Right. But I don't have any.'

'Of course you don't. But if you did, where would they be?'

'I dunno. Lowestoft, probably. London. I don't get how it relates to us.'

'It's a way of getting to know each other. Instead of taking nice holidays, we visit places that we've lived or loved.'

'So we go to Lowestoft instead of Tenerife?'

'Sort of.'

Still, Tom didn't get it, so insisted that Esme start. She chose a trip to Leicester, taken in February 2008, which took in her old school, the library she spent so many hours in, as well as the café she had run away to when her Oxford acceptance letter arrived, so she could open it away from the prying eyes of her parents.

Tom, for his part, had chosen Norwich. The scene of his best gigs in amateur bands, his first Saturday job in a branch of a music shop, and the hill he had careered down out of control on a skateboard, before colliding with a parked car and breaking his nose, the result of which remained in the form of a slight bump on its bridge.

Later, a tour of Lowestoft comprised primarily of his old schools, friends' homes and the sites of a few carefully selected childhood moments. Birmingham told him more about Esme's teenage years in the Midlands.

Every one of these day trips would start with a journey around the chosen town on the top deck of a bus, followed by a visit to three or four important places, like former homes or sites of significant events. Budget tours for people who wanted to know each other inside out.

This time they were in University Parks in Oxford. Standing on the bank of the River Cherwell, where Tom was trying (and failing) to skim stones.

'Shit,' he said, as another stone clipped the water and sank immediately.

'I think that might've been two bounces,' Esme said cheerfully.

'Stop being so nice,' he said, picking up a perfect skimmer: smooth, round, about the size of a watch face. He threw it, watching on in hope as it flew fast, and sank instantly again.

'But it's just so tragic standing here watching you try to skim stones. It's like some sort of mating dance.'

'Thank God it isn't. I'd be an eternal virgin.'

'Tom! People might hear you.'

'What? We're at a university full of clever people who were good at school. I'd say a good proportion of them are worried about being eternal virgins.'

She punched his arm, more shocked and embarrassed than before.

'I just can't work out why I can't do it. Some people just chuck any old rock and it bounces, like, twenty times.'

'I'm not sure why you care.'

'Neither am I,' Tom said, trying another, with the same result.

'I think you're trying too hard.'

'It said online—'

'You looked up how to skim stones online?'

'Um...'

'Bloody hell, Tom. That is quite something,' Esme said. 'Maybe it's a man thing?' she questioned. 'If you can't grow a beard, skim stones or own a shed, you'll never truly be masculine.'

'Probably,' Tom said. 'I also can't do more than five keepy-ups with a football.'

'You should stop talking. I'm finding you less and less attractive with every new revelation. I might go and try my luck with one of the lads over there,' she said, pointing towards what Tom assumed was a university sports team running sprints between two sets of cones.

'The rugger buggers?'

'I bet *they* can skim stones *and* were good at school. Brains and brawn, Tom. It's what every girl wants.'

'Hush it,' Tom said, throwing one more, so hard that it avoided the water altogether and landed on the opposite bank of the river.

Esme started laughing.

'Right. Enough of this,' he said, grumpily dumping the rest into the river. 'Where's next?'

'I think halls. Who knows, if we're stealthy we might even be able to go up to my old room,' she said, taking Tom's hand. 'This way.'

Esme led him back through the park to where the bus had dropped them off near the centre of town. They walked in contemplative silence, taking in the nascent buds on the trees, crocuses dotting the ground, and the green shoots that would soon sprout into daffodils. It was quiet, except for a few runners, dog walkers and one or two who he assumed were students.

Esme looked as happy as Tom had seen her as they strolled around the walks. Despite her claims that she never really fitted in at university, she had toured him around the city with a confidence and warmth that suggested Oxford was once a place she had found real comfort in. It was beautiful to see.

It was quite the opposite of their visit to her home city, where she'd mixed normal memories of childhood and teenage life ('here's where I broke up with my first ever boyfriend'), with the more sinister: the park in which she first saw her dad kissing a woman she didn't recognise; the McDonald's outside which three school bullies cycled past and threw a drink at her. Those bits of Esme's life it broke his heart to think about.

'The people who choose to stay in the town they grew up in are always the cool, popular kids at school,' Esme had said, after recounting that particular story. 'Everyone else has to flee, to escape the memories.'

'And the cool kids eventually become the losers, right?'

'Ideally. Maybe it's a fifteen-minutes-of-fame kind of thing. Everyone gets one period in their life when they're cool. Some people use it up at school. Some at university. Some have to wait until they're older.'

'Have you had your time yet?'

'I suppose that's for others to say,' Esme had said.

Now, as they walked onto Parks Road, Tom was sure that Esme's

98

time – her prime even – happened here. Among the architecture, the intelligence and the education she so venerated. He could easily envision a younger version of her joining societies, at which she would state her forthright position on whatever it was, from wine and books to the failure of neoliberalism under Tony Blair. He played out scenes of her walking through colleges on crisp autumnal days, scarf thrown loosely around her neck. Although he took the piss a bit, these were all things he wished he had been around to see – the very point of these day trips, really.

'Here,' Esme said, as they crossed over the road to arrive at Keble College. She immediately provided Tom with the college's potted history, taking on the mantle of an unofficial guide with a walking tour that touched on controversial architecture, the size of the student body, *University Challenge* wins and notable former students. She flashed her alumni card at a woman dressed in security garb waiting on the gate, walked under the arch of the porter's lodge and out into the pristine grass quads and Gothic buildings of the university.

'Jesus, Esme. You lived here?' Tom said, with incredulity.

'Sort of. Most people's dorms are over there,' she said, pointing at a comparatively disappointing, perfunctory new building that Tom was disappointed to see disturb the flow of the old and ivy-clad. 'We took seminars and tutorials here. It's nice, isn't it?'

'A bit *Brideshead Revisited*, isn't it?' he said, a bit shocked by his first real glimpse behind the curtain of this particular kind of elite higher education.

'You've read *Brideshead Revisited*?'

'Yeah,' he said. 'Well, half of it. You gave it to me.'

'Name three characters,' Esme said.

'Fine. I only read a quarter. And the Wikipedia page.'

Esme laughed. The happiness at being back here was writ large across her face and seemed to lift her whole body. She threw her blue, white and red crested college scarf around her neck and set off into the college grounds. They made one full circuit of the largest quad, criss-crossed through the middle of the lawns and toured the library, Esme pointing out various noteworthy features as they wandered.

'And this,' she said as they arrived at a fairly nondescript part of the college, 'is the bench where I first met Jamilla.' Esme presented the bench like a magician finishing a trick, causing the girl currently sitting on it to look at them strangely, get up, and leave. 'I thought something bad had happened to her. But really she'd just drunk a shitload of Aftershock and was trying to hide from the CCTV because she was throwing up on the quad.'

'Good,' said Tom, half listening.

'Why's that good?'

'Sorry. I didn't mean *good*. I meant—'

'Are you bored?'

'No! Es, really no. Far from it.'

'Well, you weren't really listening. We can go if you want?'

'Honestly, no. It's just that so far you've told me all about your mates, where famous people lived and that bloke in your year who became a TV presenter. But I want to know more about you, Es. Your time here. You looked so happy when we came in.'

'Okay,' she said uncertainly. 'I mean, I'm not sure there's much to say.'

'Give me a typical day.'

'Just like any, I suppose. Breakfast in halls. Tutorials. Seminars. Lunch. Reading. Dinner. Pub. More reading.'

'I'm not sure that's like any other. For a start, I doubt most students do that much reading. Or have breakfast in halls.'

'Well, no.'

'What about the societies, then? Drama, book groups, sports?'

'You know about the drama.'

'Well, where was it based?'

'Over there somewhere,' she said, throwing her arm in the direction of the city centre.

She looked strangely dispirited. The confidence and joy that was so obvious when they'd walked over from the park was gone and replaced by a kind of reticence.

'What's up, Es?'

'Look. I just don't want you to have an unrealistic view of what my time was like here,' she said, taking a seat on the bench. 'I was a bit of a swot, to be honest. I didn't go out much, only had a few friends. Mainly I came to work and I did. It may not have been the stereotypical Oxbridge experience. But it was *my* experience.'

'That's fine—'

'And I loved it, Tom. I really, really loved it. Every day. I know for some people uni is all about the experience and meeting a load of people and getting blind drunk. But I was here for the education. And I know that sounds really boring and square, but—'

'It's fine. It's good, Es. More people should be like that,' Tom said, bringing her close to him. 'Sorry. I suppose when you brought me here I was expecting all the stories of your uni days. All the things you hear about Oxford and Cambridge, like the balls and societies and that.'

'The balls are like a hundred quid to get in. Basically, only the future bankers and lawyers go to the balls.'

'I literally thought they were free.'

Esme shook her head sadly. 'Nope. Everyone else goes to the pub.'

'Come on,' she said, leading him off the bench and back onto the paths, where current students walked busily past them, talking into mobile phones or to each other in little groups. 'If you care so much I'll show you where I lived.'

As soon as she said it, Tom felt a little spark of panic. He almost regretted asking her for a more personal version of her history here. He had forgotten that it would mean doing *this* – that it would be his first time back in a university halls building for almost nine years. Tom checked his watch, half hoping that they'd run out of time, so he could suggest skipping it. But it had only just gone twenty to three.

Esme took him around the side of another Gothic building and towards a modern block, sneaking in the front door before anyone paid them too much attention. She moved through the corridors quickly, muscle memory guiding her. Their footsteps on the cold linoleum floor echoed off the scuffed walls. They went up one set of stairs, halfway down another corridor and eventually arrived at room 119.

'This was me,' she said, looking a little wistfully at the door of her old dorm. 'I used to have a little sign saying ESME.'

Tom stared at the door. Now the only feature of any note was a small scrap of Christmas tinsel dangling from a piece of Sellotape.

The similarities to his old room at university were striking. The smell of the place was familiar: bleach-washed floors and stale air. It even looked the same. The white walls, dented and marked over the years, occasionally interrupted by noticeboards advertising gigs, or displaying warnings about student behaviour and fire safety.

Although he barely remembered anything of it, there were things he'd pieced together from what others had told him: a history of that night cobbled together from guesswork and his own fragments of memory.

It happened around 10 p.m., that much he knew. He was discovered by an engineering undergrad named John. They'd heard groaning and retching from his room. Two months after the event, Tom was sent the bill for repairs to the door the paramedics had to break down to get to him.

Beyond that, he knew very little.

There was a faint recollection of a gurney's squeaking wheels; the blue-red lights and blurred onlookers.

He couldn't go back to university after that. His steady decline from party animal to suicide risk was complete. And even if he had returned the following year and surrounded himself with a new set of students, Tom knew word would work its way around. Universities were like that. Before long the quiet, introspective twenty-year-old music student would become a cautionary tale of unchecked excess – an example of the need for student counselling facilities.

Besides, he didn't want to return. That part of his life had closed that final night of term before the Easter holidays. It wasn't for him. And things were better for it, he was certain.

'You alright?' she said.

'Fine.'

'You don't look fine.'

'I'm *fine*,' he said.

'Okay,' Esme said, taken aback by the force in his voice.

Tom leant up against the wall. Esme took his hand and leant in close.

'Is everything okay, Tom? You've gone really pale.'

'I'm . . . I'm okay. Don't worry,' he said, trying to collect himself, aware that he was on the verge of ruining what had been a nice day. 'Where's next?'

'I thought I'd show you my favourite pub. It's not far. The—'

'Actually, could we not?' Tom said. 'Maybe just a coffee or something.'

Esme still looked uncertain, confused.

'Of course,' she said, taking his hand. For a moment he wished he could shake it off and run away. He had never felt like that about her before.

# CHAPTER EIGHT

**3 – 4 am**

# THE CAMPING TRIP
## August 2012 – Wimbleball Lake, Somerset

They both looked up at the roof of the tent, which sagged heavily with collected rainwater. The portable lamp Tom had fixed to the hook above them was now at least six inches closer to their noses than it should have been.

'And you're *sure* you put it up properly?'

'Yes,' he hissed.

'It's just we've never done this before.'

'I know, Esme.'

'And I did say it looked a bit... well... sad.'

'Sad?'

'Yes.'

'How can a bloody tent look sad?'

'You know. Floppy.'

'Next time you can do it.'

'*Camping*,' Esme said, bitterly, as she shuffled around on the air bed, trying to get comfortable, and Tom started to giggle.

'What is it?'

'Floppy,' he said, trying to stifle a laugh.

'It does!'

'The sad, floppy tent,' he said, which made Esme laugh as well, emitting the occasional snort that came whenever she found something uncontrollably, unaccountably funny. Gradually his laughter made hers worse, and hers his. Until they were both in silent hysterics, desperate to howl and giggle, but at the same time desperate not to make any noise. It was fart-in-school-assembly laughter, the kind that no amount of effort can suppress.

'The maudlin tent,' Esme said, struggling to get the words out.

'Underwhelmed,' Tom countered, and as she muttered 'unfulfilled' the two of them were into full, howling laughter. When from somewhere in the field, a nearby camper shushed them as if they were children.

'Sorry!' Tom called out, making Esme laugh again.

'Look, mate,' they heard from another tent. 'We've got a thirteen-miler starting at seven tomorrow morning. We'd appreciate a bit of kip.'

They laughed again as they moved their sleeping bags closer to one another, shuffling like caterpillars on a bouncy castle.

As the laughter died and they came back to earth, Tom leant over and kissed Esme. He was relieved that they were laughing about the tent, instead of arguing about it, which until ten minutes ago had seemed the more likely outcome. He knew that, had it come, rather than passing them by like a storm on a summer's day, a fight might well have put an early end to their trip. It would have been the latest in a series of squabbles, fights and rows that had culminated last week with Tom sleeping on the sofa – the first time he'd been forced to do so since they'd moved in together.

That big one was about the late hours he'd been keeping recently, as he tried to finish work on a banal but cheerful ukulele soundtrack he'd been commissioned to write and record for a payments technology company's corporate video. TotalPay had been exceptionally difficult to work for. Not least because their junior marketing manager fancied himself as a musician-cum-critic and constantly found fault in Tom's work, comparing it unfavourably to other, more expensively commissioned payments technology companies' corporate videos.

'For what they're paying you, it's ridiculous,' Esme had said, irritated by the sheer amount of time he was putting into the project. But having only recently started working with a large advertising agency and a producer who liked his work, Tom wanted to show he could do a good job and was willing to put the hours in.

He was frustrated. But recently neither he nor Esme would admit it when the other was right. So instead of trying to talk, he had chosen to shout.

'Fucking hell, Esme. I've jacked in the covers band, I've sacked off the gigging. I need to make money *somewhere*!' he had yelled, then marched out of the bedroom and slumped down on the sofa, only to realise it was far too small for any kind of proper sleep. So, instead, he spent two uncomfortable hours wondering if he should concede a little ground to Esme, if only to get back to bed. In the end he decided not to, believing that backing down would only lead to more problems. He regretted his decision the next day, when his back ached so much that he could barely sit at his desk chair for more than twenty minutes at a time.

In the manner of couples experiencing a rough patch, Tom knew 'the ukulele incident' was a fierce and personal argument about a fairly benign topic. But recently that kind of petty bickering had started to crop up in all areas: when Annabel texted him in the middle of the night; when half-drunk cups of cold tea were left around the house whenever Esme worked from home.

The scale of the offence had little to do with the scale of the row. But however bad the arguments were, Tom knew he couldn't let himself forget the last time something like this had happened. Back in October 2008, when he'd panicked and called off the relationship in a fit of self-destruction. That time the problem was proximity, rather than bickering. Esme was closer to him than anyone had been before, and he was unable to cope with it.

Of course, he realised how stupid he was almost immediately, lasting all of forty-eight hours before begging her to forgive him. However, angry and upset, Esme had kept him waiting for a week.

Eventually she had agreed to meet him at a pub in Pimlico on a rainy day in mid-autumn. Tom arrived far too early, taking his place among the regulars, with half a Diet Coke, a damp copy of the *Evening Standard*, and a broken umbrella that had done nothing to stop his feet from getting soaked on the short walk from the Tube station. The pub was an empty, grim mix of midweek drinkers and people sheltering from the rain. All of them looking out onto the rough, grey, Thames. Outside, the once-crisp golden-brown leaves covering the streets had turned to a muddy, fusty sludge – the result of days of non-stop rain.

Tom was focused on the crossword, trying to scrawl *MAGPIE* without tearing the wet page when the door creaked open and Esme appeared. He smiled and offered a half-arsed sort of wave. But as she approached he didn't know what to do.

A hug? A kiss? The former seemed a little cold, the latter a bit too much, given the circumstances. In the end, he did nothing. She removed her jacket and placed her bike helmet atop Tom's newspaper. He just about managed to avoid wincing at the half-done crossword she had just ruined.

'I still can't believe you cycle in this weather.'

'It's not that bad,' she said shortly, as she wriggled out of her waterproof trousers and hung them over the big grey column radiator.

'Can I get you something?'

'Half a London Pride,' she said. 'Actually, make it a pint.'

When Tom returned to the table, she was perched on a stool

flicking through her emails on her iPhone – her new favourite toy, and as a result, Tom's least.

'So,' he muttered.

'So,' she said, allowing the murmurs of the pub and the distant sound of the radio to make the silence between them that bit more awkward.

'Es, I'm really not sure what to say.'

'I'll just go then, shall I?' she said, making to climb off the stool.

'No, please. Esme. It's just hard.'

'Right.'

'I mean . . .' Tom began. But he had no idea what he meant, nor what to say to fix things between them. He only wanted to see her again – hadn't thought as far as explaining himself. 'I suppose I mean I'm sorry.'

'Suppose.'

'Es.'

'What? You either are, or you aren't.'

'I am.'

'Well that's good, Tom.'

'Esme, please.'

'You tell me it's over. Completely out of the fucking blue. And for no fucking reason that makes any sense. Then you invite me to this bloody pub and all you can say is that you suppose you're sorry?'

Tom went to intervene. But she was away now. There was no point.

'It's going to take a fucking damn sight more than "sorry", Tom. Okay?'

'I chose a place that's near where you live,' he said tentatively.

'What?'

'The pub. That's why I chose it. You sounded annoyed about it.'

'Right, Tom. Let's put pub choice to the bottom of the list of grievances. Why don't we start with why this happened in the first place?'

'I—' Tom stopped. He knew the precise reason why he had called it off. What he didn't know was whether admitting it would be worse than telling a lie. 'I got nervous.'

'Nervous?'

'Yeah. You know. Like, the closer we get, the worse it'll be if it goes wrong.'

'So you decided to make it go wrong?'

'Well, sort of. But then I realised that I was wrong to make it go wrong. If that makes sense?'

'Very little about this makes sense.'

'Look. We had a few arguments. Things were becoming different.'

'It's called life, Tom.'

'I know—'

'If you can't stand that, then . . . God knows.'

'I thought, if we moved in together, or whatever, and it didn't work . . . that'd be terrible, right? And I'm not exactly easy to live with. So I just—'

'Got cold feet.'

'No.'

'Yes. You got cold feet. People get them all the time. You know Christine? Before Barney she was with a guy called Jason. Two weeks before they were supposed to move in together, he got off the bus a few stops early, walked into a dodgy massage parlour and paid for sex. You know what he blamed it on? Cold feet.'

'Well I didn't . . . do *that*.'

'My point, Tom, is that cold feet is a bit of a bullshit excuse for being a dickhead. Why was it easier to tell me we're over than to say what you were actually thinking?'

After a moment, Tom said, 'Don't know,' in the manner of a school child asked to explain precisely why he had set the fire alarm off. But he was being quite truthful: he didn't know. All he did know was that he had made a mistake.

They didn't reconcile that evening, even though they both wanted a resolution. Instead, Esme made him wait a few days before getting back in touch, making it clear that this was the first and last time something like that could happen.

Tom had disrupted the trajectory of their relationship. Set things back. But while he was sad for the problems he had caused, he was strangely also a little relieved.

The camping trip was, if unofficially, another rebuilding and re-connecting exercise: five days of walking, eating and talking in the West Country. Esme had imposed a 'no social media or work email' rule; Tom promised to be less quick to anger about the small things that didn't matter. Esme told him she would, in turn, stop being too critical of his foibles.

And now they found themselves wet, cold and stuck beneath a rapidly disintegrating piece of canvas.

'Was this what you envisioned?' Esme asked as the tent continued to crumble. 'Lying awake hoping the tent won't fall apart.'

Tom thought about making a joke. But settled instead for honesty.

'I was just hoping we'd get along,' he said.

'Tom—'

'I know I've not been easy recently.'

'Please, Tom.'

'No, it's true.'

'Yes, but I've not been easy either, have I? Maybe I'm not under-standing enough about your work and how things have changed. I don't really have to think about my next career steps all that much. I'm in a bit of a bubble.'

'There is no music bubble. Or at least if there is, I haven't found it.'

'But you're good at the advertising stuff. I know it's not what you originally wanted to do. But how many people get to call themselves a composer?'

'There are levels, though. Aren't there?' Tom said, thinking back to the 'in' he'd thought he had about a year ago, when a producer of TV soundtracks expressed some interest in the music he was making. That interest died almost as soon as it was born. But through that producer he had met another who suggested he could turn his talents to advertising, mostly online. It was fine work for good money. Meeting the deadlines meant a bit of compromise. And he was actually okay with stopping the gigs, now having more reason to be at home. He was finally making a living creating music. Just not in the way he'd anticipated.

'What do you mean, levels?'

'Like, some people are composers of film scores and stuff. Some are composers of jingles for businesses who sell credit-card machines to supermarkets.'

'But *you are* a composer, Tom. That's amazing. And besides, who knows, one day you might work your way up.'

'Hmm.'

'And if you don't, I'll still be proud of every little jingle you make. I'll even listen to them in the gym.'

Tom smiled. He knew that she was probably telling the truth. Every decision he had made, from his work as a private music tutor to the wealthy and uninterested kids of Hampstead, to this new move into advertising, had been wholly supported and encouraged. Even if her certainty about her career as a child speech therapist meant she couldn't ever quite empathise with him, she was always positive about what he did.

'I suppose I should apologise, too,' Esme said quietly, after a moment in which the campers around them thought the evening's chatter had finally come to an end.

'No,' Tom said, unconvincingly.

'Tom. Come on. I know I've been ... uptight. I can't even say why.'

'Because Annabel texts really late at night?'

'Well obviously that is incredibly annoying. But it's never bothered me before. Besides, I like Annabel. She's good for you. Christ, if it wasn't for her at that party we'd never have met.'

'I like to think we would have.'

'How?' she said.

'Maybe on the Tube. You would see me reading one of your favourite novels and start up a conversation.'

'I would literally never start up a conversation on the Tube. And I cycle to work.'

'Flat tyre. And clearly you would also find me so irresistible that you had to.'

'Well, of course,' she said mockingly. 'Anyway. I know I've been uptight and grumpy. I just ...'

She paused, as if struggling to find the courage.

'What, Es?' Tom asked.

'I need to know. Are you ... okay?' she asked seriously, but before Tom could make up an answer they were interrupted by the quiet snap of a tent pole.

'Shit, get out!' Tom said, as they scrabbled out of their sleeping bags, grabbed a few clothes and fell out of the tent, the front half of which promptly collapsed under the weight of the collected water, sending it down a small slope towards the grumpy campers who had earlier shushed them. And leaving Tom and Esme standing in a wet field, wearing nothing but pyjamas and wellington boots.

'I have to be honest,' he said, as the rain began to soak through his threadbare checked bottoms. 'I didn't really look at the instructions when I was putting it up.'

'I know,' Esme said, beginning to laugh again, as the one

remaining tent pole gave way, creating a canvas outline of their airbed, cool bag and Tom's walking boots.

'Would you *please* be quiet?' came a gruff, angry voice from another tent.

'Oh, fuck off,' Esme said through her laughter, and as they both fled across the squelchy mud towards the car park, Tom hoped she'd forgotten about the final question she'd not received an answer to.

## CHAPTER NINE

1 – 2 pm

# A PARTY OF SURPRISES

## May 2011 – Belsize Park, London

'You are coming, aren't you?' Tom said, his phone trapped between ear and shoulder as he opened a packet of confetti.

'Think so.'

'Don't give me "think so", Neil.'

'What? I always said I was a maybe.'

'On Facebook you're a yes.'

'Yeah well that's Facebook, isn't it?'

'Just come, okay?'

'What's the problem anyway?' Neil said, still denying Tom the full commitment he was after.

'The room's massive. Much bigger than it was two months ago when I booked it.'

'How can a room be bigger now than it was two months ago? It's the same bloody room.'

'You know what I mean,' Tom said, looking around the cavernous function room of The Lamb pub in Belsize Park. So far, he had spent an hour moving tables and bar stools around in various patterns, put up a trestle table to display the cake and a selection of Esme's favourite foods, and strung up large blooms of blue and white helium balloons. Yet despite all of it, the room still felt much too big. 'I think I've vastly overestimated the amount of space forty people will take up.'

'Just like when you used to put on gigs in Lowestoft.'

'Fuck off,' Tom said. 'Just be here. Half past and no later. I don't want you ballsing up the surprise.'

'Fine. Take it I can bring Stace?'

Tom was about to ask who Stace was, but thought better of it. She'd most likely be the latest in a long line of Neil's girlfriends. He had the unfortunate habit of falling deeply in love very quickly – before just as quickly becoming acutely aware of his partners' unforgivable flaws. The churn of relationships was often too fast to keep up with. But that wouldn't stop Neil from becoming deeply offended if Tom couldn't remember Stace's name.

'Of course,' Tom said, and hung up the phone. 'Shit,' he muttered to himself, as he took in the ramshackle job he had made of decorating. There was now less than an hour left and still loads to do.

At least he knew that Esme liked the pub. They visited most weekends, after walks on Hampstead Heath or to sit around doing the newspaper crossword on rainy Sundays. To them, it was as personal as a place could be, somewhere they had found and grown to love in an area they'd become happy calling home. Even if he had initially been resistant to the very idea of going to a pub to relax.

For Tom, any drinking den was simultaneously tempting and terrifying, and he felt the need to constantly remind himself of what he was.

This discomfort meant that he'd cut short their first visits to The Lamb; offering Esme one of a litany of terrible excuses and lies that would give them reason to get out minutes after they walked in, sometimes even before she had ordered.

*It's too busy, we'll never get a seat.*
*Sorry. I just feel really sick all of a sudden.*

*Why don't we head home instead? Watch a film or something.*

But gradually, as with so many things, Esme's presence made Tom feel more at home with his own mind. As long as she was opposite him, maintaining sobriety as a twenty-something Londoner did not feel like such constant hard work. Gradually he began to feel normal there.

She knew none of this, of course. And now, alone with all the taps, bottles and optics, Tom felt uneasy. There was no compulsion to drink. But there was *something*. A sort of pre-temptation characterised by the knowledge that he *could* do it. Even if he didn't want to.

It was a familiar anxiety. One that occasionally rose up, and once or twice bubbled over in his teens and early twenties. And as he scattered silver *30!* confetti pieces across the tables, he found himself drifting back to the worst moments. His own history was packed full of case studies that now gave him constant reason to say no: being carried home by friends; his mum crying as his dad and sister tried to sober him up with water and coffee at 3 a.m.; alone in student accommodation, drunk and throwing up on the ancient carpet. Quitting drink once, on the pretence that his mental make-up made alcohol problematic, that the two things were incompatible. Then relapsing a couple of years later, before finally admitting to himself that he had used alcohol to cover something up – as a way of trying to cope.

The smell of the disinfectant was nauseating. Tom ran a hand over the beer tap handles. How easy it would be to fall, to let go of five years of sobriety. How easily one sip could become one pint, one session, one failure.

Pins and needles prickled his hands and neck. He tried to bring Esme to mind: her smile, the feel of her palm on his thigh when she sensed he was becoming anxious. He must continue doing this for her, Tom knew. And one day he would tell her everything. Just not yet.

Tom checked his watch. Nearly 1.30 p.m., the time he had asked people to arrive on the invitation. Esme herself would be brought to the pub at 1.45 p.m. by her friend Jamilla, ostensibly for a quick lunch after a morning in Selfridges.

He carelessly threw some more confetti around the place. Two young barmaids (one of whom he vaguely recognised) appeared at the top of the staircase.

'Looks nice,' the short, blonde girl with a northern accent said.

'Thanks.'

'Those balloons look a bit low, though. The ceilings are quite high in here – you can afford to let them go up a bit.'

'I've run out of string.'

'Well I'm sure it'll be fine,' she said, with obvious uncertainty. 'How many you got coming?'

'Forty odd.'

'And you know it's a minimum spend of two grand, right?'

'I do,' Tom said, aware of the irony that, unless his guests drank enough, his biggest ever bar tab would hit him almost a decade after he quit drinking.

'What's her name, then?'

'Esme.'

'Nice name, that. Your wife is she?'

'Girlfriend.'

'How long you been together?'

'Almost four years.'

'Well she's lucky to have you. My boyfriend barely buys me a drink, let alone organises a party.' She smiled and started cutting fruit for mixers, while Tom perched a board of recent photos of Esme atop the pub's mantelpiece.

A creak on the staircase made him turn around. It was Esme's parents, Tamas and Lena, who had made a rare trip down to London for the party. Tamas reached out and shook Tom's hand firmly, as though grip and force were measures by which to judge a man. Lena, meanwhile, hugged him tightly and planted a kiss on his cheek, leaving behind a greasy smear of dark red lipstick.

'So wonderful of you to be doing this for our girl, Tom,' she said. 'And it all looks lovely.'

'Thank you.'

'The balloons look a little low, though.'

Tom forced a smile and excused himself to greet his own parents before they came over to make awkward conversation with Tamas and Lena – because they felt they should, not because they wanted to.

It wasn't the first time the four had met. Two months after Esme and Tom had moved in together in 2009, they had decided that a small housewarming party would be the ideal opportunity for their immediate families to get to know each other. Everyone got along fine. But trying to conjure a friendship between four people in their late fifties and early sixties, with all their firmly entrenched personality traits, was more or less impossible.

Nonetheless, the four of them gamely persisted to spend entire functions together, as if it was what their children wanted. Tom knew that later his dad would describe Tamas as a 'nice fella' and his mum Lena as a 'lovely woman', with neither of them able to add any context to either statement.

'This all looks lovely, Tom,' his mum said. 'And she does deserve it, doesn't she?'

'Yes, Mum,' Tom said, as she grasped and shook his upper arm in proud excitement, perhaps expecting more from the day than she could reasonably expect to.

'Might want to let these balloons up a bit, though. Unless all her mates are dwarves, eh?' his dad chuckled, before plodding off towards the bar, no doubt with a joke prepared about London prices.

Tom heard more footsteps on the stairs. Esme's friends were

arriving, with boyfriends in tow – people Tom knew because he was always thrown together with them at parties. They were inherited mates who, after three or four meetings, would add him on Facebook and send invites to golf days or five-a-side football matches, knowing with relative certainty that Tom would decline (regardless of how much Esme encouraged him). Perhaps if these 'away days' became less about the post-event drinking, he might one day.

Laura was first to turn up, with Steve (or 'Ste'), who yelled 'on your nod then' before headbutting a balloon, which floated slowly in Tom's direction. He remembered with some relief that, according to Esme, Laura would soon be leaving Steve for a colleague she'd been sleeping with, having been up overnight with him to report on the General Election last year and letting things grow from there. Tom felt a little sympathetic towards Steve. Or as sympathetic as he could towards a man who spent all his spare time and money in Square Mile strip clubs.

A procession of friends and their partners followed. Some Tom had met only a handful of times. They were people from the more obscure regions of Esme's life. It seemed like the further she got from university, the less she saw or spoke to the friends she had made there. They variously congratulated Tom for organising the party, marvelled at how he had managed to keep it a secret and, of course, commented on the low height of the balloons.

'The pub's health and safety regulations dictate,' he eventually said a little too loudly, snapping at an old school mate of Esme's from Leicester who had innocently wondered aloud who had put the balloons up, 'that helium inflatables must be at least six feet away from the ceiling.'

Despite the balloons, the people, the hellos and the how-are-yous, Tom could not concentrate on the small talk. It was 1.40. Esme would arrive in five minutes. And as he looked around at almost everyone Esme knew and loved, he couldn't shake the feeling that when she arrived, she'd take one look around, and turn on her heel to leave.

Was this party an utterly terrible idea? he wondered.

'Just me and you. Dinner maybe. Or a weekend away at the very most,' Esme had told him when he'd raised the prospect of her thirtieth earlier in the year. It was New Year's Day and they were taking their now-traditional 1st January walk around Regent's Park to talk vaguely and flippantly about their hopes and ambitions for the months ahead.

'But it's a big one, Es,' Tom said, before backtracking suddenly. 'Not big as in, you know, the *number*. But big as in a milestone.'

'Yes. But what do I really have to mark? Everything in my life now is the same as what it was two years ago. Apart from you it's the same as it was *five* years ago.'

'One: not true. Two: it's about more than the last two years. You've done so much in your twenties. Degree, masters, amazing job, home in London.'

'We don't have a home in London. We *rent* a flat in London.'

'Yes, well you know what I mean. You've made a home in London. Or *of* London. Whatever.'

'I'm not even sure I want to live in London.'

'Really?'

'There's more than one city in England, Tom,' she said grumpily. 'This year I've done conferences in Bristol, Norwich and Manchester. All of them seem nice.'

'My family live near Norwich.'

'And?'

'If we moved there they'd be round all the time.'

'It's nice to see family.'

'But *all the time*?'

'Fine. Look, all I mean is that I'm coming up to thirty. Great. But I don't want to feel as though everything is set in stone. That

I've ticked all the boxes and my future's just a continuation of the past few years.' She cracked the ice on a frozen puddle. 'When our parents' generation turned thirty, that's just how it was. You had your job, your home, your family and your friends. And nothing changed again until you got to your mid-forties, your kids started to make their own lives and your friends started getting divorced.'

'What's your point, Es?'

'Thirty doesn't mean what it used to. I've no idea why we celebrate it.'

'So what should we celebrate instead?' Tom asked as they passed the tennis courts, where paunchy middle-aged men were striving to impress their young tennis coach with overly ambitious serves and smashes.

'The fives.'

'Huh?' Tom said, slightly distracted by the coach himself.

'We should celebrate the fives. Twenty-five, thirty-five, forty-five. That's when the milestones happen now. At twenty-five people have left uni and figured out what they want to do with their lives. Thirty-five they might have got married or had kids or something.'

'Forty-five?'

'Don't know. Still probably getting divorced.'

'How cheerful.'

'At twenty-five you look for the one. At forty-five you look for *anyone*. That's the way it is.'

'What a bleak picture of the future you paint.'

'Not bleak. Just realistic.'

'Anyway. So you'll have a party when you're thirty-five?'

'I don't really like parties.'

Tom said nothing as they crossed the bridge over the boating lake and started to walk back north towards Camden.

'Why have you gone quiet?' she asked. 'Tell me you weren't thinking about a party.'

'It might be nice. Get everyone together.'

'Just no, Tom. No. Not even a "no but really yes", like when your sister told Nathan not to buy her a Christmas present and he actually didn't. This is an *actual* no.'

'Fine,' Tom said. 'An actual no. Understood.'

*An actual no.*

The words reverberated around Tom's head as the text came in from Jamilla.

**Almost at the pub with Es. Everyone ready? X**

Tom replied with a *yes*, then picked up two glasses and knocked them together to silence the room. Immediately he felt his throat dry up, suddenly convinced that all of this was indeed a terrible idea, that it would be better to tell everyone to flee out of the back door.

'Two minutes away, everyone,' he called, as a loud cheer rose up around him.

'I don't know how these things work. But let's get the lights turned off, keep quiet and we'll just shout "surprise" when she comes in.'

The barmaid obliged by turning down the dimmer switch and casting the room into dark dinginess. Then came a creak on the pub's old wooden stairs. Esme.

Tom's heart began to thump in his chest – what would her re-action be? Affection? Or anger? Of the kind that would make her turn around and storm away?

And then, before he knew it, she was there, standing in front of him – beautiful in black jeans, a white cotton shirt, and heeled shoes with red pom poms on the toes. The look on her face suggested she'd just been plunged into ice-cold water without warning – her mouth somewhere between a smile and a scream.

Their eyes met. For a second, before the lights came back up again, Tom had Esme's complete attention. And before the people and the party took her there would be this one, perfect moment he would remember her by for years to come.

The yell of 'surprise' came sharp and loud, beginning at the front of the room and working its way back, like a Mexican wave, ending their all-too-brief time together. Esme reacted with a duly surprised scream, clasping one hand over her mouth as Laura put a glass of prosecco into the other, and immediately made to pull her towards her closest friends.

'Wait,' Esme said firmly. Wresting her arm from Laura's hand and approaching Tom instead, whose heart, lungs and probably liver were all now collected somewhere near the back of his throat.

'You?' she said, a hint of a smile creeping onto her face.

'Me.'

'All you?'

'Mostly. Are you—'

'Taking it all in,' she said. With that she leant forward, kissed Tom on the lips and was quickly dragged away from him, into a melee of those closest to her.

It took Tom ten minutes to find Esme again. By that point she was two drinks down and looking at the cake and food table, which was also stacked with presents, cards (and more bloody balloons).

'Do you hate me, then?' Tom said, taking her hand.

'Well, hate's a bit strong.'

'Annoyed?'

'Hmm,' she said.

'But do you like it?'

'Well, we're only ten minutes in.'

'Right . . . yeah,' Tom said, looking down at the floor.

'Look. Shall we go outside for a minute? I could do with collecting my thoughts.'

'Oh . . . sure,' Tom said, certain that this would be it. The moment she lost her temper with him for ignoring her and doing what *he* wanted. They worked their way through the busy ground floor of the pub, full of Sunday walkers looking for tables and well-to-do families in possession of them. Esme led Tom out of the big, heavy wooden door and onto Fleet Road, where a small group of drinkers was smoking together.

'You hate it, don't you?' Tom said, when they were alone.

'No.'

'You can just say, Es. Don't pretend. I'd really rather you didn't pretend.'

'Tom, I love it,' she said with a smile.

'Really?'

'Yes!' she said. 'It's amazing. And even more amazing that you managed to keep it a secret.'

'It was hard. Especially your—'

'Mum?'

'Good guess,' he said.

Esme kissed him. He could taste prosecco on her lips. It was not a drink he was familiar with – fizzy wine rarely the choice for people who want to get drunk with great speed and efficiency.

'You okay?' Esme asked.

'I am.'

'Did you hear what I said?'

'No. Sorry. I thought . . . never mind,' Tom said, looking over at the group of smokers.

'I said to be clear, I still hate parties.'

'Okay.'

'And the surprise thing means I've not managed to do my make-up properly. Or my hair.'

'You look amazing.'

'Tom,' she said, silencing him. 'What I mean is that I love that you did it. That all these months you've been doing stuff like inviting people and sorting out cakes and decorations. And all just for me.'

'Good,' Tom said, but he was still only half listening. He recognised one of the smokers. It was a face he hadn't seen in about ten years. One he'd hoped to never see again. Worse, the smoker now seemed to recognise him.

'One thing though,' she said. 'Those balloons are a bit low. People keep knocking their—'

'Hang on.'

'I said the balloons,' Esme said, waving a hand in front of his face. 'Tom, are you even—'

'Fucking *Murray!*' the familiar, nearly forgotten voice said, almost pushing Esme out of the way to get to Tom.

John, the smoker's name was. Or Jonno, to the friends that convened every night in the kitchen of Tom's halls at the University of Hertfordshire, before going to the student union bars or the clubs in nearby St Albans. They were all engineering students. Tom remembered their little in-jokes. Drunk was 'well oiled'. They referred to their usual crawl around three pubs as 'the track'. They were always civil to him, but never friends.

John grabbed his hand and shook it firmly. He was obviously drunk, swaying gently on the spot with a cigarette still lodged in the side of his mouth.

'How you fucking been then? Haven't seen you in time, son. You did a bit of a disappearing act.'

This was how he talked, Tom remembered. Even in his late teens he spoke like a fifty-year-old welder leant over the bar in a flat-roofed pub.

'I'm alright,' Tom said. 'I'm at my girlfriend's thirtieth, actually. We were just in the middle—'

'Happy birthday!' John said, almost shouting at Esme while shaking her hand. 'Fucking thirty, eh? Creeping up.'

'Anyway,' Tom interrupted. He was desperate to get rid of John before the conversation turned to the past, to the subject of how they really knew each other. A knot had formed in his stomach from thinking about it. Or rather, from Esme learning about it. Why did all of this have to happen today?

'We better get back. People will be wondering where you are,' Tom said, trying to move away.

'You live round here then, do you?' John said, ignoring him.

'Not far.'

'Nice. Me and the boys are on a bit of a mission round north London. Gary's just moved up Chalk Farm. Fucking fortune,' he said, adding no context to who Gary was, or what was a 'fucking fortune'.

'Yeah,' Tom said dismissively. 'Look, we'd better . . .' Tom said, trailing off as he took Esme's hand and moved towards the pub. She looked confused by the whole thing. 'Come on.'

'Fucking hell. Alright then,' John said, now affronted by Tom's determination not to speak to him. 'I was only saying hello. Thought you might at least give me the time of day, after what happened the last time I saw you.'

'Tom, what—' Esme said, but he cut her off.

'Sorry. We just—'

'Whatever, mate. Whatever. You just fuck off back to your party.'

Tom and Esme turned away in the direction of the pub. Before they did, however, John called out to him again.

'Good to see you're off the booze. Fucking pisshead,' John yelled, a parting shot. The rest of his group were looking over now, as was every other smoker.

Tom took Esme's hand, made for the heavy, brass-handled door and led her towards the stairs and the party. But he could feel her resisting, pulling back.

'Stop. Tom, stop.'

'What?' he said, turning to face Esme. He felt sweat across his brow. His heart was beating fast, relieved to get away from John but worried that she had already heard too much.

'What do you mean "what?"' she said. 'Aren't you going to tell me what that was all about?'

'I knew him at uni.'

'Yes. But that's not really how I'd expect you to greet an old friend. What was he talking about when he said "the last time"?'

'Nothing.'

'He called you a fucking pisshead.'

'Es,' Tom said. He was about to tell her it was nothing again. But when he looked into her eyes he realised he couldn't. Not this time. 'It's not as bad as it sounds.'

'Well tell me then.'

'After the party.'

'Now, Tom. I want to know now.'

Hesitant though he was, Tom spoke.

'We were at uni together,' he said. 'I had some problems . . . in my first year.'

'Problems,' Esme said. He could see her joining the dots together. Connecting the things he'd told her in the past with what just happened outside the pub. 'With alcohol?'

'Yeah. With . . .' But Tom couldn't bring himself to say it. 'It's why I don't drink. When I was younger I used to drink too much.'

'Bad experiences.'

'What?'

'You told me you had a couple of bad experiences.'

'I did,' Tom said. 'But . . . it was more than . . . it was more than a bad experience.'

Esme was looking at him. She seemed almost scared by what he was saying.

'There was one night when I took a few pills,' he said, unable to meet her eyes. 'John found me.'

'Found you? For fuck's sake, Tom. Come on. You're giving me half a story.'

'Fine... just let me...'

'Let you what? Tell me what happened,' she said forcefully. A few people at the bar were looking at them, while at the same time trying to not get caught gawping.

'I'd stolen his beers from the shared fridge because I didn't want to go out to get any. Apparently when he came to ask me about it he couldn't get in my room. He heard something unusual. So he kicked the door in. I was there, out cold... then John called the ambulance.'

'Unusual?'

'Like retching. I think.'

'Tom, are you telling me what I think you're—'

'No,' he said firmly. 'Es, no. I was just drinking too much.'

'Because it sounds like you—'

'Esme, no,' he said. Tom was determined now. Intent on pulling her away from thinking it. 'I just wanted to be out of it. I found the pills and that was it. You know?'

'Not really, Tom, no. I've never felt like... *that*.'

'Es.'

'And that's why you dropped out?'

'I struggled with uni, okay?' he said firmly, aware that other people in the pub were watching. 'I'm sorry that happened, but it was the right decision to leave.'

'And were you *ever* going to tell me this, Tom? For four years I've thought that you're sober because you didn't like how it made you feel.'

'I don't!'

'And now this.'

'Es, I was going to tell you. Just not now.'

Esme looked up at him. Tom had never seen her like this before. He couldn't tell if she was angry or sad. Either way, it confirmed his decision not to say any more. Not yet, anyway.

'Some surprise,' she said.

'Es, I'm sorry.'

'Let's just go back.'

Esme turned away and started back up the stairs. He was about to call out to her, when the door opened and John stepped in. They looked at each other for a moment.

'Es,' Tom called, turning away.

When he got back to the party, Esme was already with her friends on the other side of the room. He wanted to go over and see her, but knew that doing so would make things worse. This would have to wait. Maybe later that evening they could talk. Although Tom hoped that she wouldn't want to. Things had gone far enough already.

He was looking over at her when he felt a push in his back.

'Sorry we're late,' came a voice from beside him. It was Neil, accompanied by a thin, pale-skinned girl with red hair. 'You remember Stace, don't you?'

Tom nodded, unable to concentrate. He was still looking over at Esme, who was chatting and laughing and drinking as if nothing had happened downstairs.

'Everything alright, mate?'

'Fine.'

'Right. Good to chat as always, Murray. We'll go get a drink,' Neil said, turning to his girlfriend. 'Watch out for those balloons. Some dickhead has hung them too low,' he said, at which Tom marched over to the bar, picked up a pair of scissors, and began to cut the ribbon of every balloon in the pub.

# CHAPTER TEN

**5 – 6 am**

# ANOTHER BED,
# TWO MONTHS BEFORE WE MET
### April 2007 – The Royal Free Hospital, London

'Hey,' Tom croaked, when he noticed her stirring. She opened her eyes with what looked like great difficulty, as though someone had glued them shut during the night. But just as soon closed them again, refusing to wake up.

'Annabel,' he said. Still nothing.

He swallowed what little saliva he had to lubricate the back of his throat.

'Visiting hours don't start until nine, love.'

'Seriously?' came her croaky reply. Annabel stretched out and sat up a little groggily. 'You're seriously making a joke now?'

'Sorry. Gallows—'

'Don't even think about finishing that sentence. I'm not in the mood for jokes, Murray. Fuck knows why you are.'

Annabel had been asleep on an avocado-coloured, faux leather armchair. She was dressed like she was going out, in tight fitted dark blue jeans, a white shirt and a jacket, her hair ruffled and untidy. She looked so uncomfortable, Tom thought – she surely couldn't have been sleeping on it for more than a couple of hours. As she came round, she looked surprised to see him awake. Or perhaps she was just surprised to find herself in hospital at five in the morning.

It was still dark. In the silence he could hear footsteps and trolleys in the corridor, the sounds of a hospital getting ready to tackle the morning. Before long the doctors, nurses, visitors would gather around his bed to talk about him as if he wasn't in it.

'You're up, then?' Annabel said.

Tom nodded. He couldn't bring himself to speak again. Instead he offered a little wave, lifting his hand out of the itchy blanket that had been draped over him.

Annabel stood up and walked to his bedside. Tom pointed at the plastic cup full of water, a white straw sticking out of the top. Annabel offered him a sip, which he took. The feeling of the water on his mouth and throat was shocking and welcome – the first drops of rain on heat-parched ground.

She dragged the armchair across the room, towards his bed.

'You don't have to—'

'I know,' Annabel said. 'I want to.' She took the cup and replaced it on the table next to his bed. 'How are you feeling?'

'Terrible. My throat . . .'

'They said it would hurt.'

'It does.'

'I'm supposed to tell a nurse that you're up. They almost didn't let me stay.'

'Give it a minute,' Tom said, looking into his best friend's eyes.

As he did, he tried to piece together what had happened. Yesterday afternoon he had returned to his studio flat with a bottle of vodka. Time was it would've been two. But now, after years of sobriety, one was enough. The visit to the little shop near his block had been the only time he'd left the house in five days, since returning from a music lesson with a fourteen-year-old boy with an expensive grand piano placed in a bay window that looked out over Primrose Hill. He'd spent the entire lesson unable to concentrate, feeling dizzy and uncomfortable, hot and nervous. Sick and nauseous for no reason that he could explain.

'You alright?' Joel, the boy, had asked.

'Fine,' he had lied.

As before, it was the anxiety that came first. Twitchiness and panic. The feeling that he wanted to scream and smash things, to tear the skin from his bones. To run and hide.

Try explaining that to an over-privileged teenager who didn't even want him there in the first place.

Soon after came the creeping self-hatred. The feeling that he couldn't trust anyone else around him; a retreat into the four walls he knew the best. All he wanted was to close himself off from the world around him, to subsist instead of exist.

This episode had followed the pattern of the others before it. However, unlike before, he had lost his old method of self-medication: the thing that would not so much dull the edges, but remove them entirely. For Tom, anxiety and depression meant alcohol. But he was sober, and had been for years.

At first, the bottle had only been an option – a way out, should he choose to take it. But, vulnerable and alone, the unscrewing of the cap seemed almost inevitable. He remembered how it happened now. How he had sat there with it open for a good half-hour, testing his own resolve.

*Are you strong enough to resist, Tom Murray?*

Of course, the answer was no. The answer was always no. A hard-maintained iron will was the only reason he ever stayed on track. But he was rarely able to seek help when he felt anxiety coming on in the face of oblivion.

The first taste was hideous: noxious and chemical. Just as he remembered it. The second sip was no better. But within a few minutes of sitting on his bed, drinking from the bottle, he became accustomed to it again.

It didn't take Tom long to feel drunk. The last thing he remembered was hazily walking into the bathroom, where he found the box of paracetamol pills. One deck half used. The other three complete.

Then, nothing.

'How many did I take?' he asked Annabel.

'Enough,' she said, smiling at his incompetence, sad that she had to smile. 'Apparently your lack of tolerance for alcohol meant you blacked out before you could get very far. Lightweight.'

He looked away, ashamed.

'Funny that it was booze that saved you.'

'As in funny ha ha?'

They fell into silence again. Tom had a hundred questions, and a hundred apologies. But he could think of no place to start that felt right.

'How did . . .' he began. Before he could finish his sentence, Annabel took out her phone and held it in front of his face. On the screen was a text message from Tom:

HellP

'Got that at half seven. I was on a date, by the way. Fancy restaurant in Soho. She was very nice, but now thinks I'd prearranged for someone to text me so I could escape early. So that was good,' she said.

'Sorry.'

'Oh, you will be, Murray,' Annabel said. She was trying to joke with him, but immediately her face fell and she sobbed, turning away.

'I am sorry,' he said.

Annabel turned back, her face a little red now. She was angry,

Tom could tell. He had known her since they were both eleven and had never seen her like this. Despite everything they had been through and experienced together, he had managed to bring out this new side of Annabel.

'Do you know what it's like to find you like that?' she said through gritted teeth. 'On the fucking floor, lying in your own sick.'

Tom tried to look away but couldn't turn his head.

'I thought you were fucking dead, Tom. Dead. I thought, this time he's done it. And it's me that's found him.'

'I'm sor—'

'No,' she interrupted. 'Now you're awake and can barely talk, I want you to listen.'

Tom nodded.

'I am not doing that again, okay? Never. You try it once more and you're on your own. Fuck, I've basically lost my parents. I am not losing my best friend as well. You are the closest thing I have to family, Tom. Don't fucking do this to me. Not again.'

Now Tom was crying too.

'I'm sorry,' he said, his throat painfully dry again. He flinched as he spoke and Annabel handed him the water. She sat down next to him in the chair she'd been sleeping in. Her anger had dissipated, replaced once more by a heavy sadness. Tom hated that he had the ability to do this to people.

She took his hand.

'I know there's no cure for this. But you have to remember that there are other ways out.'

'I know.'

'There are always reasons to live, Tom. Sometimes you just have to remind yourself of what they are.'

Tom smiled. 'Very profound,' he said. 'How long had you been preparing that one?'

'Fuck off. Again.'

The moment lifted both of them, and tipped the tears over into smiles and bleak, genuine laughter. As they wiped tears from their eyes, early light began to poke through the roller blinds. The room was growing warmer.

'My parents?' Tom said.

'At a hotel round the corner. They came down last night and left at midnight when the doctor told them you'd be okay.'

Tom winced. The thought of his mother standing over his bed. The second time in her life she'd seen this. Her own son.

'What did they do?' he said. 'The doctors.'

'Not much. Pumped your stomach, gave you a charcoal treatment drink thing.'

Annabel and Tom sat in silence for a few minutes longer. The memory of all of their shared experiences seemed to hang over them. They were as far from the two awkward kids – spending their school lunch hours in the music rehearsal rooms listening to Nirvana – as it was possible to be. But there was still something of those children about them. They were a unit of sorts, albeit nervous, awkward, ill-fitting. Tom was glad she'd stayed. As awful as the situation was, there was no one he'd rather have had with him.

As dawn crept up on them and the off-centre wall clock ticked towards six, it was Tom who broke the silence.

'Thank you,' he said. 'I know I said sorry. But I should also say that.'

'You're welcome.'

'I—' he began, but needed more water to continue. 'I owe you.'

'That, I am aware of. I've actually already decided what you can do to start making it up to me.'

'What?'

'Ali Matthews is having a fancy-dress party in June,' she said. 'Superheroes. You'll be coming with me.'

'No.'

'No choice, I'm afraid. Anyway, it'll be good for you. New faces and all that. I don't want you locking yourself away.'

'I don't want new faces.'

'I don't care.'

'Can't you just join *Guardian* Soulmates?'

'I'm already on *Guardian* Soulmates. The last date I had was with a woman who was using it to meet a lesbian who'd be up for a threesome with her boyfriend. The one before that suggested we skip dessert to go to a sex party in Rotherhithe.'

Tom went to laugh, but his throat had gone dry again.

'Fine,' he said, with some resignation.

'Good,' Annabel said, standing up. 'Anyway. I've got to be in work for seven. Thanks to you I have some things to catch up on.'

She put her coat on and checked her phone.

'Get some sleep. Your parents will be here soon.'

Tom raised a thumb.

'Tom.'

'Thank you,' he said. 'And sorry. Again.'

Annabel smiled at him. She kissed two fingers and pressed them against Tom's forehead. Then she left him alone again, with nothing but the distant noises of the early-morning hospital workers, and the gargled cooing of the pigeons that briefly settled on his windowsill.

# PART 3

# CHAPTER ELEVEN

6 – 7 am

# FINDING YOUR OLD PHOTO ALBUMS
## December 2013 – Knighton, Leicester

Doing his best not to disturb Esme, Tom let one leg fall out of the bed, immediately feeling the icy air crawl up his thin pyjama trouserleg. He cursed Tamas for permanently being too hot, and so keeping windows open and the heating off – even during the winter. He thought that things might've changed after he got sick, but no.

Carefully, Tom crept out from beneath the duvet and two blankets that enveloped the two of them and found his slippers and hoodie among their half-unpacked overnight bags. Using his phone light as a torch, Tom negotiated his way through the bedroom to the door and slunk out onto the hallway.

It was early on Christmas morning, a few hours before he and Esme would start on their drive east to Lowestoft, and he'd been awake for a while, simultaneously thirsty and desperate for the toilet: a consequence of the salty, rich food of the day before, and the gallons of grape juice he'd consumed. Every Christmas, Lena's mum decanted the juice into a wine carafe so he didn't feel quite so left out while the rest of them glugged several of the dusty bottles of claret Tamas only brought out from the garage for special occasions.

Still guided by the light of his phone, Tom stepped gently down the hallway, avoiding the floorboard creaks as best he could. On the staircase, gold-plated, wooden and plain black picture frames interrupted the magnolia-painted Anaglypta – almost all of them containing photographs of Esme, each depicting a significant life event or a cheesy, staged photoshoot her parents forced on her in early childhood (he remembered her telling him about the strange, creepy man who ran the little studio in Knighton, and his showroom that detailed both his work with children and in the glamour-model industry).

It had taken Tom five years to get onto that wall. There he was, smiling awkwardly in a family shot taken on London's South Bank, in between graduation photos from both of Esme's ceremonies.

The timeline continued as he descended. A few steps down he arrived at her teenage years: Esme wearing a white shirt graffitied with well-wishing messages in pink and blue highlighter pen on her last day of school, her smile full of train-track braces; taking a bow at the front of a stage, after a performance of what Tom guessed might be *Oliver!*. Then a small gap in time (which Tom supposed signified the unspoken-of two years when Tamas absented himself from the family home for his new, ill-fated relationship with Noelle) before the chronology recommenced with an image of Esme and three unknown friends dressed as Sporty, Ginger and Baby Spice.

He had seen all of these photos a hundred times, but that morning it was as if he was seeing them for the first time. As he went, Tom imagined what Esme was like between these photographs: the theatrical, showman Esme, born in her mid-teens, carried to university and then abandoned soon after her one stint on the Edinburgh Fringe; the forthright, politically charged Esme who arrived at her graduation ceremony, aged twenty-one; the versions of her told by

Laura, Jamilla and Philly, friends who knew the woman she had become and the things that made her her.

But was there ever a sullen, teenage Esme? Angry at her family for reasons that were understandable, and the world for reasons that were not. Or was she polite, conscientious and hard-working? The kind of teenager every parent wants but few seem to get.

Finally, Tom arrived at the bottom of the stairs, and Esme as a baby – the photos he'd laughed at the first time he came over, after an embarrassed Esme had said, 'Oh ignore those!' Even back them her eyes, in particular, were distinctly *hers*. A noticeable thread that ran from her earliest years, whether she'd been snapped sitting on the lap of a grandparent, or standing in her old bedroom beneath an Idlewild poster.

'Which is your favourite?'

Lena startled him. Holding the bannister, she began to walk down from the landing, wrapped in her pink fleece dressing gown, her hair messily tied up.

'I don't know. It's hard to choose. I suppose it's just interesting to see her through the years.'

Lena picked a photograph off the wall.

'I love this one,' she said. It was Esme at maybe five or six years old. She was wearing a pink, flowery dress and standing in front of a rose bush. 'I took this at her cousin Peter's wedding. She was five. It was the most brilliant time. She started school that year, was reading, had friends. She had become a proper little girl. It was the first time that I felt like we had done a good job as parents. I stopped worrying for maybe an hour.'

Tom smiled. He had never given much thought to what that might feel like. That sense of achievement. Of life's most significant job having been done well (or well enough for it not to be socially awkward). Perhaps it was because the parents he knew, even his own, were far less outwardly proud of their offspring than Esme's. Gordon and Anne Murray rarely made public declarations of his brilliance or their happiness to have played a role in it, preferring to keep their pride private, reserved for special occasions like the Christmas china. Tamas and Lena were the opposite.

'Are you up now?' Lena said to Tom, rehanging the picture on the wall.

'I am. Couldn't sleep.'

'Good. Go into the kitchen. I'll show you some more. Merry Christmas, by the way.'

'You too,' Tom said.


Lena came into the kitchen carrying a stack of red leather photo albums, each two inches thick and the size of an LP. They reminded Tom of the books given out by Michael Aspel at the end of *This is Your Life*, though with beaten edges and chipped, burnished gold embossing around the edges. She dropped them down heavily onto the table in front of him and went to put the kettle on.

'Tea?'

'Please,' Tom said, and picked the album on the top.

'That one is when she was a baby. I think it ends around her first birthday. I worry that the photos are fading. Tamas always says he's going to scan them into his computer. But he never will.'

Tom opened the cover. In the top left-hand corner was Lena in a hospital bed, her hair dark and thick with corkscrew curls she could only have got away with in the eighties. In her arms was a puce little thing, its face pressed hard against its mother's chest.

Lena put Tom's far too milky tea in front of him and sat down at the table. Pulling the album towards her, she folded over six of the polythene-coated cards that housed the photos at once.

'These are my favourites,' she said.

It was a double-page spread of photos taken in and around a

cottage by a lake. In the corner, someone's hand (Tom presumed Lena's) had written *Lake District 1982. Three generations!*

'This was the only time my grandmother came to England. Our flat in London was too small for my parents, Yanya and the three of us. So we found a cottage in the Lake District. We'd never been before, but someone Tamas worked with told him it was nice. We were there for a week and it rained for five days. This, I think, was the Thursday. The only sunny day. Tamas took his camera out and started taking photographs. Three generations of my family together for the first time,' Lena said, stopping for a second, possibly to think back on that time together. 'Yanya only met Esme three times. The other two were in Hungary and she was so old by then that she could hardly remember my name, let alone Esme's.'

'Is that why her middle name is Anya, then?'

'Sort of. Yanya is the Hungarian name for grandmother. Short for Nagyanya. We thought it was a nice touch.'

Tom blanched a little, embarrassed not to know these things about Esme. Parts of her history he should perhaps have asked about, or seemed interested enough to be told about, long before now. Better late than never, he thought.

'What was she like as a baby, then? One of the quiet ones, or really noisy?' he said, thinking of his sister Sarah's newborn, who by all accounts was the latter.

'Happy. I mean, she cried and we had some terrible nights with her. But mostly she was a cheerful little thing. Very curious, too. Always trying to look out of her pushchair. She fell out once in the town centre because I hadn't strapped her in tight enough.'

'She still is curious. Always looking over strangers' shoulders to see what they're typing on their phones.'

Lena smiled and said, 'Maybe people don't change much from cradle to grave.'

'I don't know,' Tom said hopefully, taking a sip of his tea.

Lena turned a few more pages, smiling at the memories the photos evoked. It was nice for Tom to see this. A journey back to a time when a photograph meant something.

'So tell me what you were like,' she said, looking up from the book. 'I can imagine a thoughtful little boy.'

'I don't know, actually. Never asked.'

'You should! Babies always take after one side. Who knows what you might end up with.'

To Lena, it was probably a throwaway comment. But for a moment it derailed Tom.

'Oh . . . yeah. Well I mean . . .'

'Sorry,' Lena said. 'I shouldn't have said that. It was presumptuous of me.'

'No. It's just we . . . or I . . . We haven't talked about it, really. I don't think,' he said, which was true. Kids was not a conversation they'd had, except when nudged into non-committal maybe-one-days by Laura, for whom family, marriage and moving away from London was permanently front of mind. Besides, Tom didn't think of himself as especially parental. He struggled to imagine himself as the kind of person who could shape the life of another.

But now, all of a sudden, he was thinking about it. Looking at the baby photos and wondering what his and Esme's child might look like. How much of him it might inherit and how much of her.

'Of course,' Lena said. 'You're young and I am an old fool who wants to be a grandmother one day.'

'Well . . . maybe,' Tom said.

'They are a blessing, though. I will say that. Sometimes I wish we'd had more. I suppose there's always plenty of time until there isn't,' she said, getting up from the table. 'More tea?'

Tom was just about to say yes when they heard another set of footsteps on the cold hardwood floor of the hallway. Esme shuffled sleepily into the kitchen.

'What's going on here then?' she said, covering a yawn.

'I'm reminiscing with Tom. I found him looking at some photos on the stairs and thought I'd take us back in time. Tea?'

'Please,' Esme said.

'You're up early,' Tom said.

'I thought you were going to come back. I came to look for you.'

'You were fast asleep.'

'I know. But I can tell these things,' she said. 'Woman's instinct. Oh bloody hell,' Esme said, noticing the photo albums. 'Not these.'

'Tom had never seen them.'

'For a reason.'

'They're nice,' Tom protested.

'They're embarrassing,' she said, bringing the album towards her at the table. 'Oh, Mum, why?'

'He was interested. And these things are important,' Lena said, which was met with a quick, sharp stare from her daughter. 'I think I can hear your father. I'll take him up his tea.'

Alone in the kitchen, Tom edged closer to Esme. She had picked up the second album, this one chronicling her threes and fours. A little girl with shoulder-length brown hair and a happy, enquiring look about her. She wore a selection of dungarees (yellow, blue and orange), with either wellington boots, sandals or trainers. Occasionally they would come across a picture of the whole family. Usually these were taken either in the Midlands on a day out, or on an English beach holiday – Tamas's old blue Volvo estate almost always in the background.

Tom liked looking at how the hairstyles and fashions changed. He laughed at Tamas's moustache, grown in the summer of 1986 and gone again by Esme's birthday in 1987. Every so often a friend would appear, whom Esme would name and wonder what had become of. Most were the kids of her parents' friends who had drifted out of their life in the decades that passed, relegated to their far-too-infrequently updated Christmas card list.

'Your parents must have photos,' Esme said. 'We should have a look when we go up tomorrow.'

'I've never seen them.'

'Liar.'

'I haven't! They've got one of Sarah and one of me on top of the telly. But that's it.'

'Well, they must exist. Your parents will have more than one photo of you, Tom. Maybe even a video,' she said, playfully nudging him in the ribs. 'Little Tommy running around.'

'I was *never* Tommy.'

'I bet you were. I'd love to see it.'

'I wouldn't.'

'Oh, so that's how it is then? All very well leafing through my dodgy old photos but yours are off-limits.'

'Exactly.'

Esme turned the page onto a spread titled *Benidorm '88*, which began with a photo of a rental car, the inside of a Spanish apartment, and a swimming pool. Then Esme in arm bands and a My Little Pony swimming costume, and Tamas sitting on a deck chair with a cigarette and a beer.

'It's nice, isn't it? Looking back.'

'It is,' Tom said. 'Do you ever . . .' he began, trailing off.

'What?'

'Huh?'

'Do I ever what?'

'Oh, nothing.'

'Come on,' she said, trying to tickle him under his ribs.

'Fine. I was going to ask if you ever wonder what it'd look like. You know, if we had one.'

'Oh,' Esme said, silenced by him. 'I don't know, really. Do you?'

'Not really. But then this morning I sort of did. When I was on the stairs looking at those old photos. I thought about what it might be like if we were three.'

Esme said nothing for a moment. She took Tom's hand under the table, linking her fingers through his.

'It's something I've thought about,' Esme said, still staring at the photo album, refusing to break her gaze. 'I always wondered if you—' she continued, but was interrupted by the sound of a loose-fitting slipper slapping loudly against the cold wooden floor in the hallway.

'Your father,' Lena announced, marching into the kitchen, 'has decided that we should all go for a walk before you leave. The lake, he says, and you two can go on to Tom's from there. So showers whenever you're ready.'

'Bloody hell, Mum,' Esme said, unlinking her hand from Tom's and looking up at the clock on the microwave. 'We've got to be on the road by nine.'

'Well you should hurry up then,' Lena said. 'By the way, that timer is slow. I can't work out how to change it.'

'Well I need to wash my hair,' Esme said, closing the album and getting up from the kitchen table.

Tom wanted to go after her, grab her and say, 'I do.' But she was out and away before he could move. *Later*, he told himself, *tell her later*. He took out his phone, opened the news app and went back to his tea.

# CHAPTER TWELVE

**10 – 11 pm**

# THE NIGHT THAT COULDN'T CHANGE YOUR MIND
## July 2014 – Balham, London

The applause was a relief. Even though Tom had been expecting it. Weddings were always the easiest crowds: a bunch of merry drunks, predisposed to happiness. Except for the one he'd played five or six years ago, when the best man's speech had given most guests reason to believe that he and the bride had once slept together.

Tom unplugged his guitar, placed it back in the padded case he'd thrown behind the DJ's booth and climbed down from the small riser that functioned as a stage. Esme was waiting for him. During the song she had been stood at the back of the dancefloor. Where she always was when she watched him play.

'How was it?' he asked.

'Beautiful, Tom. Really lovely.'

'Really? I thought I sounded a little flat,' he said, prompting her to find a flaw in his performance.

'Well, I didn't notice. And before you say anything about my being tone deaf, neither could anyone else.'

'I saw everyone slow dancing. It's a shame we couldn't.'

'I'll survive,' Esme said, draining her glass.

Before Tom could speak again he was interrupted by Sam, Annabel's new wife, who was a little drunk and immediately threw her arms around him.

'It was *perfect*, Tom!' she cried theatrically, which Tom didn't take much from because, being an extremely flamboyant actress-cum-drama tutor, Sam did pretty much everything theatrically. 'Just perfect. I was crying. *Literally*, mate, tears down my cheeks. Annie was the same. Tell him, Annie.'

'I was,' Annabel said. 'It was really wonderful.'

Annabel hugged Tom and thanked him again, this time 'for everything'. Because as well as performing a slow, acoustic rendition of Fleetwood Mac's 'Landslide' for their first dance, Tom had also been Annabel's best man, and the assembler of the wedding playlists. He'd even given her away, too, after her parents had decided that they could not countenance their daughter's decision to marry another woman.

Tom excused himself from the little group to press play on the laptop controlling the second of three mixes he had pieced together for the evening. Immediately, the disco lights he had borrowed from Mogs, one of his old covers band mates, began to swing around the small upstairs function room of the Balham Bowls Club, half a mile from Annabel and Sam's flat, where they would later host an after-party for their closest friends. Knowing it would be full of drink and probably a few people taking drugs, Tom had already decided he wouldn't go. He compared being the only sober person at a thing like that to being celibate at an orgy.

A pub-crowd-esque cheer greeted the first song. It was the start of the eighties hour he'd put together. He loved to hear the reaction to music he played or curated. That was one of the things he missed most about playing live now that his work was almost entirely teaching and composing.

In the past, Tom would have been one of the first on the dance-floor, kicking off the fun stage of a wedding with verve. But this time he wouldn't be joining in. Instead, he went to find Esme, who was standing by the buffet table next to a silver foil tray of sausage rolls, gently tapping her foot.

'You love this song,' he said to her.

'It's alright.'

'Springsteen. We could . . .' he said, nodding to the ten or so people throwing their arms around like in the music video.

'It's okay,' Esme said, taking a seat at a big round table, opposite two bored kids stacking used party popper shells on top of each other.

'You look uncomfortable,' she called over the blaring noise of 'Dancing in the Dark'.

'It's the bloody suit.'

'Let me guess. You hate wearing suits?'

Tom frowned and nodded childishly. Though if he was honest, the suit was not so much the problem in and of itself. Instead he was concerned by how much tighter it suddenly felt, and that after years of being 'naturally skinny', he might be developing his first paunch. Esme meanwhile looked beautiful in a floral dress that fitted tight over her thighs that she'd joined three gym classes to reduce the size of, but which Tom hoped would remain. Her hair was flowing freely, with light curls down to just below her shoulders. And she was wearing her purple horn-rimmed glasses for the first time at an event, after an eye infection stopped her from using contact lenses. She had complained about it. But Tom always found the glasses quite sexy.

'Third fucking time this year,' he said.

'You don't have to wear it to Philly and Adam's if you don't want to.'

'And be literally the only man there in slacks and shirt?'

'I wouldn't mind.'

'I know you wouldn't. It's Philly I'm worried about. She's probably got bouncers and a dress code,' he said, referring to how Esme's friend had recently told her erstwhile bearded future brother-in-law (and fiancé's best man) that he was under no circumstances to arrive at their wedding with any more than three millimetres of hair on any part of his face, otherwise he would be excluded from the official photographs.

Tom and Esme sat there for a little while longer, until the song ended and the next began, greeted by a cheer from the already drunk dancers who would likely be pounding their feet against the floor until closing time in a couple of hours.

They were often like this at weddings. A duo. Two of them set against an institution they wanted nothing to do with, occasionally fending off questions around when it would be 'their time'. Because of that, they never quite enjoyed the occasions. Or at least Esme didn't. Tom still found some joy in watching two people pledge their lives to one another, then watching their friends dance and laugh.

'It's basically a load of admin so your friends can get pissed,' Esme had once said, when Laura questioned her over her vehement and quite public aversion to getting married.

'Very nice,' Laura said. 'What about you, Tom?'

'Well, I quite like weddings. But I only really see the good bits.'

'See! *Tom* likes weddings. What about the official stuff?' Laura asked. 'You know, the certificate, the recognition of it all. You don't have to have a big flouncy do,' she said, obliquely referencing her own very big flouncy do, complete with doves, ice sculptures (in July) and, for no reason anyone could understand, a mariachi band playing before dinner.

'More admin. State sponsored, though,' Esme said with a mischievous smile, knowing how it would irritate her marriage-minded friends.

154

She had repeated these kinds of statements a hundred times over. Especially during the peak of wedding conversations a couple of years ago, when some of her friends spoke openly about what her wedding to Tom might be like, as if trying to change her mind.

Tom's friends, meanwhile, told him about the various bits of wedmin they'd taken on, as though heroically bucking a system that dictated women should care more about the particulars of the big day than men. Mostly things like booking bands and cars. Rarely flowers or favours.

But even now, when they were both well into their thirties, the occasional wedding question might be thrown in front of them. Most recently at a barbecue at Laura (again) and Aman's house in an outer London market town they were always overly keen to extol the virtues of.

'Are you two still on the anti-marriage bandwagon then?' Laura had asked, while bouncing their daughter Tallulah (or Toots) on her knee and making horse noises.

'I don't see how there can be a bandwagon for *not* doing something. Surely it's you who is *on* the marriage bandwagon.'

'Yes fine, Esme,' Laura said, taking the tone she did when trying to castigate her friend's argumentative intellectualism. 'I'm just asking if you've changed your mind about it.'

'No more than you have.'

'Hmm,' Laura said, with a look round at Aman that suggested a change of heart about their marriage might not be entirely inconceivable.

Of course, Esme and Tom *had* talked about marriage. Early in their relationship she had voiced her objections to it: citing how unnecessary it felt in a changing world; how religious ceremonies were bombastic, overblown and based on veiled threats made to couples who would likely not set foot in a church again until a christening, funeral or wedding called for it. How, with their lack of bombastic, overblown veiled threats, secular ceremonies felt thin, regardless of how much the two protagonists puffed them out with readings and poetry (and, on one occasion, asking the congregation to sing 'I Love You Just the Way You Are' in some ghastly echo of a romantic comedy).

But these complaints, Tom knew, were a smokescreen. Her real problem with marriage was neither the ceremony nor its relevance. Instead, Esme's idea of a binding connection between two people, at the expense of all others, was shattered in 1993, when her father left the family home to pursue a two-year affair with a recent university graduate named Noelle.

Tom had learned of the affair six months into their relationship – the knowledge of it was like a military badge, only bestowed after so much service.

'Ever since then I've known I could never do it,' she had told him. 'From the moment I saw those suitcases piled up in the hall.'

'But he came back.'

'After two years,' Esme had said firmly, the pain of it still clear and fresh. 'It was so fucking tawdry. This older man shacking up with one of his former students. Like something from a dodgy European film.'

'Did you know her?'

'I spent every weekend with them until I was fifteen. And one holiday in Ibiza. She was the worst. She used to take me to see kids' films and critique them as though they were Merchant fucking Ivory.'

'What was it like? When . . .'

'He pretended like none of it had happened. Called it his "blip". And Mum just took him back.'

Tom stopped talking about it there and then and hadn't mentioned it much since, knowing that to do so would be to pick at a scab that would probably never heal. Esme's idea of family, and particularly marriage, would never be the same again after that. It had become something people could pick up and put down at will. If one partner was willing to leave the door open, the other was free to wander in and out like a bored cat.

Although her relationship with her dad repaired over time, a vulnerability had been exposed. As much as he liked him, Tom wasn't sure if it was something he could ever forgive Tamas for.

Tom placed his hand on Esme's and watched with a smile as the kids' party popper stack collapsed, sending the colourful plastic rolling across the table.

The dancefloor had hit peak busyness by the time his first hour of songs was almost up. Annabel and Sam were at its centre, barefoot and passing a bottle of prosecco back and forth. Neil, Pod and Ali had their ties around their heads, dancing like bad facsimiles of Mick Jagger while their partners looked on with weary, loving acceptance. A heavily tattooed blonde girl elicited a great cheer as she delivered a tray full of shots.

When Esme got up to go to the loo, Annabel made her way over to him, taking the seat she had just left.

'It's still a great big no then?' she said.

'Probably.'

'When was the last time you spoke about it?'

'About two months ago. Laura asked.'

'I mean just the two of you. Not at a party or something.'

'No idea. Probably years ago. It just doesn't come up.'

'Maybe it should.'

'How do you mean?'

'I mean maybe she'll change her mind if you actually ask. She looked happy today. During the ceremony and that.'

'She looked happy because she likes you. Not because she likes marriage all of a sudden. She's barely spoken for the last half-hour. She's thinking about her dad. I can tell.'

'All I'm saying is that you never know, Murray. She's changed you. There is the slightest possibility that you've changed her, too.'

With that, Annabel was pulled away by Sam, back to the dance-floor for the beginning of Tom's Britpop section.

Meanwhile, Esme was walking back over to him. He handed her a glass of red wine he'd poured from the bottle left on the table, and took a sip of the sweet fruit juice he was drinking, wondering as he did how much his high intake of sugary, alcohol-alternative drinks was to blame for the gut that was pushing a little too noticeably against the buttons of his white shirt.

'Seriously. Do you want to dance?' he asked, as the final strains of Suede's 'Animal Nitrate' rang out. 'Because we're really getting towards the good stuff now.'

'Maybe in a bit,' she said. 'I'm enjoying watching other people. They look like they're having fun.'

It may have been what Annabel said, but for some reason Tom thought he could sense something in her voice. A note of envy, perhaps?

'They are having fun.'

'You've done well today,' she said, kissing him on the cheek. He could faintly smell the red wine on her breath. 'I'm proud of you.'

'Thanks.'

'And sorry if I was a bit of a grump a minute ago.'

'It's fine,' he said, knowing he didn't have to say any more. Tom listened as the first strains of 'Don't Look Back in Anger' bounced around the room, and a delayed, drunken cheer rang out.

'Es. Do you ever—'

'Tom. Not tonight.'

'I just—'

'I'm not going to change my mind. You know that, don't you?'

'I do.'

'Because I thought we were—'

'We are.'

'Are we, though?' she said, turning to look at him.

'We are,' he said again, unsure if he had sounded convincing enough. Equally unsure if he wanted to sound convincing at all.

He pulled out his phone. It was 10.59. Tom looked back at Esme, who was staring across the dancefloor, that blank, almost sad look on her face again.

'Good,' she said, taking his hand.

## CHAPTER THIRTEEN

**Midnight – 1 am**

# UNHAPPY NEW YEAR
### January 2015 – Covehithe, Suffolk

'Happy New Year!' Neil shouted, popping a cork and filling seven tall, thin crystal-cut glasses with champagne.

Everyone stood. Kisses, hugs and handshakes were exchanged, as Neil went over to the bi-fold doors that led out onto a wide, brightly lit and lightly frosted lawn to let the new year in. One by one, his friends joined him, as his wife Karin hit play on the wireless speaker which now belched out 'Auld Lang Syne'.

All except Tom, who remained on the big grey couch in front of the wood burner, hoping that the rest of them would be so drunk that they wouldn't realise he hadn't joined them.

He had been feeling it for an hour. He knew the symptoms immediately, even if they had become like strangers to him after such a long absence.

First came the restlessness; the inability to get comfortable or to concentrate on anything for more than a few minutes. And the feeling of confinement, as though the walls in Neil's kitchen were closing in on him. Then a dizzy sensation took him away entirely – like being drunk but without drinking.

His heart was beat, beat, beating away in his chest.

The worst was coming, he knew it.

He desperately needed to run away.

He tried to concentrate on the large oak coffee table, laden with wine, spirits and mixers. Sipped his non-alcoholic beer, but it tasted acrid in his mouth. He craved something more.

In a strange way, it made sense to him that it was happening. This was the pattern things followed: the lack of sleep, the low feelings. The desperate hoping beyond hope that it might fade away like a common cold or headache. It was all a familiar song Tom had heard before. Each day taking him a little lower, riding down in an elevator with no ground floor.

The things he could tangibly hold on to in the world one by one slipped away. The pit was opening up and he could do nothing to avoid sliding in. Dread, nausea, palpitations. One fear perpetuating the next and the next and the next like dominoes falling. Rational thinking, logic and reason all gone.

The question was, now sober, how could he block it out?

Tom was acutely aware and embarrassed that this was happening around people. Friends. That they'd witness him losing control of his body.

They were halfway through the second, vaguely mumbled verse of 'Auld Lang Syne' when Esme noticed that Tom hadn't joined the rest of them.

'Are you feeling alright?' Esme said, leaning over him. Her voice was quiet.

The year was less than ten minutes old. Tom didn't want it to start this way.

'Not really.'

'Okay. Are you going to be sick? Do you think it's something you ate?' she said, pressing the back of her hand against his forehead. It was cold from the outside air. 'I said you shouldn't have eaten those—'

'No,' Tom said. 'I just feel . . .' he said, but drifted away before finishing his sentence.

'Feel what?'

'We should go,' he said, trying to stop himself from crying.

'But it's just turned—'

'I said we should go,' Tom snapped.

Immediately, Esme grabbed his hand and pulled him off the sofa.

'Okay,' she said, ushering him towards the door, without offering an explanation to anyone at the party. 'You're okay.'

Together, they left Neil's house – a barn conversion he'd pretentiously named 'Vanha Talo', which apparently meant 'old house' in Finnish, despite his lack of Finnish connections – and found their red Nissan Micra sitting out on his gravel driveway.

As Tom got into the driver's seat, he saw Esme run back to where Annabel was standing in the doorway. They spoke for a second before she returned to the car.

'What did she say?' Tom asked, his voice urgent and abrupt.

'Nothing,' Esme said. 'You forgot your coat. Do you want me to—'

'No. I will,' Tom said, turning the car on. He reversed out of the driveway with a screech and pulled onto the road that would take them towards Lowestoft and his parents' house. But he managed barely a mile before pulling over to a stop to take deep, panicked breaths – one after the other.

'Tom, what is it? Tell me,' Esme said, trying to keep her voice measured and calm.

'Nothing.'

'It's not nothing, Tom. Please just say. Did something happen?' She tried to place a hand on Tom's arm, but he threw it off.

'Okay. It's okay. Do you need me to drive?'

Tom didn't answer again. Instead the breathing continued.

'I need to go home.'

'I know, sweetheart. I know. It's not far—'

'I mean home.'

'London?'

Tom nodded as the breathing continued.

'Okay. But it's midnight and—'

'I know,' he said, sounding pained, as tears began to form in the corners of his eyes and his breathing began to shudder.

'We can, Tom. If you feel okay to drive home you know we can,' Esme said, remaining calm to counteract his panic. 'Or, if you want, we can try to get back to your parents tonight. And I'll drive us home tomorrow. But only if you want.'

'Maybe,' he said. 'Maybe that.'

Ten minutes later, with his breathing finally measured, Tom turned the ignition and began the twenty-minute drive back to his parents' house.


It was during that week and a half over Christmas that he had felt the first pangs of it. The low moods. The desire to be inside rather than out. The discomfort when around people, noticeable everywhere he went – from the Christmas morning charity swim, to the pub where he'd met family on Boxing Day.

But he hadn't said a word about it, defying his understanding of himself in the hope that it might fade away. Maybe things might be different this time and it would lift, as though his depression was a passing cloud rather than a full-on storm.

In the past when he'd felt anxious about leaving their home in London, Tom had passed it off as 'feeling a bit sick' – unable to quantify *why* he was experiencing this dread, and what was its cause. He'd successfully sequestered himself in his childhood bedroom, could barely bring himself to move. As far as Esme and his parents knew he was working. They wouldn't think to bother him.

Much of the time Tom found it remarkably – even scarily – easy to hide how he was actually feeling.

And through it all, he couldn't escape the sense that it was all wrong.

This wasn't supposed to happen now.

Not when he was supposed to be happy.

For years, Esme's presence had precluded this from happening. The conditions for depression to manifest – whether loneliness, anxiety or self-hatred – did not exist when she was around.

So why had that all changed?

That night, sitting on Neil's sofa and feeling as though the world was shutting down around him, Tom realised he'd been foolish enough to look for reason where none existed.

This thing needed no reason.


After a twenty-minute drive they arrived at Tom's parents' house. Esme helped him up to his bedroom, sneaking him away from his parents, aunts and uncles who were chatting in the living room. They'd all insist on a New Year's kiss or handshake, and human contact was the last thing Tom needed.

Esme left him to undress and crawl under the covers before she turned the light off. She asked no more questions and closed the door behind her as she left.

Alone, he lay there for a few minutes before he heard voices in the hallway outside. His mum. Had she noticed that something wasn't right? He should've known that she would. It was unlike Tom to ignore everyone, to not walk into their dining room and start picking at the leftover cheese and crackers. Unlike him to be so distant over Christmas. His mum knew that best.

'What is it?' he heard her ask Esme.

'I don't know. He just came over all ... funny, I suppose. We were at Neil's and suddenly he just shut down.'

'Can I see—'

'Not yet. Maybe tomorrow. We should let him rest.'

'Nothing's happened, has it? He's not had a drink.'

'No. Why would he? It looked like a panic attack or something.'

'Oh God,' Tom heard his mum say, a tearfulness creeping into her voice. 'I didn't think this would be back,' she said, and Tom began to panic. Would this, he wondered, be it? The moment. What would his mum say to Esme?

'What?' Esme said. 'Am I missing something?'

'His . . .' she started angrily. '*Sadness.*'

*Sadness.* Tom considered the word. It's what she always called it. So often unable to call it by its real name. Even way back when he was away at university and his depression was at its worst. Tom would never forget the time he had stood in their family kitchen, screaming the word over and over while his mum cried and his sister begged him to stop. Depression, depression, depression. How terrible he felt when he'd discovered the reams of online articles about depression and anxiety disorders printed off and left under her bedside table, along with a stack of NHS pamphlets and a book about the condition she'd ordered from the library. Nor could he forget his dad's pain and desperate good intentions when trying to talk to him about it, unsure and awkward.

'Sadness?' Esme said.

'You know, I really thought that this time things might be different. You've been so good for him. I always thought that with you . . .' Anne said, her voice failing her. 'And he was on such a good . . . It's been, what, nearly ten years—'

'Anne, sorry,' Esme said. 'I'm really not following you. Could you tell—'

'*Depression,*' Anne snapped. 'Okay? You don't have to make me bloody say it, Esme.'

Then, for a moment, there was nothing. Silence. Tom could

picture Esme's face, taking it all in. The realisation that her boyfriend, the man she lived with, had this thing, this illness.

And that she had no idea all this time.

Tom curled up in the bed, keeping his ears trained on the door. How much more would she reveal to Esme, and how much would she leave for him to tell her himself the following morning? The red digits of the chunky eighties alarm clock on the bedside table next to him cast a little light onto his face. 00:47.

'Tom has depression?' Esme said quietly.

Again, the silence. This time it felt longer.

'Oh, Esme,' Anne said. 'I'm . . .'

'He's never said.'

'He hasn't?' his mum said, the realisation setting in.

'What's been ten years?' Esme said firmly.

'I don't know if I—'

'Anne. I have a right to know.'

'Tom tried . . .' she tried to speak. But the words wouldn't come easily. Tom had seen this before, when she had tried to ask him why, to understand the disease so she could look for the cure. 'He tried to . . . harm himself.'

'Self-harm? Like cutting?'

'No.'

'Suicide?'

'Esme, please,' she said, her voice breaking and cracking.

'When?'

'It was before he met you. That spring was the second time. And—'

'Twice? When . . .'

Tom could almost hear the penny drop. A new understanding of Tom and his past drift over Esme like a raincloud covering the sun. It wouldn't take her long to fit the pieces together. When he went strange on her in Oxford, John outside the pub at her thirtieth birthday party, the teetotal life he led.

167

'At university,' she said. 'That's what happened at university.'

'I'm sorry, Esme,' his mum said through tears. 'I really thought he'd told you. He promised me.'

That was the last thing his mum said. After that, he heard sniffs and the rustles of clothes as the two of them embraced, or so he assumed. Followed by footsteps on the stairs and, faintly, his dad's voice asking, 'What's wrong?' Then the turn of the door handle, as Esme stepped inside.

'Tom,' she said. He pushed his head down into the pillow, longing for sleep. For oblivion of some sort.

'Sorry,' he said quietly.

She sat down on the bed next to him. He desperately wanted her to show some sign of affection. A hand on the shoulder, a kiss on the head. But nothing came.

'I'm sorry, Es.'

'Tom,' Esme said, as the red lights of the clock changed, signalling the end of the first hour of the year. 'I want you to tell me everything.'

# CHAPTER FOURTEEN

**1 – 2 am**

# WORKING ON MYSELF
## February 2015 – Stansted Airport, London

The voice over the address system announced the further delay. Her flight was now due in at ten past one. He took a seat on the hard, metal chair and took out his phone. There were three or four others around him. Kind souls who'd offered to pick up their loved ones despite the late hour – all of whom were, like Tom, probably worrying about how tired they'd be at work tomorrow. They all cast glances up at the display screen that confirmed the bad news.

**RY074 GLASGOW 00.46 DELAYED 01:10**

Tom wondered if he should even have come to the airport at all. Esme would never have expected him to. But tonight (or rather this morning) was intended to be a surprise. A show of how far he'd come after what happened on New Year's Eve, and the weeks that followed. They had come back from his parents' house, Esme still shocked, angry and devastated at what his mum had told her, and Tom had shut himself away – beginning a six-week period of acute anxiety and depression so bad that he couldn't leave the house.

It was a new thing to him. Never before had he felt so low that an unnameable, yet all-consuming dread prevented him from even so much as walking around the block. What was more, it was the first time he'd been forced to cope with a such a serious dip in his mental health without alcohol, the thing that conquered all his social anxieties, at least for a few hours. And the moment he stepped over the threshold of their flat on the afternoon of 1st January, Tom could not countenance the idea of going back over it again.

It wasn't as if he hadn't thought about it. Alone, standing at their kitchen window, Tom had watched passers-by sheltering under coats, scarves and woolly hats as the weather grew colder and more fierce. When it snowed later in the month he looked on at the nervous commuters navigating ungritted paths, and at the few wealthy north Londoners who owned snow boots usually reserved for annual skiing holidays. He himself had experienced none of it. Almost missing an entire season was quite something.

He had gone over and over how it would be to leave.

One step.

Two steps.

The end of the house.

The beginning of the path, through the small front garden.

He had thought about the particular noises of their corner of north London. Buses, slow-moving cars, the whirr of a racing bike, ridden by some squidgy forty-year-old in multicoloured lycra. The shouts and calls from the noisy shop owners and delivery men, the telephone conversations overheard. All of which would grow louder as he walked to the end of Islay Gardens and towards the much busier West End Lane. Then the smells: musty, foetid leaf and grass mulch from the garden at number forty-two, so vibrant in spring and summer; the faint drifting scent of fried food from the best-avoided kebab shop on the corner. And the feel of the end-of-winter air on his cheeks and on fingertips that would poke from the top of his mitts, a reminder of his dislike of the cold. The stiff leather of his shoes after weeks of wearing slippers. The firmness of the pavement, instead of the comfortable cushion of carpet and rugs.

In the end, it wasn't a bit like that. The things he thought he'd notice he didn't. His fears remained.

Tom shifted on the seat and glanced at the fat, bald man next to him.

'Fucking typical, ain't it?' the man said. He had a paper sign face down on his lap. Tom wondered if he should've made one. Was that the done thing now? Or was it only for cabbies and chauffeurs?

Tom smiled back at him.

Earlier in the day he had been sitting on the tatty armchair in his little office box room, a piece of furniture much used in recent weeks. Especially now Tom no longer walked around north London listening to the music he produced. Instead he played things back while slouched in that armchair, staring blankly at the Bruce Springsteen poster on the wall opposite – one of the various habits that had become his new normal since he and Esme had returned from the New Year's Eve party in Lowestoft.

Magnus, their cat, was on the floor in front of him, looking up occasionally as if questioning what Tom was doing with his life, while the ukulele chorus to a vegan dog-food jingle played out around the room.

But Tom was unable to concentrate on the irritatingly chipper voice singing about 'good things for good dogs' and 'the first ever ethical treats made from baobab and ginseng'. Instead, he was thinking about that day's session with Christine, his therapist.

She came to their flat once a week, charging extra for a home visit. Esme had insisted that he seek help, after he had refused medication outright.

He and Christine had talked about this recent anxiety-induced agoraphobia, but were no closer to dampening the fear he felt at the idea of going outside, of being so exposed and vulnerable. What could he tell her about a nameless dread? An aching sickness? A fear that was so real and yet apparently rooted in absolutely nothing? He had been trying to explain similar things to himself for almost fifteen years without success.

'I feel sick every time I think about it. Then the sickness makes me panic,' was all he could really manage. 'And it all makes me feel worse.'

Christine had nodded and written something down in her notebook.

'Explain worse,' she had said.

Their sessions were an incomplete, basic summary of a life continuously interrupted by bouts of depression and anxiety. One that was getting close to becoming little more than a collection of near-catastrophes – of various support structures built up and later destroyed. Recently, in her more frustrated moments, Esme had questioned whether Christine was 'any good'.

'I can't change therapist now, Es,' Tom had said. 'We've made progress.'

It was a half-truth. He and Christine had made progress. But not necessarily in the right direction. While they should have been talking about the root of his problems, most of their time together was spent on Esme. And how he could save what they had together after all his concealing and lying.

Hours had been lost to talking about her kindness, her supportive nature, her forgiveness and her selflessness. Echoing something Annabel once told him, he contrasted her nurse-like caring with his clichéd artistic self-absorption (despite it being increasingly difficult to paint himself as an artist with each corporate video he soundtracked).

He had spoken at length about how he was undeserving of her understanding and empathy, all the while praying to some nameless God that he would never lose it. And of how she was often the one thing that kept him from returning to his oldest and most destructive crutch: alcohol.

Going through it all again that afternoon, Christine had diligently listened and nodded. She had told Tom that he was lucky, and that he had all the right things around him to repair himself.

'But *you* have to do the repair work, Tom. She can be your support. But she can't be your answer to everything.'

'I know,' he said. 'I think I'm trying to say that it's holding on to what we have that makes me want to break the cycle.'

'If that's what it takes,' Christine had told him. It was the end of their session and he could see her wanting to wrap up, probably with half a mind on the traffic. 'Whatever works for you, Tom. But that can't always be the answer.'

As Tom had sat in the tatty chair, her words swirled around in his head.

*If that's what it takes.*

*Whatever works for you.*

Esme was the only thing that worked for him. From the day they met until today, it was all her. After everything that had happened, he wouldn't blame her if she decided she'd had enough. He had pushed and pushed and she had stayed through it all. The drive home from Suffolk might've been her last straw, perhaps. But instead she had questioned herself, had asked him why he couldn't trust her to know the circumstances of his suicide attempts. She begged for him to tell her if he found her unapproachable or lacking in empathy. It was all nonsense, of course. To Tom's mind, he was the problem, and she was always the solution.

Esme didn't know it, but Tom had found himself standing by their closed front door ten or fifteen times a day during the past few weeks. Making the trip from the sofa or his office, then back again. He had listened to Esme bustling around in their cluttered hallway, searching for headphones or shoes, and thought about following. He had wanted to stop her and tell her to wait for him every time he heard the screech of metal on metal as she turned their broken door handle to leave the house.

But each time he said nothing and stayed inside. The impetus to go out was always overridden by something holding him back, the return to familiarity infinitely more comforting.

His retreat had made reconciliation with Esme slower than it might've been, he was sure of it. There had been nights spent in separate beds, as she made the distance Tom had put between them real. At times he'd hoped she might be over everything, or at least have forgiven him enough to allow their relationship to re-find the equilibrium it had up until the end of last year. Then, out of nowhere, it was as if something would remind her of it: a throwaway line from a television programme; a song on the radio. Enough to bring back to her mind the meaninglessness of a guarantee from Tom Murray.

He sensed her frustration and upset. Something had to give.

It was four hours after Christine left, and while he was listening back to the terrible ukulele music, that Tom decided if things were to repair, he would have to try to ignore certain nagging parts of himself. He knew he could never shake anxiety. Nor depression. But equally, he knew that his best chance of happiness was bundled up with his love for Esme. And that despite her caring and kindness, she would have a limit, beyond which the difficulties of his life would begin to create difficulties in hers.

It was not possible to ignore things, Tom knew. But he could try to suppress them, to push them down into the deepest recesses of his being, in the desperate hope they remained dormant. And, maybe, that would give him the best chance of thickening the line he was trying to draw under the things she'd learned on that night outside his childhood bedroom.

Sitting up, Tom had looked down at Magnus and said, 'I should go, shouldn't I?'

Tom looked out of the window towards the brightly lit runway. A plane was approaching the strip, its landing lights cutting a path through the night sky. It must be Esme, he thought. There were only two other arrivals on the board after hers.

His heart jumped a little at the thought of her touching down. Behind him the last of the arrival lounge shops pulled its shutters down, making him jump. The fat man beside him swigged at a bottle of Coke and got up from his seat.

What would he tell Esme about his first time outside? Maybe about the cold and the thin layer of ice that lay across the scratchy, patchy grass out the front of their flat. Or how it had taken a moment for him to realise what he had done, the step he had taken. That he had escaped from the only place he'd found safe for the past month and a half.

Then Tom heard the familiar voice behind him and turned around.

Esme.

She was talking to the fat man, who was now picking up the small suitcase she always took to conferences. Tom could see the other side of his sign now. It read ESME SIMON, below which was the logo for North West Cars, the minicab firm whose business card was permanently stuck to their fridge.

'Es,' he called. But she seemed not to hear. The two of them were making for the doors. 'Esme!' he called again.

She stopped and turned.

'Tom?' she said, loud and surprised, running over to him. 'Fucking hell. Tom!'

They hugged tightly, in a way that they hadn't for months. It may have just been his imagination, a hopeful thought interrupting the recent darkness, but things felt different.

'I was waiting,' Tom said. 'I thought I'd seen you land.'

'We were a bit early. Well, a bit less late.'

'I'm so happy to see you, Es,' Tom said, kissing her cheek, still cold from the walk from the plane to the terminal.

'You almost gave me a heart attack.'

'Sorry. It's just that—'

'You're out!'

'I know!'

'You're out,' she said again, throwing her arms around him.

'I'm out.'

'How does it feel?'

'Fine. Well, so far. I didn't really have time to think about it. I sort of just got up and ran from the house.'

'Oh, Tom,' she said, sounding as if she was on the verge of tears. 'Tom, I'm so proud of you.'

He didn't say anything back. The emotion of it, the achievement of something so huge but so mundane was overwhelming him.

'And you feel okay?'

'So far, so good.'

'Not, like, unsettled or anxious or anything? Because I can drive,' she said, speaking quickly. 'We can take our time.'

'I'm fine, Es,' he interrupted. Though, in truth, there was an element of him that was ill at ease and had been since he'd got to the airport. Thankfully it hadn't been busy. Even now, knowing he'd be happier indoors was less important to him than the knowledge that he was doing the right thing. For Esme. For both of them.

If that meant pushing himself a little, he was happy to be pushed.

'If you're sure,' she said, taking his hand in her mitten. 'But you have to tell me, Tom. If you start to feel bad. Just say. Okay?'

Tom nodded, but Esme wasn't satisfied with this.

'Promise me, Tom. Baby steps, not giant leaps, okay?'

'Promise.'

'Okay.'

'Excuse me,' a gruff voice said, interrupting the two of them. 'Is he here to take you home then?'

'Oh God,' Esme said to the minicab driver. 'I'm so sorry. It was a surprise.'

'Fucking hell,' he said, shaking his head. 'Almost two in the fucking morning.'

'I'm sorry.'

'You still have to pay,' he said. 'You know that, right?'

'Oh. Of course,' Esme said, opening her bag to get her purse. 'Ninety, wasn't it?'

The driver nodded, took the money, stuffed the ESME SIMON sign in the bin and marched off towards the exit.

'I'll pay for that,' Tom said.

'Yeh you will,' Esme said in return, leading him towards the sliding doors that opened into the cold night.

As they went, Tom focused on the things around him that would keep him in check. Five things he could hear, see and smell. It was a tactic Christine had told him to employ the first time he went out – something to root him in the safety of the world around him.

In this case, it was the closed fast-food kiosks outside the terminal. The smell of the night air, a mix of jet fuel and bus exhaust. The uneven, grey pavement and how it felt against the soles of his feet. All things that were certainties. Reliable parts of the world that couldn't possibly be unpredictable, and so would never be cause for alarm.

After a few steps, Tom stopped.

'Everything okay?' she said.

The answer was no, but Tom swallowed it down.

'I think so. Just need a second.'

'Take as long as you need,' she said and he wondered if she meant it in every possible way. He had been so het up on his way to the airport that parts of the anxiety were masked. Now, with Esme again, the surprise over, Tom felt things coming back.

'We can go back inside if you want,' Esme said. 'It doesn't matter what time we get home,' she said, checking her watch. Tom could see it was almost two. No matter what she said, Esme would be worried about having so little sleep before a work day.

Tom drew a breath. He knew from experience that he would never feel entirely settled about it. As ever, there was no proper fix, and no guarantee that he would ever wake up in the morning and not feel the rising in his chest, clammy palms and unexplained sense of dread.

But he had to be an active participant in getting through it.

'I'm okay,' he said, convincing himself as much as her.

'You sure?'

'I'm sure,' he said, taking a determined step forward, and forcing a better version of himself back into life, piece by piece by piece.

# CHAPTER FIFTEEN

9 – 10 am

# A DYING MAN'S WISH
## November 2015 – Knighton, Leicester

Esme put their shared overnight bag in the boot of the car and went back to the house. Her mother was waiting in the doorway, an old maroon cardigan unbuttoned and wrapped around her body, standing on the threshold in a pair of grey slippers. A light rain was falling, the last remnants of the storm the Simons' usually perfectly manicured front garden had endured the previous night.

'How long will it take you to get home?' Lena said.

'Couple of hours,' Tom said from where he was standing at the driver's door, reaching in to affix the mobile phone holder to the windscreen.

'Sorry we can't stay longer,' Esme said. 'We'll be back, though.'

'It's fine, darling.'

'I sometimes wish we lived closer.'

'Nonsense. You have your life. We're fine here.'

'We'll come back next week.'

'I'm fine.'

'I know you are, Mum. I just want—' Esme said, her voice cracking before she could continue.

'I know,' Lena said, embracing her. 'You should go and say goodbye.'

Esme disappeared into the house, as Tom checked the car over, ready for this latest drive down the M1 back towards London – a journey they had made six times since Tamas's diagnosis for prostate cancer a few months before.

It was the second time he'd been given it. The last coming a couple of years ago, when a routine doctor's check-up revealed abnormalities. One operation and a round of chemotherapy had led to the all-clear, and seemed to give him new life and a new enthusiasm for it.

This time Tamas was out of luck. The cancer had spread to his kidneys and lungs. His whole body gradually surrendered to the disease. Initially he had been given four months to live, eight if he was lucky.

But things had deteriorated rapidly, as if the knowledge that the end was coming had caused him to give up fighting. Now Christmas was a target for him. February looked ambitious. But Tamas and those around him were keenly aware that each new day might be his last.

Most of the time Esme and Tom came on the pretence of providing help – supporting Esme's mother by cooking meals, doing the shopping, tidying the house. Though in truth Lena was managing just fine. The regular visits, Tom knew, were Esme's long goodbye to her father, even if she couldn't bring herself to admit it.

'How is Esme coping?' Lena said.

'Fine,' Tom said, almost instinctually. 'Well, not *fine*. But she's okay.'

'I just wish they would talk. She carries so much about him with her. She never forgave him like I did.'

'I know. She will,' Tom said hopefully. But he and Lena both knew that his thinking was more wishful than realistic. Esme still bore the scars of the walkout twenty years ago. The spectre of Noelle – the recently graduated student he had a six-month affair and two-year relationship with – cast a constant shadow over the two of them.

'I'll go and say goodbye,' Tom said.

Esme was leaving Tamas's bedroom with a handful of mugs when he arrived at the top of the stairs. She dabbed the cuff of her dark blue lambswool jumper against the corner of her eye, smudging the mascara.

'You okay?'

'Fine,' she said, as she passed him to go back downstairs to her mother, leaving Tom to take her place.

The bedroom was overly warm and airless. Suited to the needs of the patient, who was feeling the cold more with each passing week. A vase of purple sweet williams sat atop the pine dressing table opposite the bed, adding some colour to the plain magnolia and beige room.

Tamas was propped up on a stack of four pillows, beside him the same breakfast-in-bed tray he and Lena used every Sunday for tea, marmalade on toast, and the weekend paper. On the bedside table was a small stack of *The Economist* back issues (a subscription Esme and Tom had bought him and which Tom suspected he never read), and a collection of pill bottles.

'I've just come to say goodbye,' Tom said, trying to steal his attention from a recording of last night's *Match of the Day*, playing on the small television in the corner. Tom hoped the football would not spark yet *another* retelling of Tamas's 1993 meeting with Ferenc Puskás in Dublin, when Hungary played the Republic of Ireland.

'Shut the door,' Tamas croaked.

'Sorry?'

'The door,' he said impatiently. 'And turn this shit off.'

Tom did as he was told.

'Is there something you need?'

'I need five minutes,' he said, clearing his throat.

Tom wondered what would be worse: one of Tamas's serious 'chats' or a request to attend to some medical need for a man he did not want to get that familiar with.

'Before I go I want to talk to you about Esme,' he said, weakly pushing himself up on his pillows. 'Sit if you want.'

Tom decided to remain standing, unable to think of anything more awkward than perching next to Tamas on six inches of spare mattress.

'What is it?'

'You make her happy, Tom,' he said, with a little cough. 'I know everything isn't always easy and normal for you. But she likes to care for you. And says you care for her.'

'That's . . . good,' Tom said, unsure of what to say and slightly irritated that his problems were being summarised as 'not normal'.

'I didn't always make her happy. As you know. It's hard to live a long life without making mistakes. Even big ones.' Another cough, though Tom suspected it was forced this time to allow for a swift move away from the difficult subject he still hated to talk about. 'Anyway, I had hoped I might have a bit more time to spend with her and Lena. But life has other plans. So now, it's up to you.'

Tamas reached for his glass and took a small sip of water.

'I spent thirty years trying to make my daughter's life as good as possible. I don't think I always did a great job. But I tried. Then you come along and finish the job. I know Esme. She is happier than ever. More content. Talks less about moving to different countries, new careers, big ideas,' he said, surprising Tom, who had never heard Esme talk about living anywhere except the UK. 'If I have learned one thing,' Tamas continued, 'it's that always looking for something else doesn't make us happy.'

'No. Of course,' Tom said still not entirely sure what he was getting at.

'I want you to marry her, Tom,' he said quickly. 'I know you want to. So, before I go, I am telling you that you have my blessing.'

'Oh... okay. I mean, I'm not sure she wants to. Es has pretty much always been anti-marriage. Ever since we met—'

'You've changed her. I can see it. Lena can see it. We talk about it sometimes. Esme is very firm in her beliefs. Maybe she doesn't want the stupid big white wedding. But I know she wants you, Tom. We can see it. I won't be there. But I want to die knowing that it will happen.'

Tom was shocked. Firstly at the idea that Esme might have changed her mind about something she was so virulently against – the thing he had just assumed they would live without for ever. And secondly that it was Tamas's wish, as though it was something he'd accidentally left out of his will.

'I really... I don't know,' Tom said, struggling to find the right words. Was he supposed to thank the old man or correct him?

Tom was about to speak again. But voices from the stairs warned him that Esme and Lena were on their way back to the room. He quickly slipped out as Tamas turned away, passing Lena, who was holding a tray laden with a bowl of tomato soup and a buttered brown roll. He made his way downstairs and walked out into the cold spring morning to run over what had just happened. And to ask himself whether there was any validity in it.

Or if what just happened was little more than a dying man trying to right a wrong.


They were barely on the road out of Knighton when Esme started to cry, the image of strength she had presented over the past couple of days falling apart as they drove home to London. Something within her had shifted, and Tom imagined it to be more untreatable than anything he himself had suffered.

Tom reached over to her side, taking his hand off the gear stick to take hers for all of twenty seconds, before the traffic slowed in front of them and he had to shift down. The car smelled damp, the result of old window seals that let in water which worked its way into the material of the seats.

Over the past few weeks, since Tamas's diagnosis, he had listened with understanding when she complained about the doctors who treated him after his first bout, convinced that better work *then* would've prevented the cancer from coming back with so much more aggression *now*. Esme jumped spasmodically between heaping praise on the NHS staff and damning them with a bitterness that was so unlike her.

'It's the fucking doctors,' she'd said. 'Not the nurses. The nurses are fine. But the doctors couldn't give a shit. It's all about targets for them. Numbers.'

Tom knew she didn't mean it. Working in the system herself meant that Esme was all too aware of the hard work, strain and limitations that weighed down on the people helping her dad. But keeping up with her moods, her ups and downs, was difficult. Although not something Tom had much of a right to complain about.

'You alright?' he said, as they drove past the huge shopping centre that came just before the motorway.

'I will be.'

'If you need to talk,' Tom said, leaving the offer hanging there.

'What were you and Dad talking about earlier? When we came up.'

'Oh,' Tom said, unsure of how much to divulge. 'Nothing, really. He was telling me about when he met Puskás.'

'Again?'

'I know,' Tom said, trying to sound irritated by it.

He drove them onto the motorway, accelerating to overtake a slow truck on the slip road. The rain was getting heavier, beginning to obscure his view. Tom turned the radio up. A reality television star was being interviewed about his autobiography. They carried on for a few minutes before he pressed mute.

'He also talked about us. Your dad.'

'Us?' Esme said, distracted from looking out of the window at the grey sky, bare trees and hard shoulder.

'As in you and me. He wanted to ask me some stuff about our future.'

'Like what?'

'Well, I suppose it was more like advice really.'

'Ha,' Esme said bitterly.

'Es. Come on.'

'Of all the people to offer fucking advice,' she said. 'Follow what I say, not what I do.'

'It's been a long time, Es.'

'It still happened, Tom,' she said. 'He can't just rub it out of our family history because he's dying.'

This was the other thing about Tamas's illness. The consistent resurfacing of things he had done, all of which were made worse by his burying of them in silence. No matter how much the family tried to ignore it, his affair was a reminder that he was not perfect, perhaps not even fundamentally good. That any eulogising of him as a family man at his funeral would be entirely untrue. Tamas had made mistakes that would forever dent his daughter's memory of him, a bitter, devastating chaser to any love she felt.

'Can I suggest something?' Tom said, as they passed a huge road sign that read LONDON and THE SOUTH.

'As long as it's not another one of those grief coping things you found online. You know one of those links was just a Mumsnet forum?'

Tom ignored her. 'Forgive him,' he said. And when Esme looked up he didn't know whether she was going to break down in tears or throw her bottle of water in his face. 'He was a good man, Es. I know he made a fucking clanger—'

'A *two-year* clanger.'

'Fine. A long fucking clanger. But he cared for you. Massively. You were everything to that man and he did a lot for us. He gave us that money for our deposit when we bought the house,' Tom said. Her dad's first punch-up with cancer a couple of years before led him to cash in his pension, savings and stocks to gift Esme the money that would allow them to put a down payment on their first place together in West Hampstead.

'Only because he thought he was going to die.'

'Even so. I just think there's a time to let things go. People can be good *and* do bad things. Life isn't all just split into binary things where one cock-up – however massive – makes you a bastard for ever. And you like being around him, Es. I've seen it. You love to talk to him, to play games. Fuck, why would I have been to Leicester God knows how many times if you didn't like *both* your parents?'

'I know,' she said, matter-of-factly. 'I know you're right. It's just that it made a perfect marriage imperfect. There'll always be that thing hanging over it. *Noelle.*'

'A perfect marriage? Come on, Es.'

'Look, I'm sorry if I don't sound particularly forgiving about it. But I've had a pretty shit year, what with this and—' Esme stopped before she could say what they both knew she was thinking.

*You.*

They drifted back into silence. Tom turned up the radio again to hear the reality TV star pick his favourite all-time record (which was less than six months old).

'You're right,' she said finally, her voice more forgiving and gentle. 'I know you are. It's just they were together for so long before it happened. Every time I think about it I imagine what my mum must've felt at the time. And I wonder how she can still love him and stay married to him.'

'Till death us do part is bloody ages, Esme,' Tom said, wondering if it would open up the path he wanted to go down. 'Thirty, forty years. People are bound to have bad moments. Maybe it's better to forgive than to give up. Like your mum did. When you've put in all that time.'

Esme said nothing.

Tom wanted to tell her to reconcile the man she loved with his mistakes; to see his life as a whole, rather than a series of incidents she could sort neatly into 'good' and 'bad'. Maybe with that, he thought, some of her old self might return.

'How long though?' she asked, as they drove past junction twenty, the rain becoming more deliberate.

'What do you mean?'

'How much time do you have to invest before you can forgive something like that?'

'I don't know. Ten years?'

'Fifteen,' she said. 'Maybe more. Not enough can happen in ten. Look at us. What are we, seven?'

'Eight! Which I suspect you knew,' Tom said, looking at Esme who had that playful, mischievous look on her face that came out every time she wanted to play a game, wind him up or ask a difficult question.

'I'm sorry. About all of this. You've got enough to worry about.'

'It's fine. It's understandable. I've never been in your position.'

'Except that you are now. My dad is basically your father-in-law, no?'

'I suppose. I've never really thought of that before,' he said.

'You're family, Tom. As good as, anyway. All that's lacking is the bit of paper.'

Tom feigned a laugh. Was there some truth to what Tamas had said earlier? Was she changing her mind about marriage?

Tom looked over to her in the passenger seat. It seemed trite to say that he saw a girlfriend sitting there. The word implied a certain juvenility. Inexperience. Youth. Esme was more than that to him now. They were a million miles from the two people who'd met at a fancy-dress party in Stockwell. She was a different woman from the one he'd approached when her friend went out for a cigarette at just the right moment.

Tom thought back to what Tamas had said. She had changed, but had he changed her? Annabel said something similar before and had a point. Esme felt differently about so many things. Art, politics, how much time they should spend in front of the telly each evening. Why not this?

Maybe it would even be good for them. A way to repair some of the dents that had been dealt to their relationship over the past year. And a way for Tom to protect what they had together, what he knew he'd need every day of his life.

The events of the year had pushed them to the limits. And through it all, Esme had stood by him and supported him. But how long would she continue to do so? The next time something happened – and there always would be a next time – there might be nothing tethering her to him. She may have once said a marriage certificate was just a bit of paper, but what if it was the thing they needed most?

'You alright?' she said, bringing Tom back around again.

'I'm good. You?'

'Fine,' she said. 'I was just wondering how long we've got left together.'

It took Tom a moment to realise that she was talking about her dad.

'As long as possible, I hope,' he said. And as the song on the radio faded to make way for the news, Tom's mind was made up.

# CHAPTER SIXTEEN

7 – 8 pm

# THE WRONG QUESTION TO ASK YOU

## September 2016 – Laura's house, St Agnes, Cornwall

The beach was nearly empty, their only company that evening an elderly couple holding hands and walking barefoot across the firm sand and salty puddles of the evening's low tide. The chilly breeze whipped around his bare legs, as he pulled his ratty, dark blue hoodie around him and zipped it up. Cold seawater spilled over the tops of his flip-flops and toes.

'It's beautiful, isn't it?' Esme said.

'It is.'

'Do you ever think you could live somewhere like this?'

'I think the *thinking* of it is easier than the doing. It's a big change. I think you'd go mad outside of London.'

'*Psh.*'

'The other day you got annoyed because you had to wait three minutes for a Tube train. Out here you'd be waiting three hours for a bus.'

'I could adapt. It's a slower pace of life here.'

'That it is.'

Tom looked around. They were very nearly getting to the spot. He had found it two nights ago on a run around the cove. A little inlet between two patches of rock that formed its own sun trap at around ten past seven. There would be a little bit of seawater still covering the sand. But that would be okay.

It had been a struggle to even get her to come out that evening. She had been sitting on the decking in Laura's garden sipping a gin and tonic and reading a book. Tom had to pretend that he was restless, fancied a walk and a chat. A bit of time for just her and him.

'Can't we just do it tomorrow?' Esme had said, closing the thriller she was reading in that slightly irritated manner she had when Tom interrupted her halfway through a sentence.

'I'd really rather go now. I think it'd be good to get out,' he'd said. 'I'm feeling cooped up.'

'You're in a lovely garden in a quiet part of Cornwall and all we can hear is the waves. How on earth are you "cooped up"?'

'I don't know. But I am,' he said insistently.

Eventually he talked her round enough for her to abandon her drink and her book. Although Laura's kids running out into the garden in their pyjamas might've helped his cause.

Now, Tom led Esme over a little rocky wall – and stopped.

'Here,' he said.

'What do you mean *here*?'

'Just this little spot. Nice, isn't it? I found it earlier. Thought I'd show you.'

'Suppose. It's a bit wet, though,' she said, looking down at her submerged Birkenstocks. 'The tide's coming in. We'll be knee-deep in a minute.'

'Well, yeah. But . . .' he trailed off, half losing track of what he was saying. His heart had started beating faster and there was a touch of panic in his voice. 'Just sit down there, would you? On that rock.'

'Why would I sit on a rock?'

'I want to show you something.'

'Tom, are you alright? You're being like Toots,' she said, referring to Laura's attention-seeking daughter who often forced Esme to sit down and watch while she danced or sang, or told long and elaborate stories about people in her class at school.

'I'm fine.'

'You're acting strangely.'

'I said I'm *fine*,' he insisted. 'I've got you a present. Now sit there and close your eyes.'

Cautiously, Esme did what he told her to, as Tom rummaged around in the side pocket of his cargo shorts.

It was when she heard the splash of his knee dropping into the water that Esme opened her eyes.

'*Tom.*'

'Esme. Now, I know—'

'Tom, what the fuck are you doing?'

'Es, please,' he said, looking up at her. She seemed taller than she might, the camber of the beach sloping down towards Tom.

'No! I can see what you're doing and I'm telling you not to.'

'But—'

'Don't you even dare say what you're about to, Tom. Don't open that box.'

'Esme,' he said, pleadingly. But she was up now, over the little rocky wall – now fully submerged in seawater – walking quickly away from him back in the direction of St Agnes. He shoved the ring into the pocket of his hoodie and followed, calling her name and begging her to stop. Until, after a few minutes, she turned to face him.

'What?' she said. They'd almost reached the small row of shops and huts at the top of the beach, with the smell of frying chips and the distant bubble of noise from the pub.

'I just—'

'What, Tom? What? You just thought you'd throw out a quick proposal? Just thought you'd see what I think about the idea? Just thought you'd go and buy a bloody ring and plan this little walk, hoping I might change my mind about the whole thing?'

'No, I—'

'I don't know how many fucking times I have to tell people, Tom. This is not some little whim I'm likely to go back on because I fancy a nice piece of jewellery. I thought you of all people *might* understand that,' she said, turning to walk away, then turning back to face him again. 'Does Laura know about this?'

'No.'

'Because I *fucking* swear—'

'Esme, no one knows.'

'My mother?' she said, to which Tom said nothing. 'Are you telling me that my mother knows you were going to do this?'

'No... Well, not really. That I know of, anyway.'

'Tell me, Tom.'

He looked at her, hair blowing in the wind that came across the Cornish cliffs to shake the gorse bushes and fan their scent around the heathland. Her cheeks were red in the gloom, eyes big and set firm on him. He could see that she was angry.

'If I find out that you and Mum were in on this together,' she continued, 'then I'm getting in that car and I'm driving straight back to London,' she said, pointing in the direction of Wales. 'Alone.'

Tom hesitated for a moment. Unsure if what he was about to say – what he *wanted* to say – would make things worse or better. But he was here now. And there was really no point in telling her anything but the truth.

'It was your dad.'

Esme waited a moment, taking it in. 'My dad?' she said. 'What do you mean?'

'That time he spoke to me, the day before he died, remember?'

She took a second to process it. Remembering back to the previous November, when they were up visiting her parents in Leicester. At five the next morning, Esme received a call from her mum: Tamas had collapsed at the top of the stairs, apparently ill from the chemotherapy. By seven o'clock he was gone. Esme had arrived at the hospital half an hour too late.

'You asked his *permission*?' she said, incredulous. 'So all that shit about me forgiving him, and how great long marriages are – that was just to get me to come around?'

'No—'

'When does it stop, Tom? For years we had people asking us about it. I thought by now it'd be a closed book.'

'Esme, you've got it wrong.'

'Answer me one thing,' she said, ignoring him. 'Is this about last year?'

'No.'

'Because I swear, if this is your way of apologising for *lying* to me for *years* about your . . . your problems,' she said, searching for the word, 'then you've just made things a lot worse.'

'Esme, listen!' Tom said firmly, grasping both her hands as if to stop her from lashing out at him. He took a deep breath. 'Your dad told me to marry you. He thought that you didn't really mean all the anti-marriage stuff.'

Esme said nothing. Gradually hurt began to replace anger. Her eyes looked watery, though that might have been from the wind.

'He said that he wouldn't be around to see it. But he wanted to know that it would happen. So . . .'

'My dad,' she said sadly, as though every unreconciled emotion and issue that had been bubbling around since his death had all come back to the surface in that moment. 'So you're doing this for him, then?'

'No, I—'

'Or are you doing it for you, Tom?' she asked, to which he said nothing. 'Because I really need to know why you've put me in this position. Is it something you actually want? Or are you trying to appease my dad?'

'Both. I suppose,' he said, looking down to see the water around their feet again, the tide encroaching a little further on the land.

'So, it was just me, then? All this time? Just me who didn't want all that bullshit. Me who thought that we could be just as happy without it. And every time I was asked about it, or you were asked about it, you were actually thinking "Ah she'll change her mind soon enough. She'll come around."'

'It wasn't like that!'

'What, then? For nine fucking years we've said we didn't need it. We were just fine as we were. And you knew all along why that was. But now here I am, standing in the fucking sea, realising that every word of it was a lie.'

'Esme,' he said desperately. 'It wasn't.'

'How?' she shouted. 'Tell me how you weren't lying... Tell me how you weren't simply lying *again*. I thought we were a team. You and me. Esme and Tom. We did things our own way.'

'We still can.'

Esme turned away from him again, starting towards dry land. Tom went after her.

'Do you not see how he wasn't saying that for me or for you? He was saying it because he blamed himself for me not wanting to get married, and was arrogant enough to think he could fix it before he went.' She wiped her nose on her sleeve. 'And you, like some bloody patsy, just go along with it. Because, if you're being honest, Tom, it *is* what you want too.'

'And what if I do? What if I think we need this? If I need it?'

'Then you're going to be disappointed. I've said so many times that I—'

'And what about *me?*' Tom yelled over the noise of the waves. He was surprised to hear himself say it. 'This whole thing has been about you.'

'What whole thing?'

'Marriage, Esme. You have never once, literally not once, asked me what I think. You said no, and that's the end of it.'

'I don't want to get married, Tom. Why is that so fucking difficult for you to understand?'

Tom didn't answer immediately. He knew what he wanted to say. But was unsure if it would be wise to say it.

'Well?' she said.

'Because I think it would be good for us, Es,' he said, matter-of-factly. 'Things have been . . . well they've been a bit shit. With my . . . stuff. And your dad. I think that maybe this is what we need.'

'I don't.'

'If you'd just think about it.'

'I *have*. I've thought about marriage a million times. On every hen do. Every time a friend asks me about it. Every time your bloody mother drops it into a fucking conversation thinking I won't notice.'

'Fine.'

'No, it's not fine, Tom. It's anything but fine. You knew how I felt.'

'And now you know how I feel.'

Esme and Tom stood apart from one another, each looking into the other's eyes. Tom understood then that he was in fact looking at the same woman he had met at a party all those years ago. She had remained consistent, certain of herself and her life. He questioned if he was the same man. And if not, who was she looking at?

'I'm going to go,' Esme said. 'I don't want you to follow me.'

'I'm not sorry I did it,' Tom called out as she walked away.

'I am,' she called back. 'I never wanted to turn you down, Tom. But I didn't think you'd ever be stupid enough to ask.'

*

Fifteen minutes later, Tom was sitting alone on the few rocks that hadn't yet been claimed by the sea. He was wondering where he would sleep, given that Esme would almost certainly not want him in her bed. And how would it be when he arrived back at Laura and Aman's beach house? Awkward and silent? Or would the four of them gamely press on with the evening, playing cards and chatting, pretending that the day – the whole week – had not been ruined?

Maybe there would be a room at the pub. Though Tom knew that today of all days was not the time to spend a night above taps, bottles and optics.

Inside the pocket of his hoodie he fingered the rough velvet of the small, black ring box. Part of him wanted to toss it into the water, to let the gentle waves of the Celtic Sea consume it. Another part knew that he couldn't. Something unseen and unknown tied him to it. Instead of selling, returning or junking it, he would take it home, place it at the very back of his desk drawer and leave it to gather dust. He would allow the gold band to slowly tarnish over time, its pointless emerald to become dulled with disuse.

'IDIOT!' Tom heard called from behind him. He looked around to see Laura walking across the sand towards him. Since moving here she had become every bit the middle-class English woman at the seaside. Blue and white Breton top, tight khaki trousers rolled up at the ankle, Salt-Water sandals. Her blonde, wavy hair bounced on her shoulders. She permanently wore the relaxed look that Tom now associated with escaping London, having quit her job at the *Telegraph* before Christmas last year to move to the coast and work on her children's books.

'Mind if I sit?' Laura said, dropping down onto the sand next to him before he could answer. 'So. Are you going to stay here all night?'

'I was thinking that the sea might eventually carry me out. I could start a new life in . . . wherever's over there.'

'Ireland.'

'Probably not far enough.'

'I don't think things are *that* bad, Tom.'

'Well,' Tom said, stretching his legs out in front of him, feeling the coarse sand on the backs of his legs. 'Right now I'm not sure how they could be much worse.'

'Tom,' Laura said, as though asking one of her kids to be reasonable.

'How is she?'

'She's okay. Bit upset still. I left her reading a Doctor Seuss story to Mo with a G and T.'

'He's old enough to understand Doctor Seuss?'

'Not really. But he likes the cartoons and Esme does the voices.'

Tom thought of her sitting on the couch in Laura's big living room, surrounded by expensive wooden furniture, decorative driftwood and garish plastic children's toys. He could see her with the two-year-old boy on her knee, arms around him as she read over his shoulder. He imagined her voice reading, how she would take care to give each character a distinct tone and accent, slipping from one to the other to delight the child.

'I love kids, but I'm not sure,' was Esme's stock line when they spoke about the prospect of having children. His too, unsure of whether he'd made too much of a mess of his own life to convincingly curate another's. They were never quite ruled out, never quite planned in; he could see a child in their future just as easily as he could see them growing old together without one. Typically, it was another thing they'd never really had a proper talk about; allowing the busy bustle of life to obscure bigger decisions year after year. They'd skirted around it in the way other people might discussions about putting in a new kitchen.

'It's a bit fucked, isn't it?' Tom said.

'No!' Laura said, allowing a long pause to set in before she continued. 'I mean, it's not *brilliant*. But . . . I don't know, Tom. I see where you were coming from.'

'I'm glad someone does.'

'When did you change your mind? I always thought you didn't care enough to push it.'

'Her dad told me to do it. Just before he died.'

'Yes, I know her dad told you. But how many times do you think they actually discussed marriage, him and Esme?' she asked, making Tom feel a flash of sympathy towards the various politicians she had, as a journalist, determinedly grilled over the years.

'Well, clearly never.'

'Exactly.'

'But the thing is that talking to him made me realise that I wanted to as well. That's the bigger problem.'

'You'll get over it.'

'Maybe. But it'll always be there, won't it? I want to. She doesn't.'

Tom dug his feet into the sand, enjoying the feel of grit between his toes.

'It was a stupid idea. I should've known,' he said.

'If it helps, I know why you went for it, Tom. God, there have even been times I thought she might change her mind, because it's you. But you know Esme.'

'Yeah.'

'She's really determined about these things.'

Tom nodded and recrossed his legs.

'I know she always says that it's just a piece of paper. But some pieces of paper are worth more than others,' Laura said, once again nailing her colours firmly to the pro-marriage mast. 'No matter what Esme says.'

'Degree certificates.'

'Huh?'

'The pieces of paper she values most: degree certificates.'

Laura smiled.

'You are good together,' she said. 'You know that, don't you?'

'I liked to think so.'

'Tom,' she said. That tone again.

'Things are such a fucking mess now.'

'And you'll get through it. There are some couples who just work. They click. That's you two. Everything you lack, she has. Same the other way around. You're like two bits of bloody Lego or something. You make it work.'

'I always thought that about you and Aman.'

'Tom. Come on. I love Aman. But sometimes things between us are a total shit-show. My terrible racist of a dad *still* isn't totally comfortable with the fact that I married an Asian man. And Aman hates it when I go away for work, but he'll happily fuck off to give a keynote at some techie nerd conference in San Francisco at the drop of a hat. Where, by the way, I am almost certain he flirts with every young reporter who asks him a question. We barely have sex, and at least once a month have an argument that I think is going to end the marriage.'

'It all looks fine from where I'm standing.'

'Well, it isn't. We keep it on the rails because we love each other. Despite all the reasons not to,' she said with a laugh. 'You and Esme are nothing like that.'

'We used to be.'

'What do you mean?'

'You know about everything, don't you? From last year. That . . . episode.'

Laura nodded.

'Since then it's been hard. She found out some things . . . from my mum of all people.'

'I know. She said.'

'Then her dad.'

'Tom, you'll—'

'The thing is I'm not quite there, you know? Better, I mean. I still get these moments.'

'Does Esme know?'

The two of them sat looking out at the waves for a minute.

'Tom,' she said, prompting him.

'That's why I did it. The proposal. So she wouldn't leave. If there's a next time.'

'Does Esme know this?'

He hesitated before he spoke. 'Not really. She thinks I'm better than I am.'

Laura got up, brushed the sand off her backside and took a long, deep breath of the sea air.

'I can't be the one you talk to about this. I love you. You know I do. But I can't.'

'Laura—'

'I'm going back,' she said firmly. 'It's Mo's bedtime.'

'Please.'

'Talk to her,' Laura said, looking back at him. 'For fuck's sake, just talk to her.'

Tom waited a minute for the sea to get a little closer to him. The pub was in full voice tonight. They had a band on. He thought back to the last time he'd played live music to a crowd. It would be a nice thing to get back to – and he needed the money.

In the distance, a church bell began to chime. He took the ring from his pocket.

# CHAPTER SEVENTEEN

**10 – 11 am**

# THE WORST PART OF THE HOSPITAL

## January 2017 – The Royal Free Hospital, London

Esme tapped her foot against the floor. It was as if there was music playing somewhere and she was swept along by the beat. Every few seconds there it was: *tap, tap, tap.* The hard, stubby heel of her shoe against the cold, pale blue linoleum of the hospital. The cold, bare corridors seemed to make it much louder than it actually was, each *tap* echoing down past the maternity and early pregnancy units.

He noticed that she'd barely looked up as they walked through, past all the expectant mothers and nervous fathers. Since they'd been told by the GP that there was a problem she'd found it impossible to so much as glimpse a young child or baby without welling up.

'It's never a good sign at this stage,' the doctor had told them the day before. He was an old man who they both suspected had lost faith in the medical profession years ago. 'But we'll send you for a blood test. See what comes back.'

The results of the test were rushed back to the clinic in West Hampstead, and confirmation that her HCG levels were low meant

Esme was immediately booked in to the early pregnancy unit for later that day.

'How low?' Esme had asked.

'There's no exact number, I'm afraid. But at this stage we'd be expecting them to double every couple of days or so. And it doesn't look as though they are.'

After cancelling her appointments, Esme spent the rest of the morning scouring the internet for good news stories of women with low HCG levels and bleeding in early pregnancy. She was looking for hope in the doom-laden forums. All she found was acronyms and empathy.

Tom, meanwhile, had been feeling it all coming on again. It was as if there was something inside him, around his lungs or stomach perhaps. Something real, as if he reached his hand in behind his rib-cage he could grab at it and pull it free. But through it all he had adopted a four-word mantra that he repeated to himself: *Don't let Esme know.*

He hoped it would pass with the weather, later in the year, when the winter lifted. And in the lowest moments he tried to rationalise it all, to tell himself that he wasn't worthless, that life wasn't hopeless. Yet still, there it was. The feeling that he might break down any second.

When Esme had showed him the positive test, Tom decided that there were more important things to think about. It was time for him to be a man – to protect and persevere rather than malinger and suffer.

'But it says "pregnant" doesn't it?' Esme had said, climbing onto their bed, where he was scrolling through his phone, trying to distract himself. She was confused because her period had arrived on time.

'Yeah.'

'So,' Esme had said, a broad smile spreading across her face.

'So . . .'

'You're going to be a dad,' she had said.

Tom had smiled, laughed and cried. But behind it all was that deep fear again. How could a man who struggled so much to care for himself care for a child? Tom had searched online for articles about whether depression and anxiety could be genetically passed on.

At the same time, he worried about bringing a baby into a relationship that had struggled recently: the blow of Esme's father's death; *that* day in Cornwall. Although they had celebrated and promised a new start on New Year's Eve, it was hard to see where it would come from when the beginning of 2017 looked so much like the end of 2016.

But maybe, beyond everything else, a baby – created between the two of them – offered the hope they needed as a couple. The hope Tom had thought he could offer through his proposal.

Though he would not admit it, a child might prove to be a restorative. Something to bring him out of the mire. Something to reconnect the two of them.

'Esme Simon?' a chubby, red-cheeked nurse said, poking her head out of a paint-chipped grey door. The two of them looked up at her. 'We'll be with you in a minute. We're just finishing up with another lady.'

*Yet more delays.* Time had been a curse in the whole thing. The uncertainty and prevarication of various GPs had allowed it to run on for three weeks, when it could so easily have been a closed matter within a few days. The first of them had all but ignored Esme's concerns over the bleeding, passing it off as 'implantation issues' and referring her directly to the midwives for an eight-week appointment.

'I reckon he was thinking about getting to lunch,' she had said, later in the process.

It was only Esme's continued concern that led her to try again, to book another appointment with him. Then, more visits, more tests, more setbacks.

Finally, there was some urgency. And now this.

Tom reached over and took Esme's hand, which was shaking lightly.

'You okay?'

'I'm scared, Tom,' she said quietly. 'Really scared.'

'I know. I'm here. We'll do this together. All of it. Like I said.'

She grasped his hand with both of hers.

'You're not in this alone, Es.'

Esme looked down at her feet. She took a deep breath and the door opened again. The same nurse as before held it open for a shocked-looking young Asian couple; the man placed his hand on his partner's back. In her hand was a small stack of hospital notes.

'Esme,' the nurse said.

She got up and went ahead. Tom followed and said 'hello' to the nurse, but she ignored him. Esme was led behind a curtain and introduced to the sonographer, Sue, who would be conducting the scan. He, meanwhile, found a seat in the corner of the room, and sat there with their coats and her bags.

'Now, love,' the nurse began, a comforting northern edge to her voice that Tom hadn't noticed before. 'You've got what we call a non-viable pregnancy. Now this means—'

'I know what it means,' Esme said bluntly. 'Sorry. I've been reading up on it.'

'Okay. And you know what the treatment is at this stage?'

'No,' she said, her voice a little shaky now.

'Well, at this early stage, we'll be looking to see if the egg dissolves by itself. If it doesn't, then a doctor will discuss the options with you.'

The nurse went on to matter-of-factly tell Esme what to watch out for, and what to do in these circumstances, before giving her a leaflet explaining what had happened and what she should do next.

Then they were both ushered out of the door where another couple was waiting.

Tom led Esme down the corridor and away from the unit, trying his best to obscure her view of pregnant mothers where possible. Moments later they were out of the hospital and into the cold January sunshine.

'Are you—'

'I'd like a drink, please.'

Tom checked his watch. It was a quarter to eleven; unlikely that any of the pubs around here would be open and serving.

'Es, it's not even elev—'

'I don't care, Tom. Just find me a drink,' she snapped. 'You of all people should be able to do that.'

He took the hit without a word. Now wasn't the time. He reminded himself that this wasn't about him. Indeed, he couldn't make it about him, no matter what else was going on privately in his life.

Instead, Tom took out his phone and quickly searched for the crap pub he knew nearby. If any was likely to throw open its doors mid-morning, it would be The George.

'Okay. I know somewhere,' he said, taking her arm, leading her up the hill away from the hospital, to where Pond Street met Haverstock Hill. As he did, he became aware that she had started crying. Tom pulled her towards him as a bus stopped next to them with a hiss.

'It's alright,' he said quietly.

Ten minutes later, they were on two sofas beneath a fifty-two-inch television showing Sky Sports News. Over at the bar was a drunk on his first of the morning. The fruit and quiz machines flickered and bleeped in the corner. The barmaid, setting up for the day, turned on a radio station that was playing 'There She Goes' by The La's. In front of Esme was a hot chocolate with a dash of rum in it. In front of Tom, the straight version. Part of him was envious of her drink. He tried to suppress the feeling.

Esme took a sip and leant back in her chair. She fixed Tom with a look of love, exasperation and sadness.

'You alright?' he said, to which she nodded. Even though she wasn't. Tom meanwhile was asking himself where this left them, and where it left him, knowing that something else was eating at him, day after day.

But, again, he said nothing.

The barmaid finished taking chairs off the tables where they were stacked overnight, and turned the sign on the door to 'Open'.

# PART 4

# CHAPTER EIGHTEEN

8 – 9 pm

# THE NIGHT BEFORE OUR 10TH ANNIVERSARY

## June 2017 – West Hampstead, London

Tom read the rules over again.

*Welcome to Our Life in a Day. A new game devised by Esme Simon, for Tom Murray, to celebrate our ten years together.*

*Each Post-it note represents an hour. You have to think of twenty-four of the most significant moments of our life together. One for each hour of the day.*

*There is only one rule: the moment had to have taken place roughly during the hour shown on the note. For example:*

*3–4 a.m. When Esme had to pick me up from Milton Keynes station because I'm an idiot and fell asleep on a train (March 2011, if you remember?).*

*The game is only complete when you have a moment for every
note. At which point you will receive your prize . . .*

*Have fun! Love you, Es xxxx*

He looked up at Esme, her face lit by the candle between them and
a broad, satisfied smile. He hesitated for a moment. Then looked
back down at the Post-its.

The twenty-four most significant moments of their relationship.
Not the best moments, she had been careful to write in her rules.
The most significant. Which meant . . . well . . .

Looking at her, Tom found himself questioning for the first time
if she did in fact know. If she had known all along – ever since it
happened. Maybe someone had been in touch or she'd met them in
the street. Maybe this was her way of twisting his arm behind his
back and forcing him to talk, whether he wanted to or not. Instead
of confronting him directly, she was going to help him bring about
his own downfall.

Tom glanced at the deck again, and then back up at Esme.

'Ready?' she said.

Tom said nothing.

'Tom?' Esme said, prompting him.

'Hang on.'

'If you need me to explain—'

'No,' he said firmly. 'Sorry, no. I'm not ready. What is this?'

'I told you. It's a game. You write down the twenty-four—'

'I know what you said,' he snapped. 'I mean this evening. First it's
a little dinner before we go away. Then you're all dressed up and there
are presents and some stupid little game. Now I have to remember
every fucking thing that ever happened to us. It's ridiculous. It's like
I'm being set up or something.'

'Set up?'

'Yes, set up, Esme. What are you trying to get me to do? Open up to you?'

'I never thought—'

'So why put me on the spot?'

Stunned, Esme said nothing. She just sat there opposite him, staring with the kind of hurt on her face he had only ever seen once before: early one morning a couple of years ago, when her mum called to tell her that Tamas had passed away while they were driving up to see him. Gradually, her eyes began to fill with tears, creating rivulets down her face, cutting lines through her foundation.

'A *stupid little game*,' she repeated quietly. And immediately Tom knew that this would be the end of their evening, that no apology would rescue it.

He was wrong. She didn't know any of it. She had no idea what he had done earlier that year and all the things he was suppressing in himself and keeping from her. Our Life in a Day was a bit of fun to bring some light to an otherwise difficult period of their lives. He could see that now. But knowing it didn't make him feel any better.

'I didn't mean . . .'

'I'm *trying*, Tom.'

'Es.'

'I really am. After everything it's amazing I even want to celebrate. Ten years, and what have we got?' Esme motioned around her, battling back tears in a way he had seen her do many times before, when she didn't want to openly show that someone had bothered her. 'A little flat in West Hampstead and a fucking cat.'

Tom didn't try to contradict her. He didn't bother to convince her of their good fortune to even have each other. Nor did he mention how lucky they were to have the kind of relationship everyone around them had once been envious of.

'So what, you agree then? Ten years and we've got nothing.'

'No, Es—'

'That game was a bit of fun. That's all. Just a reminder that we've got *some* nice memories, if nothing else.' She pushed her chair back against the wall and stood up from the table.

'Please,' Tom said, reaching out his hand to stop her. But he knew he had gone too far and that he would not be able to pull this back, at least for now.

She ignored him, marching past on her way to the kitchen. He heard the opening of the oven door, then the crash of a dish, their anniversary meal, on cold, hard, black kitchen tiles. Then came the muffled sobs he so hated hearing, let alone causing, and finally the slam of the bedroom door.

Alone now, he stared from the basket of bread to Esme's miniature bottle of red wine. The small stack of Post-it notes, 'Our Life in a Day' written across the front – the small drawing of a clock.

Tom picked up the stack and flicked through it again.

As he did, he asked himself which moments he would have included. The night they met, obviously. Maybe their first anniversary and that disastrous trip to the coast. Esme's thirtieth birthday.

But what, he wondered, were the other moments that had defined them over the past decade – those less obvious moments that only become profound, meaningful or influential with the passing of time; the conversations that go on to have far wider connotations than is first apparent; that things change the dynamic irrevocably.

What about all the incidents and accidents she had no knowledge of; his betrayals and mistakes that he had protected with silence? Or the things he had lied about?

Esme had created a game that she thought would be fun. But Tom knew that to play it properly meant it couldn't possibly be. Now, everything around him was a reminder of something that could go on one of those Post-it notes. Good or bad. From the photo on the wall, taken on that ill-fated camping trip in Somerset, to the mug she used to drink tea in their first place together (now a pen pot).

Tom needed to get out, to think.

He stood up from the table and walked as quietly as he could through the flat, down the hallway past the kitchen (where Magnus was happily eating the scattered remnants of the lasagne Esme had thrown to the floor) and past the bedroom door – firmly closed and off-limits for now. He put on his running trainers and a light jacket to protect himself from the rain, and opened the front door.

Just as he was about to step out into the small communal area that would lead him onto Islay Gardens, Tom noticed that he was still carrying Esme's game in his back pocket. He took it out, gave it one final look and dropped it into the bottom of his battered satchel before closing the door behind him.

## CHAPTER NINETEEN

**4 – 5 am**

# THE HOTEL ROOM
## February 2017 – Albert Dock, Liverpool

His phone was buzzing away again on the ugly, patterned carpet of the hotel-room floor. Face down, having fallen out of his back pocket earlier that morning, so he couldn't see the flashing light of the screen, her name and the photo of the two of them that came up every time she called. The unanswered phone's buzzing stopped, sending her away to voicemail and adding another mark to the growing missed call tally. Then silence for a few minutes before she tried again.

The person she was calling was still out cold, dead to the world, oblivious to everything around him.

He eventually became dimly aware of the noise just after four. But it still took him another ten or fifteen minutes to reach down off the tall, uncomfortable bed and pick it up. Surprisingly, it had lasted the night without having been anywhere near a charger. He pressed the button on the side to see what had woken him up to find notifications for sixteen missed calls, four voicemails and nine unread text messages. Every single one of them from Esme.

Tom unlocked his phone and began to scroll through. Reading

the first, sent at midnight, up to the most recent, which arrived ten minutes ago.

> Tom. When can we talk? I know you've been working all day but you must be finished by now. Did you not even get a break? xx

> I really want to go to bed. Horrible day. Please call me xx

> Is everything ok?

> Tom this is fucking ridiculous. It's 1am and I haven't heard from you all day.

> I'm getting really worried Tom. Please just text.

> I can't sleep. I'm in tears. You shouldn't have gone. This was a mistake. Please call me xx

> If I don't hear from you in half an hour I'm calling the police.

> I'm really worried Tom. Whatever's happened please tell me you're ok.

> I'm calling the police. Please call if you're ok xx

He dropped the phone and shut his eyes tight.

He began to feel the familiar, almost nostalgic consequences of last night. The furry, stale-tasting mouth. Aches from limbs now unaccustomed to such abuse. Prickly heat of skin trying to sweat it out. A sense that his blood was lethargically sluicing through his veins. Inescapable nausea and the beginnings of a crushing headache.

A hangover. Albeit dulled by the fact that he was still a little drunk at the same time.

It was something he'd not experienced in almost ten years, since that morning he'd woken up in hospital two months before he met Esme – something he had promised himself he would never experience again, not wanting to ever let her down. And yet he had been increasingly aware of these . . . cravings. They had begun again last month, with more clarity and keenness than he had known for almost a decade.

With the right tools he might've been able to deal with it. But Tom hadn't picked any of them up. His own fault really. Again.

Suddenly, he became aware of something else. Of breathing and twitches and movement – of an arm that was not his own on the pillow, a sinking in the mattress next to him.

Part of him wanted to shift around. To see if he was right about who it was and where she was. But the knowledge of her presence was enough.

'Fuck,' Tom whispered. He sat up on the hotel bed. He was wearing only boxer shorts. His legs felt weak, shaky, as if he was at the end of a bout of flu.

Looking over at Louisa again, sleeping quietly, he wanted to pull back the duvet to check what she was wearing; hoping that she was fully clothed, but knowing that she might well not be. This kind of thing had happened to him before. A vintage Tom Murray mistake from an old playbook long since discarded.

Gingerly, he made his way to the toilet – past the desk piled with coins and coats, above which the television and the stock watercolour print hung on the wall. He could feel the pile and weave of the flat carpet on the soles of his feet, hyper-aware of each and every feeling and sensation he was experiencing. When he turned the light on and stepped inside the bright, white, clinical bathroom, he was hit by an overwhelming stench of vomit. There, in the bath, were his clothes from last night: jeans, a Ben Sherman shirt – balled up and stuffed into a corner of the tub. The shirt was still wet and stained with sick, but the jeans were fine. He pulled them on and took the T-shirt he would've worn to bed from his overnight bag.

Tom fought to remember the gig.

How had he played the guitar in such a state? Back in the day, he was always alright when he'd had a few. Sometimes it even gave him a little more confidence, made his solos that bit bolder – and his stage presence, too. But it had been fifteen years since he last played a gig with a drink inside him. He very well could have been awful, letting the audience and the band down. Perhaps even costing them their fee, having ruined the party. But he could remember nothing except for the first song – 'Country House' by Blur – and the pogoing audience on the dancefloor in front of him.

Opening the hotel-room door as gently as he could manage, Tom stepped out of the room and into the hallway. The smell of cleaning products hit him so hard he almost retched. Ignoring his senses, he carried on through, towards the lift. What had the guests in the rooms bordering his heard from the night before? Did they know more than he did right now?

The night clerk on the reception desk looked surprised to see him. Or perhaps just surprised to see anyone so early on a Sunday morning. Tom nodded dutifully at her cheery 'Morning!' and stalked through the brightly lit, windowless lobby. Beyond the sliding glass doors he felt the slap of cold, fresh air, and the smell of sitting water from the dock.

Tom walked away from the hotel, towards the Tate building. As he passed the bobbing boats, tourist cruisers and one yellow submarine, he wondered if what he was about to do was the right thing. Or would he just be compounding lies with more lies, adding deception and foolishness to his litany of mistakes? Would it, he wondered, be better just to come clean? To admit the lapse? Or, rather, lapses?

But the timing . . .

Last night, of *all* nights.

With his back to the gallery building, he took out his phone, opened his email and started to write.

Hey Es,

Sorry you haven't heard from me since yesterday. My phone and wallet were stolen at the gig. I'm sending this from the computer in the hotel reception. Sorry it's so late (or early). Only got back half an hour ago after doing the police report. Will be back around 1 p.m.

Hope you're okay.

Love you,

Tom xx

He deleted the *Sent from my iPhone* wording from the bottom of the window, hit send, and sat himself down on the dock wall, legs dangling.

Despite a strong history of self-loathing, Tom hadn't hated himself more than he did in that moment. He knew Esme would be angry that it had taken him so long to get in touch. But at least that was the kind of argument they could get over, one that perhaps would only last a couple of days. The truth, on the other hand . . .

With the guilt and the remaining alcohol coursing through him, Tom turned his phone off and threw it into the water of the Albert Dock. For a second, he watched it float – shiny black screen on shiny black water – before it disappeared beneath the glassy surface, taking his secrets with it.

\*

Tom woke Louisa when he arrived back in the room, the slam of the heavy door shocking her out of sleep. She pushed her body up onto the pillow and looked at him in the half-light. He noticed that she was wearing a T-shirt, but that her jeans and bra were scattered on the floor by her side of the bed.

'Hey,' she said sleepily. 'Where've you been?'

'Getting some fresh air.'

She nodded. 'Feeling any better?'

'Not really.'

'No,' she said. 'I'm not surprised. Sober for, what, ten years?'

'Almost,' he said, a little taken aback to hear it out loud. 'Who told you?'

'Mogs. Eventually, anyway. Couldn't really stop you by that point, though.'

'Fuck.' Tom moved to the couch and put his head in his hands. 'Was the gig okay?'

'Errm.'

'Oh fucking hell,' he said, fighting the impulse to throw up again. 'How bad?'

'Well, you haven't been paid.'

Tom began to thump the heel of his hand against his forehead.

'Don't, Tom,' Louisa said. 'You can't blame—'

'I can,' he snapped back. 'I really can.'

The two of them waited for a moment. They were no more than acquaintances, now reunited and with a new, unwanted proximity. Tom had to know what else had happened. What he – or they – had done. But before he could ask, Louisa spoke.

'Look. I'm sorry I didn't sleep over there. I tried. But it was just fucking uncomfortable. And I didn't really fancy the bath either, for obvious reasons.'

'It's fine,' Tom said, taking a moment to realise what she'd said and what that meant. Or at the very least: what it might have meant.

'Sorry, Louisa. I know it's awful but I have to ask. Did we . . .'

'Tom.'

# CHAPTER TWENTY

**4 – 5 pm**

# MY LOSS OF CONTROL
## February 2017 – Hanover Street, Liverpool

He noticed her as soon as he stepped inside the venue, carrying his two guitars and a holdall full of his stuff for the night. She was on stage, tuning her bass guitar and laughing with her bandmates.

Tom hadn't seen Louisa in almost ten years. The last time had been at a gig in Cheltenham, when the Oasis tribute band he occasionally formed part of shared a bill with her 1980s act. That time, it was a Christmas party for a huge engineering firm whose staff were smashed by 9 p.m., and who felt it their place to join Tom's band on stage whenever any of them felt the urge to pose like Liam Gallagher and bellow tunelessly into a microphone.

As ever, Tom and Louisa had caught up like they always did when they met on the circuit. There was always a little spark of something between them. But the timing was never quite right. He had recently got together with Esme; she was engaged to a tax accountant she knew from school, and who she had reconnected with online. Both of them were in the process of winding down the time they spent playing gigs, preferring the home lives they were gradually building.

'He poked me,' she had said of her fiancé. 'It sort of all went from there.'

Not long after that gig Tom stopped playing with Supersonic. Inevitably, he and Louisa lost touch. She drifted from his memory and whatever friendship they once had faded.

So he was surprised to see her now. And found himself drifting back to another time, as she launched her band into a note-perfect version of 'Manic Monday' by The Bangles.

Tom took a seat at the back of the venue and watched as she played. Louisa hadn't changed an awful lot in the years since they'd last seen one another. Her hair was slightly longer, in an untidy bob, and the pink streaks were gone. The bell-bottom jeans and tight T-shirt depicting the logo of one of Hole, The White Stripes or Ani DiFranco, had been replaced by tight black jeans and a plain white cotton Oxford shirt. He wondered if she still had her tongue piercing, which she would stick out of her purple-painted lips whenever there was a camera around.

The song drifted to a clunking, grinding close mid-chorus, as the singer complained about the levels of the monitors. He was about to get up, wave and go over to interrupt their soundcheck. But before he could, the band members he would be playing with later that evening began to filter through the door, carrying their guitars and drum bags.

He'd not seen any but one of them since his last gig with them seven years ago, when he'd stepped in at the last minute because their regular guitarist's wife had gone into labour. Tom would occasionally run into the drummer, Steven Moggach – or Mogs – while watching Arsenal games in any one of the dwindling number of crap north London pubs that favoured their Sky Sports subscription over tapas and craft beer. It was Mogs who kept him up to date with the band and who had asked Tom to fill in tonight.

'The gig's in Liverpool,' Mogs had announced, while rolling a thin cigarette. 'Two hours of nineties covers crap for a bloke who owns a chain of restaurants. It's his fortieth or something. Neil's at

EuroDisney with his kids and his ex-wife. You're still on the roster, if you fancy it?'

The timing was awful. But they were short of money and it was £1,000, plus expenses. So Esme told him to take it before Tom had to admit that all he wanted to do was to go, to be surrounded by that world of bands and live music he'd lost sight of years ago. To forget about who he was and what he was struggling with, under the glare of stage lights and in front of a singalong crowd.

He accepted Mogs's offer.

'Tom!' Louisa said, in the high-pitched posh voice he had all but forgotten. She had finished the soundcheck and was climbing down from the stage at the Social Bar. He was chatting to his bandmates, catching up. 'Tom *fucking* Murray!'

Louisa threw her arms around Tom, hugging him tightly, as though he was an old friend returning from years spent abroad.

'How the fucking hell are you?' she said, Tom remembering her habitual, casual swearing in all and any circumstances. 'What are you even doing here?'

'I'm good, thanks. I'm part of the nineties tribute band for the evening.'

'Shit, Tom. I thought you left the circuit ages ago.'

'I did. This is a brief return. One night only,' he said. 'Anyway, what about you? I thought you'd given up, too.'

'Yep. Gave it all up for marriage, two kids and a messy divorce. The lot,' she said. 'And now I'm back. So maybe think of this as some sort of mid-life crisis.'

'The old band back together then?'

'Sort of. Tonya's a yoga teacher in Amersham now, so we're a three piece. Forty-five minutes of eighties classics before you guys go on.'

'A warm-up act for a fucking party?'

'Oi,' she said, whacking him on the arm. 'Co-headliners. I get the sense the host likes to throw his money around. Anyway, where are you now?'

Tom was about to answer when he heard his name called from the stage. Just as well, because he didn't know where to start when talking about his own life, let alone the questions he could ask about Louisa's. Why the divorce? How old are the kids? What went right? And more importantly, what went wrong?

'Look. I've got to soundcheck. But wait around. We'll catch up afterwards.'

After playing 'A Design for Life' on loop for twenty-five minutes, Tom found Louisa at a high, round table near the bar. In front of her a cold, clear drink was bubbling away. The glow of her smartphone illuminated her face as she scrolled through.

'There he is,' she said, as Tom climbed onto a stool and took a seat in front of her. This was the part of life as a gigging musician he could never get comfortable with. The endless hours of hanging about before stage times. 'So, you first. Tell me about the last ten years.'

And Tom told her most of everything. About Esme, how they met, their home in London and his work composing music for business videos and teaching the children of rich parents and private schools. The life they had settled into since he had drifted away from the live music scene he and Louisa once shared.

But as he was speaking, Tom realised that much of what he said were half-truths. When he spoke about marriage, he omitted his botched proposal the year before. And he'd decided not to share that things had been hard of late, that the reason he was in Liverpool was because all the composing and soundtracking work had dried up, and their mortgage payments were all on Esme.

He knew as he was doing it that he was making up a different version of his life. The one he wanted people to see when they looked at him and Esme. Not the actual one they were living. Complete with all its unhappiness, secrecy and heartbreak.

Then, when Louisa asked if the two of them had any kids, Tom replied: 'Not yet.'

It was true, of course. But those two words concealed so much more than Tom was letting on. They didn't tell Louisa that three weeks ago he and Esme were still having a baby, that the accidental pregnancy they learned of shortly after New Year's Eve was, for a short while at least, the joy their relationship desperately needed. 'Not yet' didn't tell her about the bleeding, the blood tests, the irregular HCG levels. It omitted the doctors' appointments and the language: non-viable, high risk.

Tom gave no indication to Louisa of his devastation at the miscarriage, or that in trying to be Esme's rock, he hadn't allowed himself to grieve. Just as he'd not admitted to Annabel how it made him feel, when Esme suggested that he talk about it with a friend.

On the surface, Tom was keeping calm and carrying on. Below he was struggling. Knowing that money was tight, Tom stopped seeing Christine under the pretence of feeling better. But his recovery from the breakdown he had suffered on New Year's Eve two years ago was incomplete. This recent loss on top of everything else had pushed him further towards the brink. And in the chaos of their lives, Tom had successfully hidden from Esme his worst slide into depression and anxiety in years.

'Not yet,' Tom repeated, and Louisa shrugged it away, telling him that he was better off out of it, making a joke about the stress of raising her own kids that she couldn't possibly have known the insensitivity of.

He faked a laugh and tried to forget the whole thing. Tom hated that he had to be that person. The guy who was wracked with anxiety-inducing thoughts about what could've been and how to get past it. The guy who couldn't admit he was struggling, because he worried about what it might mean for his life with Esme. The guy who was crushed by the weight of the world he had built around himself, and which he increasingly found hard to make sense of.

Instead, he wanted to be a previous version of himself. Someone whose primary care was playing guitar, making people dance and finding the after-party. Who would sit around in bars and chat and laugh.

As Louisa spoke, Tom watched her sip her gin and tonic and remembered how it felt. No matter how many years passed, Tom would always be able to recall what it was like to drink. His first one the loosener; the second savoured, more enjoyable. The third the sign he was settling in. The problem came when the numbers continued to rise. But he wasn't thinking about that now.

Tom was confused and anxious. Unable to trust himself. His heart was beating hard and fast. He wanted to calm himself down. He knew the best, most efficient way to do that. But it was a big step.

For a second he wanted to say 'stop me'. He could tell Louisa how he was feeling and what was about to happen. And she would step in and help him. But rationale and sensibility were slaves to pure, blind will.

She was midway through a story about one of her kids destroying a dining table when Tom got up from the table without a word. He rushed past the guitars leant up against chairs and stacked drum bags, desperately trying to employ some of the tricks that helped to alleviate it all: concentrating on the feeling of his feet against the floor; listing in his head five things he could hear, smell and see; focusing on the reality around him.

But none of it worked.

He stepped outside, on to the busy street, where he dialled the number and listened as it connected – but instead of Esme's voice on the other end, Tom got her voicemail message. He dialled again, and getting the same result, punched out a text message.

**Call when you can xx**

The reply came immediately:

**Not now! Busy. Stop calling x**

Tom stood still for a moment, while the early-evening city crowd bustled past him in the rain. He took a deep breath, but it felt as though the air couldn't reach his lungs.

Just ignore it, he told himself. He wanted to, but didn't know how.

This was it.

As the rain worsened, Tom dropped his phone into his pocket and retreated back inside, where Louisa was waiting for him at their table with an empty glass in front of her.

'Everything okay?' she asked, as Tom took a seat.

'Fine,' he said. 'Carry on.'

'Oh right,' she said, clearly put out by how blunt he was being.

Tom thought about apologising for being rude. But was too distracted. To the extent that he barely listened as she went through it all – her marriage, divorce, kids, house. Occasionally he nodded and forced a smile, before he stopped her abruptly.

'Can I get you another drink?' he asked.

'Please. G and T. Probably shouldn't have too many more before I go on. But fuck it. We're only the warm-up, eh?'

Tom smiled, grabbed her glass and made for the bar. He ordered Louisa's gin and tonic without so much as looking at the barman. Instead, he was fixated on the high-up optics. Some of the bottles were familiar, some new to him after years off the game. He could sense what he was about to do, as if he was somewhere else in the room, watching himself do it. Finally, all good reason to say no – to stop on the precipice and turn back – had dissolved.

It was too late. There was no stopping him.

'And . . .' Tom said, both his voice and the twenty-pound note in his hand shaking. 'I'll have a whisky and ginger.'

'Any particular whisk—'

'No. Any,' he said quickly.

Tom watched as the barmaid poured the drinks, then handed over the money.

'I thought you were teetotal?' Louisa said, her eyes on the glass in front of him. He studied his drink, beaded with condensation. It pooled on the table. A single slice of lime bobbed merrily among ice cubes.

'I was for a little while,' he lied, unable to meet her eyes. 'I have a few every now and then, though.'

'In that case,' she said, innocently oblivious to what was happening in front of her. She raised her glass. 'To old friends.'

They clinked, she smiled, and Tom drained his glass.

# CHAPTER TWENTY-ONE

**Midday – 1 pm**

# THE WRONG TIME TO TALK
## April 2017 – Camden Town, London

Looking up at the red bricks of his old building, Tom wondered who might be living in the studio now. Whoever it was would likely have no idea of what that small room meant to others who'd passed through it. For Tom it signified a turning point: his first move away from Lowestoft, aged just twenty-two, his parents having driven him down to London in a small yet still sparsely filled van they'd rented solely for the occasion. Tom knew that he was taking a step out on his own and that in doing so he was taking a big risk.

For two years after his attempted suicide brought about a rushed, early exit from university, he had been living in his old room, picking up bits of work as a covers musician and teacher. It was a life of parts: the child driven to medical appointments by a harried, worried mother; the adult seeking independence; the boy in recovery, unsure if he would ever feel able to cope with it all. So when he put his key into his own front door for the first time, it was perhaps a more significant moment than the impatient, pimpled estate agent could ever have imagined.

This was Tom Murray 2.0. Sober. Hopeful. Nervous.

He thought back to his tearful mother on that day, about to leave her son alone and only able to keep repeating the words 'you'll be alright' – as much to reassure herself as him.

He had gone to Camden today after a therapy session in nearby Chalk Farm, ostensibly to remind himself of what Annabel had told him all those years ago:

*There are always reasons to live, Tom. You just have to remind yourself of what they are.*

He wanted more than anything to confirm in his own mind that he couldn't knowingly do to Esme what he had done to his best friend all those years ago; that he would never let her be the one to find him on the floor, with that ugly slick of vomit trailing from his mouth. Having her be the one to call his parents to say that it'd happened again, and that, maybe this time, he'd been successful.

Esme, he knew, had always wanted him to be honest with her. Proactively so. But it wasn't the case. Before every piece of eventual honesty, there had been a withholding; him so desperate to see her as an answer to his problems that it took him far too long to understand what the problems actually were.

'It's my fault. All of it,' he had said in his therapy session, talking again about Liverpool, about the relapse. He recited the same story every week, convinced it could have been prevented if only he had been honest from the outset.

'Are you going to tell her?' Christine, his counsellor, said.

'It's too far gone.'

'Only you can decide if that's true,' she said.

Tom started back towards Camden and found a bench on the towpath. He took his new phone from his pocket and scrolled through photos backed up over the last couple of years: Esme on beaches and in city centres; selfies on Hampstead Heath; meals he had cooked that looked far better with the naked eye than they did through the lens of a smartphone. Every one of them had some small story behind it. A snippet of shared happiness, laughter, fun.

These, he thought, are the blocks a life is built with.

Moments to be alive for.

To *stay* alive for.

The photos and the memories they evoked were a catalogue of why Tom loved Esme and Esme loved Tom. Nights on the couch, sitting next to one another in shabby jogging bottoms and hoodies, watching cookery talent shows. Mornings in bed pretending to read broadsheet newspapers.

One of them took him back to New Year's Eve in 2016. They had seen in the year together sitting atop Primrose Hill, after dinner at the new Chalk Farm flat Jamilla had bought with her boyfriend, Chris – a research scientist, whose work looking into blood defects in cancer treatment always made Tom feel a little inadequate. Around them on the hill that night the families of north London let off Chinese lanterns. Parents sipped strong drinks from hip flasks, while their children ran around and slipped in the mud.

Tom remembered precisely what happened when the hour finally turned. He and Esme faced each other, both sensing that they were ready to start a new year with a clean slate.

'I love you. And I'm sorry about everything,' he'd said, as a lantern narrowly avoided colliding with a bare tree behind them.

'I love you too,' she said. 'Maybe let's have fewer sorrys this year?'

They kissed. They embraced. Then, as with of all twenty-first-century record keepers, she suggested that they take a selfie capturing the fireworks in the distance behind them.

That shot was taken less than six months ago. But it felt like a lifetime had gone by since. Aside from their familiar faces, they could be entirely different people. Tom remembered an article he'd read about how the human body supposedly completed total cell regeneration every seven years; how each and every particle becomes completely different from what it had once been.

So what about the mind and soul? he wondered.

Barely three weeks on from the selfie they were on an early pregnancy ward. Esme had her scan, where the bad news was confirmed. When they got home and she went for a nap, Tom locked himself in the bathroom and sobbed on his knees for fifteen minutes.

When he came out of the bathroom, he pretended none of it had happened.

Sitting there, overlooking the canal, Tom knew that if they were going to survive then something had to change.

Before he had a chance to overthink it, he dialled Esme.

'What are you up to?' he said, eschewing any sort of polite greeting.

'Paperwork. Why?'

'I wondered if you wanted to meet up? I'm in Camden. We could go for a walk in Regent's Park, or get a coffee.'

'Right,' she said, sounding confused. 'Tom, is everything alright?'

'Yes, fine,' he said, trying to remain upbeat. 'I just thought . . . I mean, there's some stuff I want to talk to you about.'

'Stuff? Do I at least get a clue?'

'No. No clue.'

'It's just you've literally never done this before. In ten years of you working at home, and me in town, you have not once suggested we meet for a coffee in the park.'

'I know, but—'

'Sorry. That sounded as though I don't like the idea. I do. I'm just, well, surprised I suppose.'

'I was thinking maybe it's a thing we could do sometimes. Meet up and that.'

'I do like how you think a couple meeting up is a new idea.'

'Do you want to, then?'

'Okay. Yes. I'll see you outside the Tube in twenty minutes.'

'I'll be there,' Tom said and hung up the phone, the butterflies and vague sickness rising up with the realisation that this imminent conversation could go one of two ways.

Since he had arrived back in London from his trip to Liverpool with no phone and a raging hangover, Tom had been wondering if he should tell Esme. He knew that making a mistake did not make him a bad person. But this was somehow beyond all that.

Tom stood outside Camden Town station. All around him people buzzed around the shops and cafes, sipping coffee and avoiding the punks giving out flyers for gigs. A celebrity he vaguely recognised (a TV character actress, or perhaps a gameshow host?) passed in front of him, and a busker playing the violin warbled the opening strains of an Oasis song.

It was a bright, sunny spring day – the kind that tricks people into putting on their summer clothes. Tom himself was a little cold in his dark green T-shirt, jeans and a button-less cardigan.

Esme was uncharacteristically late, and so he reopened his email.

From: louisamctell1979@geomailer.com
To: tommurraymusic@geomailer.com
02/04/2017

Re: Sorry

Hey Tom,

Look, I don't know how many times. YOU DON'T HAVE TO KEEP APOLOGISING TO ME.

I know something bad was going on with you that night. I'm just glad I was there to help. To be honest I'm sorry for making you think that… *that* happened. I wanted to sleep on the couch but I have this shit back problem and I really can't. Even had my funny expensive pillow with me in my room (I know – getting OLD).

Anyway. How are you Tom? I know it all went a bit shit but it was really nice to see you up in Liverpool. It's been a while. I really hope we can keep in touch.

Lou x

PS: FYI I am NOT Louisa McTell anymore. Just using my old email address. Last bit of post-divorce admin. Louisa Scott is very much back in the game.

He hadn't replied yet. The question 'How are you?' had become so difficult to answer in recent weeks that it was easier not to.

'Texting other girls already? Jesus, I'm only five minutes late,' Esme said.

Tom turned around, hurriedly closing the email app, locking his phone and shoving it into his back pocket, before properly looking up at Esme. Although he noticed the change, it took him a second to really process it.

'Your hair?' he said, to which she nodded. 'Bloody hell, Es. When?'

'Well I might have lied about having an early appointment today. And I *might* have taken the morning off to visit the hairdresser.'

'Today, then?'

'Well, if it was yesterday I'd have hoped you'd have noticed.'

'Yes, stupid. Sorry,' he said, staring at her, taking it in. In the time they'd been together, Esme had never had more than a variation on the same shoulder-length, slightly wavy haircut. And now the vast majority of that was gone.

'Tom, I'm quite aware that you've not said if you like it or not.'

'Oh ... shit. Sorry. No. I love it. It's, like ... really ... I don't know. Really ...'

'Short? It's called a pixie cut,' she said, straightening the fringe a little, unable to stop messing a hand through it.

'Well yes, short. But it suits you.'

'Really?' Esme said, turning to look at herself in the dry cleaners' window. 'It's a bit drastic, isn't it?'

'Good though,' Tom said, with what he hoped was a reassuring tone.

'*Good* drastic rather than *bad* drastic?'

'Exactly. How long had you been planning to ...' Tom began, unsure of what he was going to say.

'Since the weekend. But I thought I'd surprise you.'

Esme smiled and kissed Tom full on the lips. Then took his hand and led him away from the station, across the busy crossroads that led them towards the park. As they walked, Tom began to feel that today might not be the right time to talk. She was too happy and upbeat, turning her own corner. To bring her down would be selfish.

But then, if he put it off now, the stone would only gather more moss. Was it better to get it out of the way?

After a few minutes of walking together in silence, Esme spoke again.

'Sorry if I sounded a bit grumpy earlier. About coming to meet you.'

'It's fine.'

'It isn't really, though. I'm glad you suggested it. I remember when we first started going out,' she began. 'We used to wander around here almost every Sunday. I'd wonder who could actually afford to live in those big stupid mansions in the park. Then you'd complain that there were never enough seats in the nice cafes, and we'd end up in that dodgy little pub by the station.'

'There is nothing wrong with The World's End. And they served a delicious hot chocolate.'

'It was powder from a packet, and we only ever went there so you could watch the football over my shoulder. I think they called it The World's End for a reason. Anyway. I'm just trying to say that this was a nice idea.'

'Good,' and just as Tom was about to continue, about to use a sombre, serious 'look, Esme' to pivot from nicety to gravity, Esme spoke again.

'While we're here, I think it's probably a good time to talk.' She was looking down at her dark blue Converse All Stars, scuffing the path and sending tiny stones scuttling around them.

'Right,' Tom said apprehensively.

'I think we both know that this year has been pretty shit. And maybe that for a while before things weren't that great either.'

Tom didn't reply, instead allowing Esme to take his silence as tacit agreement.

'And I've been thinking a lot about it, and about us. And I think that it may have been not ideal, but also that we can't let it define us or ruin this year, can we?'

'No . . . no, you're right.'

'We have to recover a bit of *us*, don't we? Be Esme and Tom again instead of some couple who have been dealt some pretty shit luck. I won't be defined by having a miscarriage,' she said. 'It's ten years for us in a few weeks. So I think we have to remember why most of that has been fun and brilliant. And why we love each other. I know it's only a haircut, but . . .'

Tom was on the verge of tears. But he kept himself composed enough to squeeze her hand, a small gesture of acknowledgement and support so often needed throughout their relationship.

'Basically I'm saying that we should start 2017 afresh. Again.'

'Okay. I'm not sure I—'

'Spring is the time of new life and all that. So I think that we should draw a line under the last few months and start the year again – tomorrow. The first of May.'

'Which makes today New Year's Eve.'

'Exactly.'

'Well, happy New Year,' Tom said, knowing that today was not the day to talk to Esme. Nor tomorrow.

But there would have to be a time. Eventually, one day soon, there would have to be a time to tell the truth.

# CHAPTER TWENTY-TWO

**11.am – Midday**

# OUR 10ᵀᴴ ANNIVERSARY

## June 2017 – Stow-on-the-Wold, Gloucestershire

'A relapse?' Esme said, standing over Tom, who remained sitting on the end of the bed.

She looked shocked. As though just told about the sudden death of a family member. This erstwhile certainty in her life – his sobriety – had been removed. Whipped out from beneath her. Leaving Esme to process and respond to it as quickly as she could.

He had told her almost as soon as they got into the hotel room.

'When?'

'February. In Liverpool,' he said. And again there was the shock and the almost visible processing. The going back through what he told her had happened, what she now knew had really happened and the gap between the two.

*He was there when I . . .*

*He told me that he . . .*

'Okay,' she said, trying to sound calm, elongating the end of the word.

'I'm sorry I didn't tell you before. I just—'

'You just what?' she snapped. 'You just thought that ten years of sobriety ending like that wasn't worth mentioning?'

'No, I . . . I tried to say.'

'When?'

'That day in Camden. When you—'

'That was still two months after it happened! I'm talking about the day after, Tom. The day. Fuck, even the night of. Why did nobody call me?'

'I told them not to.'

'Who? Who did you tell not to?'

'You don't know them.'

Esme turned away from him. For a moment, he thought that she was going to leave the room. That this would be it, the end. When she did turn back, her eyes were full of tears. Her face full of anger and hurt, somehow magnified by the fact that it was no longer framed by her wavy hair.

'The last time you drank, you tried to kill yourself. Since the day you told me that, I have worried about it happening. I mean, I don't even know if you've been feeling like that again.'

Tom thought for a moment, but said nothing.

Almost immediately her anger became sadness and Esme fully broke down. Tom stood up off the bed and went to comfort her, but the hand on her shoulder was brushed off as though it belonged to a stranger.

'I'm sorry, Es.'

Esme swallowed and looked up at him.

'It's not enough,' she said.

'What do you mean?'

'Sorry. You lie and lie and lie. And all you can say after is sorry.'

Tom went to speak, but Esme cut him off.

'Everything I have worried about for ten years happens. And instead of telling me, you lie—'

'I didn't lie,' he interrupted.

At this, she turned and made for the door. Tom called for her to stop.

'Why should I?' she shouted. 'Why should I not just go now?'

'Because we have to sort this out,' he said, adding a hopeful, 'Don't we?'

Esme thought for a moment and stepped away from the door.

'And what if there is nothing to sort out?' she said, the words emptying all the colour from Tom's face.

'What do you mean?'

'Come on,' she said, almost scoffing at him. 'How little respect do you have for me – for *us* – if all *that* happens and you can't bring yourself to tell me?'

'It's not like that.'

'Well, what is it like then?' she snapped. 'You're not telling me anything. All I know is that you started drinking again while I was getting over a fucking miscarriage.'

'We,' Tom said.

'What do you mean?'

'*We* had the miscarriage. We always said that I didn't want you to manage it alone.'

'Yes but it is *I*, Tom. Isn't it? *I* was carrying the baby. *I* lost the baby. *You* were just there. "You're not in this alone", wasn't it?' she said, recalling what he said to her outside the early pregnancy unit. 'Well that was fucking bullshit, wasn't it?'

Esme turned away from him and stalked across the room. Part of Tom was angry about this sudden division, the instant breaking of a promise they had made to one another about how they would deal with the loss and carry on after it.

'Did anything else happen that night?'

Tom said nothing to this. Unsure of what he could say.

'Es...'

'I want to know!' she said. 'I mean, I don't think I can stand to hear it all. But I want to know what happened that night.'

And so Tom told her.

He told her about how his depression had crept back into his life, and by proxy, theirs. And that instead of telling her about it, he had tried to close the door on it, breaking the verbal contract they had made years ago, that he would always let her in.

He told her that he had been feeling on the verge of some precipice – endlessly, teeth-grindingly anxious for months. But that he had tried to carry on as though it were something he could ignore. Lapsing into the behaviour of an entire former generation, when anxiety was solved by pulling one's self together and stiffening the upper lip.

Crying openly now, he told her about the bar in Liverpool, the urge. How he had tried to call her. How he had stepped outside to try to bring himself down. How none of it was enough.

Then came his attempted kiss with Louisa, the waking up next morning, feeling her beside him. Worrying about what else he might have done. Not being able to remember if he did, and being relieved when he discovered that he hadn't. This was the hardest part.

Finally, he told her about coming home – how it all felt different suddenly, and everything grew worse and worse. How his self-hatred snowballed with each new remembrance. How he had found himself lurching towards the lowest ebb again, desperately trying to pull himself back with therapy sessions and AA meetings.

Esme listened without blinking. She did so seemingly without judgement. Tears came sporadically – perhaps at the idea of Tom suffering alone, at his pushing her away, at the vision of him drunk and helpless.

When Tom finished, Esme's face was wet from crying, and red from the irritation of wiping her eyes with the back of her hand.

'I'm sorry,' he said, and she took his hand. 'I don't know what to do next.'

'Neither do I,' she said.

They sat together for a moment, both of them silent until Esme released his hand and stood up.

'I'm going to go for a little walk. I need to process this all.'

'Okay. Do you think—'

'Don't ask me what I want to do, Tom,' she said. 'Because I really don't know myself.'

And with that, Esme turned away from him and left the hotel room, leaving him sitting on the end of the bed.

Now, on his own in the room, Tom wondered if this might be it. The end. Ten years. He confessed about the relapse shortly after they arrived in the bedroom at Byron House, the luxury hotel she had booked for their anniversary. When they came out, the words were urgent, having been building up in him for almost half of the year.

But it wasn't necessarily that need to speak that made him do it. Rather, it was a series of prompts from the moment they left Islay Gardens to the moment they arrived. The memory of the last time he was in a hotel room, and what happened in it.

He had watched Esme bustle around the room, excited as she always was when they stepped into a hotel – their home from home for the night. She was pointing out the fresh ground coffee, the roll-top bath, and the posh toiletries. But he was barely listening. Instead, he sat on the end of the bed, looking down at the floor with his bags at his feet.

'Tom,' she said, emerging from the bathroom. 'Is everything okay? Do you feel alright?'

Tears formed in his eyes as he looked up at her. 'Not really, Es. There's something I need to talk to you about.'

Now he could see her outside, sitting on a bench that overlooked a small green where two children were throwing a ball to one another. Though he knew she needed time, Tom couldn't bear to give it to her.

He got up from the bed and hurried through the hallway, away from their room and down into the lobby, busy with waistcoated staff sycophantically fawning over weekending couples. Ignoring a 'Can I help you, sir?', Tom ran out of the double doors and onto the high street. She was not far from him now. He could see her looking up at the sky, her short hair fluttering lightly in the gentle breeze.

Esme turned as he neared, and the look on her face immediately told him he'd done the wrong thing.

'You couldn't give me five minutes?'

'Es, I—'

'You what, Tom? Thought that my thinking about the future of our relationship could be hurried along?'

'No. I just hated the idea of not knowing.'

'And I hate the idea of you fucking lying to me,' she shouted, standing up from the bench and attracting the disapproving glares of an elderly couple walking their basset hound. 'Again!'

'Esme. I didn't . . .' Tom was about to say the word *lie*. However, he knew that doing so would only make things worse. He had lied. He hadn't wanted to. But intent was meaningless now. It was all about actions. 'I'm sorry,' he said, instead.

Tom and Esme were facing each other. The sun was shining down, catching one side of her face. She had rolled up the sleeves of the Breton top she was wearing, showing her pasty white arms and the watch she always wore with the face on the inside of her wrist.

He could sense that something intangible had changed. Once a team, they were now adversarial. The years that should have strengthened them had done the opposite.

'If you need time, Es.'

'It's not about time,' she said quickly. 'I don't need to think about it anymore.'

'Okay,' he said apprehensively.

'You know just then, before you came down here and interrupted me? I was trying to imagine what things would be like six months from now. Whether I could see us getting past this.'

'And?'

'I was thinking: what if you get another gig somewhere far away? If you meet some fucking friend from the good old days. Or I'm at some conference for a while? How do I know it won't happen again?'

'It—'

'I can't be with someone I can't trust, Tom. I just can't. Part of me actually blames myself for allowing you to go. As if you're a teenager. Not a fully grown man who knows better,' she said, her voice breaking. 'Who knows he has responsibilities.'

'I know.'

'Who knows he has a life . . . with me.'

Esme pulled her sleeve down over her watch and dabbed at her eyes with the cuff. She collected herself with a deep breath.

'You promised you'd always let me in, Tom. But when it comes to it you don't say a word. Half a year you've had this. And you let me think you were just sad about the baby.'

'I was. I am. That was part of it.'

'But there was more, wasn't there? It had all come back again and you didn't say. Just like you didn't say until your mum made you. Just like you didn't say until we met that bloke at my birthday. Just like you didn't say until you fucking broke down on New Year's Eve at Neil's house.'

'Esme.'

'No. You have lied and lied and lied. I get that it's hard. I get it. But if you don't let anyone get close to you, how the fucking hell are you going to deal with it?'

Tom wanted to speak again, but for the first time he had nothing much to say. She was right.

'The baby ... the miscarriage,' he said, trying to find something, anything, that would help him. 'That did make it worse. So did ...' He wasn't sure whether he should say it, if it might make things worse. 'Cornwall.'

'Right. So the fact that I wouldn't—'

'No. I mean that when you're low, these ... *things*. They make it worse. They confirm what all the anxiety is about.'

'Well thank you for telling me this now,' she said, looking around. Then she turned to face him with a serious expression.

'I can't believe we're doing this here.'

The words hit Tom like a punch to the gut.

'What do you mean?' he said.

'Here. In a town square. On our bloody anniversary.'

'But what do you mean when you say "*this*"?'

Now Esme hesitated. She looked away from him for a second.

'I can't be the one who finds you, Tom. If you get bad again and you try to ...' she said, unable to reach the word. 'If you try.'

'Es.'

'And you can't promise me that won't happen.'

'I can!'

'You can't, though. You just said earlier. You've been feeling ... that way again.'

'But I didn't. I pulled back.'

'How far did you get?' she said, the confrontational tone gone for a moment, and in its place a sort of resigned compassion.

Tom hesitated for a moment. 'I looked at the pills. The big bottle Jamilla brought back from America.'

At this, Esme broke down: the anger, the hurt, and the guilt of being angry with him for something he couldn't control all proving too much. Tom had seen it before in his parents, that same complex mix of emotions people feel when so deeply affected by the behaviour of the depressed or anxious. The anger they are made to believe is selfish.

250

'And how much of that... How much of what you felt affected what happened in Liverpool?'

Again, Tom hesitated. But he knew the answer.

'Tom,' she said firmly. 'I want to know. Which came first. The depression or Liverpool?'

'Neither!' he snapped. 'I was feeling bad and then... that. Each made the other worse. It's not as fucking simple as one following the other. Things just magnify, don't they?'

'I don't know. I really don't,' Esme said, pulling a tissue from her pocket to dab dry her eyes and nose.

Esme looked at him. Around the square a few people were looking, albeit trying not to; it was the sort of public spectacle that was impossible to ignore. She sat down on the bench and motioned for him to sit next to her.

'I want to know what it is that's happened to us which means we can't be honest with each other anymore,' Esme said.

'What do you mean?'

'Why couldn't you say something?'

'Because I—' Tom began. For a moment he was about to say that he didn't want to make things worse. 'I knew you'd be upset. And I knew we would argue. And I didn't want that.'

She stood up again, as if to leave.

'Please,' he said, desperately and she sat down again.

'We've lost sight of each other, haven't we?'

'You mean the proposal again.'

'I mean everything. The proposal, the lying, your relapse. And I'm not saying I'm innocent here, either. Maybe when you kept telling me you were fine I should've asked more questions.'

'No. Don't blame yourself.'

'How the fuck am I supposed to do that?' she snapped, turning away from him for a moment. 'I keep thinking that it would've been better if you *had* slept with her.'

251

'Why?'

'It would make things easier, wouldn't it?'

'And as it is?'

'I don't know,' she said quietly. At which Tom got up and sat in front of her, taking her hands as he crouched down.

'Esme. We *can* sort things out.'

They had been in the Cotswolds for just under an hour, but it had felt to Tom like a whole day. As a relationship grows and ages it becomes easier to guess what a person might be thinking just by looking at their face. That was the case for Tom and Esme. They knew each other's tics, traits and tells; the minute changes in facial expressions that indicated stress or worry or hurt.

But in that moment on a bench on a green patch in a town square, Tom could not read Esme at all – she was a closed book. It terrified him.

'Can I ask a question?' he said suddenly. Esme nodded, shuffled a little, uncomfortable on a seat that wasn't meant to be sat on for more than five minutes. 'What do you see when you look at me? Do you see your partner and your friend? The person you love, and the person you want to wake up next to tomorrow and the day after that, and the day after that. Or do you see something else?'

'Tom,' Esme said, a little hesitant, a little desperate.

'This is important, Es. You must know.'

'I do.'

'And?' Tom said.

Esme went to answer. Before she could, the loud church clock sounded. And one hour turned to the next.

# CHAPTER TWENTY-THREE

5 – 6 pm

# MOVING DAY

## August 2017 – West Hampstead, London

*Tom:*
*Empty freezer*
*Pack CDs*
*Bins*
*Kitchen*
*Keys*
*New furniture*

*Esme:*
*Cat*
*Fridge*
*Books*
*Bathroom*
*Bedroom*
*Living room*
*Cupboard*

The list was pinned to the fridge door, written on a piece of lined A5 paper torn from a notebook, held up by a magnet depicting

Vermeer's *The Milkmaid* they'd bought on a 2008 trip to Amsterdam. Beside most of the listed chores were ticks to signify what had been done. Their flat was a little closer to being emptied, a restoration to factory settings, like clearing out a computer before it's junked or sold. He hated the process of transforming a home back into a house, devoiding it of the meaning it once held.

Wiping surfaces clean rarely does the same for slates.

Esme had left a couple of hours ago. With a gentle kiss on the cheek and a quiet 'goodbye' she had walked away from their shared front door in Islay Gardens, carrying the cat in a box, and into their little car, leaving Tom with her key. They had agreed to rent the place out for a year or so, until they could decide what they wanted to do with it in the long term.

There was something odd in the idea of strangers – perhaps a new couple – living in their rooms, placing new things on old bookshelves, sleeping in their bed. He didn't want to think about who might call this place home next. But it was impossible not to.

Now he was alone in the kitchen, with a few more boxes to carry to the white Transit van he had rented for the day, parked badly half on the kerb outside. By his feet were four bin bags of stuff they had both agreed could serve no earthly purpose to either of them, and which would be an insult to even the most sparsely stocked charity shop. Poking out of one was the top of a small, metal sign that bore the legend LIVE LOVE LAUGH in a flowing, cursive type, and decorated awfully with butterflies and flying champagne corks. It had been bought for Esme by Laura – one in a series of genuinely awful gifts which, for obvious reasons, never made it onto the wall of their home.

Tom remembered the night they brought it home, after dinner with Laura and Aman at the Oxo Tower, overlooking the Thames and St Paul's.

'Go on, open it,' Laura had said enthusiastically. 'It's absolutely you.'

'Oh ... *lovely*,' Esme said, gamely feigning glee as she had so many times when opening a Laura present (Tom's favourite being a signed hardback copy of one of her own books). Aman meanwhile looked on in awe and embarrassment – he'd probably given up trying to advise his headstrong wife on gifting some years ago. Tom remembered how Esme laughed as he jokingly positioned it on various walls around the house.

He had been through the bags again earlier that day, checking that Esme was not unwittingly throwing away anything that might hold some sentimental value, even if that was the very stuff they should really have been getting rid of. But it was all meaningless tat.

Tom's phone buzzed along the bare kitchen counter top. His dad was calling. He tore off the rubber glove he was cleaning with and answered.

'Dad?'

'Hello, mate,' Gordon said. Tom could tell by his tone that this was the kind of call his dad was a little hesitant about making. Most of his dad's phone calls either came in the form of traffic updates when he was on the way to Lowestoft, or for other, equally practical sentiments. Emotional conversations were usually reserved for face-to-face meetings, each of them looking awkwardly at the floor until it was over with.

'Just checking that you're okay,' he continued. 'That everything's gone ... alright.'

'Yeah. So far so good, cheers.'

'And you're okay?'

'Fine,' Tom said. 'Bit knackered. But you know.'

'I do,' he said, though both of them knew that he didn't. 'And Esme?'

'She's okay, too. Left about three,' Tom said, thinking back to the moment that she had handed her key over to him.

'Good... good. Well I'm glad that you're... good,' he said, his well of words almost dry.

Such was the obviousness of her presence, Tom could almost hear his mother there, listening in and nudging his dad to say more, to keep Tom on the line just a little longer.

'Well, it's a big day for you. So your mother and I ... well, we just wanted to know that you're okay.'

'I am.'

'Good lad. You'll send us a text when you get there?'

'I will.'

They said their goodbyes and he hung up. And as Tom dropped his phone back into his jeans pocket, the significance of what was happening magnified suddenly.

So far that day the spectre of their break-up had been concealed behind admin and process; a list of jobs that pulled a dust sheet over the renovations they were making to their lives. This was (at least for the time being) the end of his and their London life, and the start of his new one, four hundred miles north and across a border.

Tom hadn't really thought about how much life would change: the new roads to get used to, his new address, the cafes and pubs. The death of his and Esme's little corner of London.

It was only when Annabel turned up that morning that it struck him how much the fundamentals of his life were about to alter: the weeks of planning before he could see an old friend; the knowledge that he would never again run into a familiar face in one of the unlikely coincidences that London had a habit of throwing up.

'You're finally doing it then?' Annabel asked, sipping milk-less tea from one of the two mugs that had yet to be packed away, while Esme distracted her three-year-old daughter, Mara.

'What do you mean, *finally*?'

'You always said you were going to do this. "I'm fed up with London,"' she aped him. '"I might just move to Edinburgh." You threatened it more or less every week throughout your early twenties. Until you met—' she said, stopping short.

'Yeah. I remember.'

'I always told you it wasn't an answer. But really I think I was just trying to keep you in London.'

'You always were selfish.'

'Absolutely. But clearly now I have no practical use for you.'

'Exactly. So, this is goodbye for ever?'

'Probably.'

'Well, we managed twenty-odd years,' Tom said, smiling and remembering back to when he and Annabel had met at school. Part of a small group of kids, often bullied for reasons ranging from ethnicity to an inability to take free kicks in football. 'You have to come and visit, you realise? All of you?'

'Of course,' she said, at which point their conversation was disrupted by Mara running screaming into the kitchen, with Esme chasing her and making monster noises. 'What is it with you, then?' Annabel said, as Mara hid behind her thigh.

'Aunt Esme is trying to catch me!' she shrieked, then screamed again when Esme bustled towards her waving her arms like tentacles. Mara then ran back into the living room, leaving the three of them alone.

Esme and Annabel hugged. Their friendship was a hand-me-down, but no less important to either of them for it.

'Give me two minutes,' Tom said, and left them for a moment to fetch something from the bedroom.

When he came back they were chatting away about the annoyances of the moving process and the solo drive Esme was about to make up to Leicester. Esme leant up against the mottled black counter, as she had almost every evening while watching Tom cook dinner (and sort of getting in the way, though he would never mention it).

'Got something for you,' Tom said to Annabel, when a break in their conversation presented itself. 'Found it yesterday when I was packing up my office.'

'Dividing up your estate?' she joked.

'Just look at it,' he said, ignoring her and handing over a cassette tape.

'What's this? One of those mixes you used to make girls at school? They always ended with "Ooh La La" by The Faces,' she said to Esme, who smiled gamely but didn't laugh.

'Shut up,' Tom said. 'And no. It's a tape of me playing your first dance. I made it when I was rehearsing. Thought you might like it.'

'Oh, Tom. That's so sweet,' she said. 'I mean, I will almost certainly never play it because it's not 1989 and we don't have a tape player. But, you know, the thought is lovely.'

'Frame it. I know they do it with records. Maybe you could be the first to do it with tapes? You live in Stoke Newington now – why not be a hipster trailblazer?'

'Because I spend most of my time cleaning Play-Doh out of the carpet.'

Annabel looked at the tape again, the marker-pen scrawl across the front that read AW-1. Then dropped it in her bag and looked up at Tom and Esme, her eyes beginning to fill.

'Look, I have to get her to a playdate in Cricklewood. So . . .'

'Oh,' Esme said. 'Don't worry. I'll give you two a moment.'

'No. Hang on,' Annabel said, before Esme could leave them to say their goodbyes. 'I'll miss you,' she said, taking Esme into her arms.

'You too,' Esme said, as she detached herself and left Tom and his oldest friend together in the empty kitchen.

Annabel picked up her rucksack and threw it onto her back. Then took Mara's hand to stop her from running off again and beginning another game of chase with Esme. Tom had rarely seen her cry: not even at her wedding, or one month before it, when her parents told her they wouldn't be attending. Only when she was sitting beside his hospital bed.

'Need a tissue?'

'Sod off,' she said, clearly altering her language due to the presence of her child.

'You know I'll see you again soon. New Year's, we said.'

'I know. But it's not the same, is it? We moved here at the same time. You're more a part of my life than anyone outside of Sam and Mara. Now you're just going to f— *naff* off to Scotland.'

'Naff?' he said, with a smile.

'Don't.' She dabbed at her eyes with the hem of her jumper. 'Listen, Tom, there's something I wanted to say to you before you go. Given, well, everything that's happened this year.'

'Is this going to make me well up? Because—'

'Just shut up, would you? No jokes. Right. Now you remember whenever you made a stupid joke, or forgot something, or were inexplicably half an hour late even though you work from home, I used to say that you didn't deserve her? That you were both my oldest friend and most useless.'

'I do,' Tom said, nodding, holding back tears himself now.

'Well I want to say that you did, Tom. You really did.'

Tom nodded and mustered a weak, 'Thanks,' as he and Annabel embraced, Mara joining in by hugging his leg.

'You know we'd never have met without you, don't you?' he said when they let go.

'All planned, mate. Every last bit of it.'

Annabel hugged him once more, said her goodbye and left with her daughter in tow. Tom spied Esme looking on from the alcove where the kitchen met the lounge but he couldn't bring himself to meet her eyes.

Now, alone, he looked around the kitchen, all empty except for one cardboard box, into which he placed the kettle and a tin caddy filled with tea bags and sachets of long-life milk that Esme had stolen from a conference centre earlier that year. As he was about to pick it up and take it out to the van, Tom heard a knock at the still-open door and a young, cheerful voice call, 'Hello?'

'Come in,' Tom said, and watched as a young man, maybe twenty-two years old, wearing a grey pinstripe suit, white shirt and pink tie strode confidently into his house, a large leather wallet stowed under his arm.

'Will Mercer, Alder Estates,' the man said, holding out a sweaty palm for Tom to shake. 'Sorry, a bit early,' Will said, checking his watch.

Tom glanced at the screen of his phone. Nearly a quarter to six. He had been hoping to have a little bit of time in the place.

'Anyway, suppose you'll be wanting to get away. Long drive to Glasgow, isn't it?'

'Edinburgh.'

'Ah.' Will frowned. 'They near?'

'Ish.'

Tom showed Will through to the living room, where a new IKEA sofa he and Esme had bought for future renters was set up in the centre, facing a TV unit, bare except for a few mug ring stains. An empty house is a strange place, he thought, looking up at the picture hooks and nails sticking from random places on the walls. At the pure, clean white squares once hidden by their pictures, now framed by the discolouration brought by time. The hard-to-get-to and so rarely hoovered corners of the room looked dirty and unkempt – Tom's shoddy work installing faux-wood skirting boards shown up for what it was. The swirled Artex ceiling they'd never replaced was now adorned with a single energy-efficient lightbulb.

'I'd offer you a tea but I've packed up the kettle.'

'No problem. Last thing in, first thing out, eh?'

'Sorry?'

'The kettle. Last thing in, first thing out. Always the way.'

'Oh. Yes.'

'Anyway. These things tend not to take that long. We'd probably be done before it boils,' Will said, failing to grasp the profundity of the day. 'Just you, is it?' he said, pulling out three sheets of paper from his sparsely filled wallet.

'Yes. Just me.'

'Good good. So if you could just sign where the Xs are, that would be perfection,' he said, watching Tom rest the papers on his knee to sign. 'Then here for the maintenance,' he pointed. 'And this one for the keys. Two sets, is it?'

Tom nodded, a little shell-shocked by the speed and heartlessness of the process. Estate agents rarely afforded it the same importance as their customers, and Will Mercer of Alder Estates was no different in this regard.

'Well, if you get them together, I'll do my bits and give you the copies.'

The keys were both on the pale blue tiled windowsill in the kitchen, next to a large crack Esme used to cover with a permanently wilting basil plant.

He handed them over.

'Thanking you,' Will said cheerfully. 'Got a nice couple moving in. Jack and Sooz. Spelled with a double O.'

Tom forced a smile at Will, who oddly seemed to now be waiting for Tom to leave.

'Do you need a moment? Say goodbye to the place and all that.'

'No,' Tom said after a second. 'I should be fine,' turning away from the kitchen.

'Oh. Don't forget this,' Will said, holding up a dustpan and brush. 'Everyone always forgets something.'

Tom thanked Will and shook his hand, before picking up the last box and taking it out to the van. He pulled out a white shoebox and took it with him into the cab of the Transit. The Esme box. He had planned to look through it before he left, but Will's early arrival scuppered the plan.

Inside was a stack of gig tickets, photographs, cheap holiday mementos, and postcards. Most of the keepsakes were of a time or occasion he could now remember little detail about. Esme had a box, too – full of the exact same stuff. On the most basic level it was ridiculous paraphernalia to keep around – and yet all impossible to throw away.

Tom pushed a reel of fairground tokens to one side and found what he was looking for. A small stack of Post-it notes, now a little battered from months spent buffeting around in the bottom of his satchel. Esme's handwriting and drawing of a clock on the front. The thing that nudged this new phase of their life into being. That caused arguments and admissions. That made them both re-evaluate their ten years together.

He began to flick through, wondering what the moments would be. And about how lenient she would be about the exactness of time.

Tom had a decent enough memory, but he questioned how sure he could be that it was precisely 4 a.m. that their tent caved in under the pressure of all that water on their disastrous camping trip. Maybe Esme could help him verify. Though more likely it was the moments she was urging him to remember, not the exact time they took place.

He found himself thinking back to the night they had met in Stockwell. Ali's superhero fancy-dress party. The two of them the only ones to ignore the directive to turn up in costume. Esme because she didn't want to. Tom because he wasn't sure if he'd make it past the threshold. He thought about how Annabel had encouraged him to go and talk to her.

*It's Esme, right?*

*Right. And you're Tom?*

The first words they spoke to each other. Followed by his terrible joke about shoes.

Instinctively, Tom knew it would be the first of the memories in the game. But what else would join it?

Some hours would be easy to pick. Some would be a little harder. After all, a life together can't be solely defined by happy times, can it? Just as important are the challenges, the hardships that enable a couple to develop the hard shell that sees them through the years. His relapses into depression. Tamas's death. The proposal. That night in Liverpool.

He questioned whether or not it was possible to quantify the moments that define a relationship while it is still in progress. Or only once the line has been drawn under it, when it's easier to deconstruct.

Then again, he thought, maybe Esme knew that. Was she trying to draw a line under them with the game?

Part of him wanted to screw the Post-its up and throw them out of the window. But instead he placed them in his jacket pocket. They would go into the top drawer of his desk. A constant reminder of what they had, and what he lost.

With one last look back at the house, Tom turned the ignition on the van. A drivetime DJ was, for some reason, allowing a child to introduce the six o'clock news. He changed the station, put the van into gear, and drove away.

## CHAPTER TWENTY-FOUR

**11 pm – Midnight**

# OUR LIFE IN A DAY – FINALLY
## June 2018 – Barcelona

Tom took a seat on one of the benches on the northern part of La Rambla Catalunya. All around him restaurants were beginning their shutdown for the night, turning away late diners or trying to chivvy out those taking their time. The city was still busy though: tourists flitting from bar to bar or strolling idly back to hotels; street sellers still trying to flog the occasional fake Barcelona shirt with *MESSI 10* on the back. Locals peered out of high windows at the city below.

From inside his bag he pulled a padded envelope containing the letter, the notebook, and, nestled at the bottom, the small stack of Post-it notes that had sat in his desk drawer ever since he'd moved out. Until today, when they would return to the person who had created them.

Our Life in a Day. Illustrated with those little clocks. The scrawled introduction to the game on the crumpled A5 notepaper.

Tom held the deck of Post-its, beaten at the edges. He leafed through every one. All twenty-four hours.

Next was the notebook. He'd bought it especially for this. A bright red leather thing containing page upon page of half-remembered conversations, notes, memories and things she'd told him. A selective history of their time together written hour by hour – as complete as Tom's memory would allow.

Aside from the occasional piece of sheet music, it was probably the only thing Tom had handwritten in years. And now he finally had some time to spare, he began to read through the entries.

Was this it? Everything? The definitive list? It had taken him several months to compile it – and pages of scrap paper full of potential additions and removals. Entire lists of twenty-four moments that were different from the ones he now held in front of him.

Most of the hours he had thought about adding were happy ones. But that kind of list would be dishonest – to him, to her, to them.

No, this was it. Tom was fairly sure that he was more or less accurate on the times these things happened. And as he had compiled the final list that morning, sitting in a cafe in Barcelona's Gothic Quarter giving each hour a reference on the relevant Post-it note, Tom had found profound joy and deep melancholy in reliving his life with Esme Simon.

But the game wasn't done yet. There was one hour left to complete.

He checked his watch. Only twenty minutes until what would have been their eleventh anniversary.

To occupy the time, Tom reached into his bag and took out her letter. It had arrived at the end of January, almost six months after they had left their home in West Hampstead. Delivered to the one-bedroom flat he was renting in an old Georgian townhouse near Charlotte Square in Edinburgh.

He remembered finding it in the cluttered mail tray shared by all four flats; the initial shock at seeing her handwriting; the butterflies he felt at what might be inside.

And the bitter sadness at what he knew it would be.

He had taken it back to his little kitchen/living room/diner, sitting down to read as Scottish rain beat hard against the rattling windows of the flat.

*Dear Tom,*

*You asked me why. Why we couldn't carry on. Why I couldn't move past it.*

*At the time I couldn't adequately answer, or put into words how I felt. All I knew was that it was wrong for me to feel the way I did about you, and that a big part of the thing that made us us died that day. And once that thing was gone I didn't think we'd ever be able to get it back.*

*Now with a little distance I know I was right. As awful as it was at the time, we made the best decision, if not the easiest.*

*I can also tell you why I decided that it was the end.*

*There was always something that bound us together. In hindsight, I suppose it was honesty. Sometimes it took you a little while to tell me things about your past and who you were. But I never thought for a moment that you'd keep things from me like you did. It might not sound like much now it's written down. Though the more I think about it, the more I realise that it was our cornerstone. When that went, we went with it. There was no other choice for us, Tom. I'm really sorry about that. Sometimes love isn't enough. No matter how much we hope it is.*

*Anyway. I don't want this to be a sad letter. I want to say some nice things about you, too. In the hope that you're moving on and having a good life. Because you deserve it.*

*Now listen up, Tom Murray. You are an excellent person. You are kind and funny and good-hearted. You are a bit disorganised and ramshackle, but in an entirely lovely way. And you aren't bad-looking, as they go.*

*For ten years you made me very happy. And while I know it was very sad when that stopped, ten years is a bloody long time! Ten years is two and a half World Cups. Six super moons. Eighty bank holidays. You literally made me happy for a month of Sundays. (Can you tell I've been googling?)*

*What I am trying to say is that you don't make someone happy by accident. You do it because you are wonderful. The fact that we didn't make it doesn't change a thing about that.*

*Before I sign off, I want to say one last thing. That day, in the Cotswolds, when it became clear it was over, you told me that I was your reason to live, and that made me angry and upset. I now know what I should have said is that YOU are your reason to live, Tom.*

*You are.*

*Please don't ever forget that.*

*So be happy. Be content. Fall in love again. Bloody hell, you can even get married if you want to! (Joke. Too soon?)*

*Miss you.*

    *Love you.*

      *Esme x*

Tom inhaled deeply, folding the letter and placing it back in his bag. The first time he'd read it, he had spent the next hour in tears, lying on the couch, reading her words over and again until they were almost memorised. Since then, he'd been through it a hundred times or more, the heartbreak it elicited gradually reducing with each read as he tried to compose a suitable reply. His bin quickly filled with screwed-up balls of paper – all abandoned letters back to Esme. Nothing worked. No combination of words was sufficient.

Until that morning, when he had risen early for a run around Parc de Joan Miró, before returning to his Airbnb apartment to finally write back to her.

Checking his watch, Tom saw that he still had a few of minutes left of the hour. He took his letter out from the envelope and looked over it one last time, then copied it into the notebook under *11 p.m. to midnight.*

*Esme,*

*Thank you for the letter. And sorry it's taken me so long to reply. To tell you the truth, for a long while I couldn't find the words.*

*Then I realised that maybe a letter wasn't the right answer anyway.*

*So here goes something else.*

*Today – as I sit here reading my own awful handwriting – would've been our 11th anniversary. Exactly one year ago, you gave me a little stack of Post-it notes, a game called Our Life in a Day. A game that we never played.*

*Well, I finally played it, Es.*

*Inside this envelope you'll find it all. A notebook full of my scrawls. Our Life in a Day. Eleven years (!!!) of us. The good bits, the bad bits, the fun bits and the hard bits.*

*A not-so-new game by Esme Simon, finally completed by Tom Murray.*

*I think I've picked the right twenty-four. You might disagree. Either way, doing this – playing your game – has made me realise that as well as saying sorry for what became of us, I need to say something else:*

***Thank you, Esme.***

*Thank you for every happy moment, every kindness, every time you made me feel better about myself and every special moment we shared together. It might sound corny (probably is), but you made me a better person. Whatever else happened between us, I will always love you for that.*

*In your letter you said you hoped I was happy, that I was moving on. Well, I am pleased to say that I am getting there. This year I went back to university (no, not the same one). I am going to finish what I started fifteen years ago and actually become a proper qualified music teacher. No more dodgy jobs and gigging around. Tom Murray is growing up (finally).*

*More importantly, I want you to know that I'm well. I'm happy. I see a counsellor every week. I talk to people when I need to. I'm accepting who I am and what I have. I don't think I would've done any of that without you.*

*You probably know there are a million things I could've done differently. One for every minute in the day. I could've talked more, shared more, done more. I'm trying not to regret things, Es. But there'll always be one thing in the back of my mind.*

*That morning, after Ali's party. We were on your doorstep and I almost shared it all. Everything. I always think how different things might've been if I had.*

*Maybe everything would be the same. Maybe it wouldn't. Either way, I know that I lost you, you didn't lose me.*

*Anyway. All I have left to say is that I love you. And I will always love you. I hope you are happy and thriving and wonderful. The world is a good place with Esme Simon in it.*

*Love,*

*Tom x*

The hour was almost up.

Tom dropped the stack of Post-its into the envelope. Then closed the notebook. Across the front he wrote: *OUR LIFE IN A DAY. FINALLY.* And placed it inside, sealing the envelope's flap shut. He knew she would read every word. But what would she think? Part of him was desperate to talk to her about it. Another part didn't ever want to know.

As the watch on his wrist buzzed, Tom got up from the bench, took the envelope to the post box across the square and, with one last check of the stamp and Esme's new address in Dulwich, he pushed it inside.

He looked down at his watch just as the hour changed.

It was the start of another day.

# EPILOGUE

# THE WALK HOME
### June 2007 – Stockwell, London

They stepped out into the early-morning night. Although it was cold, the city retained some trace of the day's warmth. The dark grey streets and pavements were lit by the orange glow of the street lamps – the city just about still alive. A group of girls in high heels and no coats spilled drunkenly from a night bus onto South Lambeth Road, laughing as they tottered away towards Clapham. A cyclist sped past on his way north. A pair of foxes crept around the Stockwell war memorial, running away when disturbed by a pair of newly acquainted voices.

'So tell me all about you then, Tom Murray,' one of them said.

'What do you want to know?'

'How old?'

'Twenty-five.'

'Twenty-six. Good. Now, recent history. School. University, if applicable. Work and, err, any notable holidays since the year two thousand. A point for each.'

'A point?' Tom said.

'Yes. It's a game. You say something about yourself, you get a point.'

'And what do points mean, in this game?'

'You'll have to see.'

'Christ,' Tom said. 'You'll have to give me a moment to think. Can you go first?'

'Happy to,' Esme said, stepping around a kebab, dropped and abandoned in the road. 'So, school. I went to the King Richard Grammar in Knighton, which is near Leicester.'

'Benjamin Britten High School. Lowestoft.'

'Most easterly town in Britain.'

'Correct.'

'That means I get an extra point. Next. University. I went to Oxford. Studied English Language. Then an MA in child speech therapy at UCL.'

'Blimey. Get you, eh?'

'Yes. I am terribly clever,' she said, mock pompously.

'Clearly. Anyway, shouldn't it be "reading"? That's what they always say, isn't it, at those places. "I'm reading economics" or something.'

'Yes. But I'm not a horrendous arse like those people. Also, if we're talking about word choice, we might need to think about you saying "blimey" to express surprise. Unless you're actually sixty and look very good for it?'

'I normally say "fucking hell". But given the circumstances...'

'What circumstances? Is there something I don't know about happening here?'

Tom cringed a little. 'You like to take the piss out of people, don't you?' he said, as they walked under a streetlight, which briefly illuminated Esme's face as he turned to look at her.

'Yes. And I thought you were avoiding bad language? Given the circumstances,' she said mockingly. 'Anyway. What about you?'

'Oh. I just studied music in Hertfordshire. Not very exciting. Big ex-poly. No nice buildings covered in ivy, either. Half glass and shiny. Half 1970s asbestos and vinyl.'

'So you're a musician, then? That might result in a point deducted. After Matt I said no more musicians, what with the touring and everything.'

'Well, I'm more of a static musician.'

'I don't have a clue what that is.'

'I teach a bit. Play in a couple of cover bands. Though what I'd really like to do is compose for films or something.'

'Fine. A static musician should be fine. Only half a point off.'

'Very gracious of you. And presumptuous.'

'You were the one who brought up the circumstances. Anyway, so next is—'

'Hang on,' Tom said, stopping Esme before she could move onto her next mental cue card. 'I have one.'

But he didn't. Instead Tom was playing for time as they approached Vauxhall Tube station and the perilous network of roads, crossings, paths and cycle lanes that surrounded it. Avoiding having to explain more of himself or his recent past. The best way to do that, he figured, would be to turn back the dial on Esme's life, to discover more about what made her *her*, rather than reveal the things that made him *him*. At the sound of their footsteps a rat scuttled from the pavement into a drain. One of his phobias piqued, he squeezed her hand.

'Scared of rats. Good to know,' she said. 'Extra point to me.'

Tom feigned a laugh and said, 'So, I want to know more about your university days. Clubs, societies. All that sort of thing.'

'There's not much to say, really. Met a couple of interesting people. One is sometimes on the telly.'

'Who's that?'

'Laura Sutcliffe. She writes about politics for the *Telegraph*. Massive Tory, but she's nice. If you watch those programmes when they talk about politics and tomorrow's papers you've probably seen her. Pretty blonde girl. Gets quite shouty.'

'I think I know her,' Tom said, able to immediately bring Laura Sutcliffe to mind, along with a couple of the things he'd called her while watching *Newsnight*. 'So what else?'

'I don't know. Joined the uni wine society. But I really couldn't afford to keep up. Couple of reading groups. And drama.'

'Footlights?' Tom said, impressed.

'That's Cambridge. So minus one point.'

'Crap. Is that sacrilegious?'

'Only if I could give a toss. Anyway, no. It wasn't the proper drama group. That's basically for boys who intend to become stand-up comedians or guests on crappy panel shows. Mine was a little amateur group. We did stuff like *Death of a Salesman*, *The Importance of Being Earnest*. One year we took a show to Edinburgh, where I learned that the most terrifying words in the English language are "come and see my one-woman show".'

'You were on the Fringe?'

'The very *fringe* of the Fringe. One of the many hopeless hopefuls struggling for an audience. It can be a bit like "if a tree falls in a forest, does it make a sound?".'

'If a play happens without an audience, did it really happen?'

'Exactly,' she said. 'But that's it, really. Uni. Then work.'

Esme led Tom onto Vauxhall Bridge. It was almost 3.45 a.m. and still a sporadic stream of traffic passed them by. Night buses, black cabs and bikes. Small groups of drunk young people carrying bottles and cans. A stumbling, staggering, kebab-carrying man in a suit, who would likely spend the remainder of the weekend regretting his decision to stay out.

When they reached the middle of the bridge, Esme stopped and looked east to the Gherkin and the mass of cranes, busily working away at pushing new teeth into the city's old mouth.

'Okay, I've thought of another question. Then I promise it's your turn again. You need the points,' she said. 'When I moved to London it was going to be a temporary thing. Maybe a year. Maybe less if I could find a job back in Oxford.'

'And what happened?'

'I suppose you just get stuck here, don't you? Decent job. Decent wages. You get used to flat sharing. Then gradually you begin to take it for granted. The other week I got annoyed because Leicester doesn't have a Pret. I've been in London for four years now.'

'I know what you mean. Except the flat-sharing bit.'

'You live on your own?'

'Yeh, a little studio. It's not much. But I have a nice landlord who doesn't jack the rent up every year.'

'Hmm. Okay, you get a point for that.'

'Thank you. How many am I on?'

'I think that brings you back up to zero.'

They fell silent for a while, staring out at the quiet, dirt-brown river. Then Esme slowly nuzzled herself into the small crook between Tom's upper arm and his chest.

'I suppose it can be quite pretty, though, can't it?'

'Sometimes.'

'Do you want to carry on playing then?'

'Not really,' Tom said as Esme stepped away, took his hand and led him the rest of the way across the bridge.

When they reached Millbank on the other side, she let go of his hand. His spirits fell a little. But he tried not to read too much into it.

'We're nearly at mine,' she said. 'So I think we might have to dispense with holidays and go straight for the bonus round.'

'What's that, then?'

'One interesting fact each. It doesn't have to be a secret. The only rule is that it can't be obvious. Like, no saying "I have brown hair and size nine feet".'

'Okay,' Tom said, a little apprehensively, knowing as he did that the most interesting facts about him were exactly the things he couldn't tell her about; his recent history still raw.

'You first, though,' he said quickly, before she could throw a question his way.

'Fine. Well, how about the fact that I am Hungarian. Both my parents are from Budapest.'

'That is interesting. No accent.'

'None. Mainly because I grew up in Leicester, didn't visit Hungary until I was ten, and didn't meet a *single other* Hungarian person throughout my entire childhood.'

'That'll do it.'

'I'm more Hungarian by nature than by nurture. Mum and Dad don't really bother with any traditions except Christmas and State Foundation Day.'

'When's that?'

'Some time in August. Normally they just set off a few fireworks and eat this kind of Hungarian trifle thing,' Esme said, steering Tom around a corner and onto Denton Road – a street of pretty, white stucco-fronted houses with long, decorative, black and white chequerboard walkways leading to impressive front doors. All the lights in the houses were off, except for one at the very top of a three-storey house.

'You live here?' Tom said, with some surprise.

'Yes. But it looks posher than it is. I have a room on the second floor of what was once a decent-sized house and is now three fairly small flats. Anyway. You've not told me your interesting fact yet.'

'And I'm not going to,' Tom said. 'Until we see each other again.'

Esme feigned shock and anger.

'Minus a million points. Literally.'

'I don't even know what the prize was.'

'You *would* have loved it. But instead here you are trying to engineer a date.'

'No—'

'Because I would've said yes without the blackmail.'

'Nice to hear. But still.'

Esme stopped when they arrived at number 34, its numbers peeling away from the pillars that flanked the porch. She took a step up and turned to face Tom, who was looking down at his shoes. He felt something burning inside of him. Some premonition of how important this woman was going to be to him. And with that some instinctual need to be honest with her. To start things off in the right way and to continue like that for ever.

'This is it then, Tom Murray,' she said. 'You'd better give me your number—'

'There's something I need to tell you,' Tom said, interrupting her.

'What?'

He had been ready to say it. To admit that he was a recovering alcoholic, and that he had been in a hospital bed two months ago, recovering from a suicide attempt. But then he saw Esme smile. The kiss could wait. There was something greater at stake. They had time for all that. Years and months and days and hours stretched out ahead of them.

'Well?' Esme said, laughing to herself.

'Actually, no,' Tom said. 'It can wait.'

'You sure?'

'It's nothing really. I'll tell you next time I see you.'

'So we're seeing each other again then, are we?'

'Yes,' Tom said. 'Tomorrow wasn't it?'

'Was it now?'

'Yes. I'm fairly sure we agreed tomorrow.'

'And what if I'm busy?'

'Plans can be cancelled,' he said. 'That's the great thing about plans.'

Esme looked at him askance, but still smiling.

'Fine. You've won me over. What are our new plans?'

'The park, I think. We can arrange a time when we're both up.'

'You're on.'

'Perfect,' he said, waiting, hoping.

'Still no kiss though,' she said.

With that, Esme Simon squeezed his hand and said, 'Goodnight, Tom.' Then she turned away, walked the few steps to her black front door and disappeared into a hallway busy with bicycles and pizza menus.

There, outside her house, he tried to commit to memory every single thing that had just happened, before he left to begin the long journey home to Camden, not noticing Esme watching him from her bedroom window on the third floor.

**The End**

# ACKNOWLEDGEMENTS

I'd like to thank the following people, without whom this book would not have been written, published and in your hands now.

Firstly, my family, whose love and faith has been ever present. Particularly my parents, who didn't scream when I told them I wanted to go to university as a mature student in my twenties to change careers and become a writer.

I'd also like to thank friends who have read my work, offered advice and been wonderful early readers. Likewise, my colleagues and friends at Octopus Group, and the editors, writers and publishers I've worked with, in particular Craig Taylor, and Jonny Cooper at *The Telegraph*.

Huge thanks to my agent, Charlie Campbell, for his dedication, advice and tenacity. To Olivia Barber, Alex Layt, Jen Breslin and the team at Orion for their hard work on this book. And to my editor Ben Willis, for giving me the opportunity to bring this book to readers, for helping to shape it and for his incredible contribution along the way to publication.

Finally, thank you to my beautiful son Rufus, and to my wife Alice, who is my first reader, biggest fan, best friend, and whose support has no bounds. Thank you for everything.